D0666151

HIGH PRAISE FOR
DOWNDRIFT
BY JOHANNA DRUCKER

THE PRINCIPAL CHARACTERS IN THIS wildly imaginative, laugh-out-loud funny, and ultimately heartbreaking story are a 3.8 billion-year-old cellular life form known as an Archaeon, a restless calico cat named Callie who sets out from Boston, and an unnamed lion, whose shrinking habitat forces him to wander far from his home in Tanzania. . . . The Archaeon's tales of the many different animals are delivered in deliciously short chapters that build over the course of one year into a story that's by turns droll, subversive, pensive, brooding, off-the-charts weird, and wonderfully surprising. . . . Animal lovers will enjoy the antics of the beagles, bears, salamanders, cows, spiders, and other creatures, but the author's beautifully subtle message isn't just for pet owners or environmentalists. It's for all of us.

 —*KIRKUS REVIEWS*

LAUGHING OR CRYING, DRUCKER SKEWERS the current cultural moment in a novel extrapolation of epic proportions. Taken to the furthest extreme, *Downdrift* is dogged by an urgent need to understand the difference between the domestic and the wild, measure it, and recalibrate its implications for survival.

 —*FOREWORD REVIEWS*

CIVILIZATION AND ITS DISCONTENTS HAS spread to "animals"; a basin of entities performing themselves as social species and known individuals, with all the self-absorptions, neuroses, and mediating technologies of this representational age. It's an earth of assumed rights and obligations, starlets and exemplars, morals and tastes, histories and powers, and foremost self-concern—sublimating, absorbing, and masking even the most driven of animal instincts. This book is a genealogical critique of morals—a migratory picture of that sometimes comic, sometimes tragic, working out of the West's metaphysics of justice on a planetary scale.

 —RON DAY, PROFESSOR, DEPT. OF INFORMATION AND LIBRARY SCIENCE, INDIANA UNIVERSITY AT BLOOMINGTON

DOWNDRIFT

DOWNDRIFT

an eco-fiction

Johanna Drucker

THREE ROOMS PRESS
New York, NY

Downdrift
BY Johanna Drucker

© 2018 by Johanna Drucker

All rights reserved. No part of this book may be reproduced in any form or by any electronic or mechanical means, including information storage and retrieval systems, without permission in writing from the publisher, except by a reviewer, who may quote brief passages in a review. For permissions, please write to address below or email editor@threeroomspress.com. Any members of education institutions wishing to photocopy or electronically reproduce part or all of the work for classroom use, or publishers who would like to obtain permission to include the work in an anthology, should send their inquiries to Three Rooms Press, 561 Hudson Street, #33, New York, NY 10014.

This is a work of fiction. Names, characters, businesses, places, events, and incidents are either the products of the author's imaginations or used in a fictitious manner. Any resemblance to actual persons, living or dead, or actual events is purely coincidental.

ISBN 978-1-941110-61-4 (trade paperback)
ISBN 978-1-941110-62-1 (Epub)
Library of Congress Control Number: 2017960406
TRP-065
2 4 6 8 10 9 7 5 3 1

COVER DESIGN AND ILLUSTRATION:
Victoria Black
www.thevictoriablack.com

BOOK DESIGN:
KG Design International
www.katgeorges.com

DISTRIBUTED BY:
PGW/Ingram
www.pgw.com

Three Rooms Press
New York, NY
www.threeroomspress.com
info@threeroomspress.com

For Nora

DOWNDRIFT

Archaen Prologue

Reports stream in from around the world.

Kangaroos are boxing in the suburban streets of Australia. Urban foxes make eye contact with drivers, then cross traffic in the center of London. Chimps take up toolmaking in the wilds of Tanzania at the same time their captive brethren in Vancouver use files to pick at the locks on their cage doors. The humans take particular note of unusual acts of cross-species compassion. But when a predatory bear shelters a stray puppy and dolphins nurse a wounded shark, the humans only see the cradling gestures and remain deaf to the traditional songs.

Uplift is what the humans call this. They would. They imagine every adoption of their behaviors to be an advancement. I see it otherwise, as downdrift, the seepage of traits across species.

And I? Who am I?

I am an Archaeon, the most ancient creature on earth. My fossil remains are 3.8 billion years old. I hitched a ride on a comet, and arrived from interstellar space while the earth was still young and uninhabited. No other life form was here before me, so you may all be my descendants.

I have no face, no furry paws, no big eyes, or puffy tail. I'm a modest bit of genetic code enclosed by a cell wall. Hardly appealing. My individual cells are a living network, a gazillion tiny points spread over the surface of the earth, picking up information at every node. I can be in the cities, at the antipodes, in a rushing stream and a vile sink hole all at the same time, seeing, watching, reporting on the animals' emerging activities.

But you will hear almost nothing from me about the humans. After all, they are a major source of this pollution. Their obliviousness is so complete that by the time they discover the seepage of their psychic attitudes and social behavior it may be too late to stop the consequences. Eventually the influence may go the other way—they may sprout monkey hair and grow pig jowls, bark loudly, or crawl on their bellies. But that will require another account.

And me? I have been here a long time and will be here much longer. I have lived through extinctions before. I can survive extremes of toxicity, heat, dehydration, and inundation, and will thrive to tell other tales of evolution and survival when all the rest of you are long gone or are so morphed you will hardly recognize yourselves, or the world you live in.

September

Callie's Quest
Boston, Massachusetts

THE HUMAN CHILDREN IN CALLIE'S FAMILY are back in school. Mealtimes shift inconveniently and sometimes kitchen traffic threatens congestion near the food bowl. But though the house is quiet during the days, the cat is restless.

I know her, of course, in the odd way that I am familiar with every living creature. The lethargy of summer is beginning to yield to the uptick of activity fostered by the brisk air. I resent thermal shifts and their taxes on my metabolic system. Nothing is finer than uninterrupted inertia. In general, cats are sympathetic to this attitude, hence my attachment. We have a common value system.

Callie sits at the window, her calico coat catching the sun. She stares distractedly, with attention to something no one else can see or hear. The stimulus is real, but invisible. Meanwhile, she pretends to ignore a pair of squirrels tricked out in new fashions.

Something is disturbing her. Messaging is in the air, her air. She tries to calm herself with a bout of grooming, washing her face with a soft pink paw. Her restlessness remains, but she drifts into tightly curled sleep, her chin turned upward as she twitches in deep cycles of dream.

Meanwhile, half a world away, near the northern border of Tanzania, a lion, aged and weary, stretches from a nap and shakes his mane, then walks away from his pride, out on his own. An air of decline is evident in his posture and bearing, as well as in his spirit. He knows his territory is shrinking and fears for his kind. Driven by an impulse to leave, he doesn't even look back at his cubs. They have stopped wrestling in the dry grass and are playing with a deck of cards. As he moves off, he has no idea how quickly they will shift from that initial distraction to video games and personal devices. Six months later, they will nearly starve, so removed from their senses they will have forgotten how to hunt, except on screen.

As he separates from his pride, he feels a shock. A spark shoots from one feline to another, across time and space, with its own improbable force. Callie, startled awake, claws at the screen, paws at the pane, scratches at the door, and when it opens, she winds out across the threshold. Her delicate ears prick up and, tail in the air, she moves quickly across her familiar yard and through the break in the fence.

In the alley, she picks her way with fastidious steps. This is as far as she usually ventures. A pair of sparrows read aloud to each other, giggling over the messages in their Twitter stream. She ignores them, hesitating for just moment, and then moves steadily along the narrow street.

In the dry hot veld, the lion is also searching for his path. In the long grass, the dung beetles tune small instruments for an afternoon concert. Annoyed by the sounds, the lion pads through the tawny brush, a blur of motion, paying no attention to the insect orchestra.

The downdrift is underway.

Hamadryas Humor
Loitokitok District, Kenya

A SMALL TROOP OF HAMADRYAS BABOONS, on a foray out of their woodland hills, pauses at the edge of the savannah just long enough for the dominant male to take stock of his troop. To suggest he is counting would be blatant exaggeration. But he is assessing the strength and size of his group, especially the hand-picked young male he tolerates as genetic backup in case of his own demise. Nothing threatens him or them just then. Nothing overt, at least. A lion passing in the distance, with lean limbs and elbows worn bald, poses no problem. His visible ribs and tired pelt, broken whiskers, give him a shabby look that is only a pale reflection of his inner exhaustion. His eyes, dull from age and disappointment, sharpen focus just slightly at sight of the baboons.

Suddenly, the baboon smiles a strange rictus grin that tightens the lips on his hairless muzzle, squeezing the already close-set eyes even closer. He wags back and forth, showing off his expression, as if it is an advertisement for a show to come. But even this display is sufficient to send the littlest baboons into rollicking laughter, for reasons their mothers do not understand. A generational leap connects the old male and the young horde, and they share their weird insider joke until it dies out, suffused through the spirit of the group.

As fall progresses, their laughter will grow louder and more strained. Hard to see anything unusual in this—laughter is their most innocent form of social behavior. But the peals have an edge of uncanny awareness, as if the male baboon is showing off on purpose, looking for affirmation of his own behavior. Why? When has that ever been the case before? If, with my long living memory, I can't answer, then who could?

Memory in me is so old the very scale of it dwarfs the time-frames of most species. They came into being long after I had spread through fissures and cracks, attached to the heat of vents of deep sea trenches and stinking sulfur pots, in the still-fluid crust of the forming earth. I have seen the cycads emerge, the horseshoe crabs come into being, the cockroach scourge choose its flat, ugly form, and many other now ancient creatures take their first steps or slither toward what they became. But mine is a spotty record, filled with breaks and gaps, areas of intense detail and then amnesiac absences. This is the price of distributed existence and intermittent awareness.

Amphibian Agendas
Boston, Massachusetts

IN THE MUDDY SHALLOWS OF A warm, sheltered North American pond, some salamanders argue violently with a group of thin-skinned frogs. The frogs declare that a wave of deregulation has broken out, wreaking havoc with their tax-and-spend policies. But the salamanders are attacking back, taking them to task for their rampant embrace of neo-liberal agendas.

Callie pauses nearby and drinks from the cool water of the stream, but she cannot bear their shrill accusations, so she turns away in bewilderment. "Neoliberalism" is a term she does not understand, so she moves out of range in search of better conversation.

The salamander behaviors are morphing with terrifying speed. Breathing through their skins, the amphibians have gone through their social changes rapidly, absorbing bad habits like toxic nutrients.

No genetic mutation happens that fast. Downdrift has to be a cultural phenomenon, transferred through the medium of the social. Animals absorb behavioral influences through communications within their species and in connection to the larger ecosystems of which they are a part. But quantum forces are also working to synchronize these changes. The "lower" life forms, as the humans call them, those at the liminal edge of awareness, are exhibiting aggregate behaviors previously unknown, and that had its own terrifying aspects, as I know.

Slime Mold Sentience
Near Waltham, Massachusetts

CALLIE'S WANDERINGS EXHAUST HER. SHE IS not used to such long walks and has no idea where to find her food bowl. She moves into shadows under some brush in the woods and bumps into a gelatinous mass. Curious, she prods at it with her paw, then shudders as the formless shiny thing edges back at her. The specimen suddenly wraps itself around her feet, as if for the sake of comfort. She does not find this reassuring and is immediately aware of the wet colony's desperate neediness. A mass of cells expressing desire in a sticky gesture of outreach is unnerving and the touch of the chilly surface repulsive. But worse, its affective system seems to have no regard for social decorum, and it moves toward her without a proper introduction. *No thanks*, the calico says, and backs away, shrinking from its advances.

She withdraws into the shadows and lies down where she can sleep and dream on her own. The slime mold, stressed by the rejection, begins to move as a single body, not toward a food source, as is its habit, but toward an emotional one, seeking the nourishment of the cat's affection. The colony stops at the edge of the shadow and pines for the cat's affection. Callie sleeps, ignorant of the gelatinous organism's longings. She cannot respond to its crush or relieve its lonely need for affirmation. Her new awareness of the sentience of many of the creatures disturbs her.

October

Squirrel Industries
Woods near Waltham, Massachusetts

I WAKE FILLED WITH INTENSE AWARENESS. Everywhere around me the dying foliage of a North American deciduous forest exudes the steady, burning heat of decomposition. The slow, spontaneous combustion is exhilarating. I am thriving, stimulated by the acrid odors of autumn.

More is changing than the season. The stench of rotting vegetation is incredibly strong. When you calibrate your survival in relation to fluctuating atmospheres and chemical climate conditions, you get sensitive. Very sensitive. Human populations, distracted by the surface noise of politics and appetites, don't notice a thing. We, the other living beings, register the shifts and changes in the very medium of our existence.

The bright fall air is filled with clattering. The squirrels, usually conspicuous for their rampages and little fits, are dashing everywhere with needles they made from stripped twigs. They are knitting—and knitting and knitting. The characteristic busy-ness of their usual frenetic chatter, and rapid streaking up and down trees and across wires, has transferred into the endless *click click* of the tiny, sharp-ended instruments. Miles and miles of tightly knotted fabric flow everywhere. Tons of this miniature scarf material is being abandoned just like ticker tape falling from the machines of the past.

The squirrels are tired of the purpose-driven life, sick of storing nuts against the barren winter. Suddenly they are addicted to the luxury of squandering their energy in useless production and consumption.

They have gone mad, manic, obsessed to the point of neglecting their usual squirrel duties, and look a little lean in the haunches. They have crafted jaunty new clothes that set off their little squirrel bodies in the most cunning ways. One sports a tight peplum jacket that accentuates the torso and another wears a sweet, short, wide sweater in soft pink mohair that is just the ticket for a squirrel in her first fresh youth. Everything has been made in an absolutely perfect small scale.

Their scale. Not mine, not by a nano-micro-millimeter. At my scale, time and space change on the quantum level, in leaps and jump-cuts, parallel processing, not linear progress. Among these busy creatures, time is different. They live according to their metabolic rates, and speed up or down on seasonal highs and thermal lows. Just now, they are rushing on excess exuberance.

Their tiny needles create perfect little squirrel gloves and buttonholes edged with finishing stitches so small that larger beings would need an enormous magnifying glass to appreciate the workmanship. The noise is incredible. The woods are a veritable factory, a squirrel industrial zone. They are so productive that they are forced to create new markets for their output. Riding a wave of entrepreneurialism, they start a clothing line for sparrows, who are quite sartorially inclined. They try one for pigeons but it doesn't work. Those dullard birds are only interested in social media. They almost starve themselves, unable to cease their banal exchanges. "Coo coo, I'm here. Where are you?" is heard all over the landscape, a melodic note above the rapid-fire click of the squirrels' needles. No one answers the calls. Even the pigeons know the cooings are narcissistic notes and don't require response.

A group of satisfied mice, looking fine in their new squirrel-designed duds, are playing guessing games in the shadows. But for some reason, no one has ever seen a rat look good in a squirrel-made suit. Must be some kind of subtle prejudice on the part of the makers. The rats set up shop themselves and explore the potential of metallic fabrics and super-tight, body-hugging styles. These suit the rat population so well that a subsidiary industry in celebrity fashion is springing up among them—which irks the more modestly inclined squirrels.

Stylishly attired, the rats stay up all night in their clubs banging out the worst kind of crooning lounge music. The sight of those rodent hips in a slow swivel around a long, drawn-out note of low-toned vulgar music is enough to send the squirrels and mice into convulsions of laughter. But the nonstop clamor keeps the rest of the animals from sleeping. They pray for a change in rat styles and tastes. In the morning, the mice launch a whole new line of athletic gear as competition. The ski slopes are calling and pretty soon their cunning little skis will steal the show on the snow.

Callie's Transgressions
Woods near Waltham, Massachusetts

CALLIE WAKES IN A FITFUL STATE following another night outside. She stretches, tangled in a pile of leaves, and tries to shake the dew from her fur and banish the strangeness from her limbs. She considers turning back toward home, but immediacies are pressing. Hungry and out of sorts, she gives in to instinct. She stalks a young, undressed sparrow, who sports only a small tattoo on his tail feathers as any sign of deviation from the old norms. She brings him down swiftly, tearing through his throat and soft parts, not knowing that within the year this will become a violation of civic protocols and social norms. Then she disappears into the underbrush, out of sight, and washes the blood and feathers from her face before moving on, fastidious as always, but newly ashamed. Even before the civil codes are issued, they have subtle effects.

I share none of her meal, not directly. Warm blood is not my thing, and freshly killed flesh has too much vitality for my tastes, which run to fetid cesspools and heated off-gassing.

Chipmunk Tempers
Woods near Concord, Massachusetts

THE SCREAMING PUFFERY OF A CHIPMUNK chops through the still morning air, spiking it with high, violent sounds. The shrill staccato cries cut into the distant traffic noise, even slicing through the pitch of high-speed trains, the whine and squeal of their wheels and brakes. But what fury drives the spate of verbiage in this relatively peaceful clearing is unclear. Some slight, no doubt, in an early morning meeting, has left the chipmunk feeling peeved beyond all tolerating, full of vitriol and in need of release.

The chipmunk's harangue continues, a protest against a steadily emerging bureaucracy. The screaming creature feels the pressures of too many committees, tasks, unkind comments from inconsiderate colleagues. The chipmunks, energetic and hyper-vigilant on their own behalf, hate these new assignments and want to refuse them. But suddenly committee work is required everywhere. Whose idea was this?

The chipmunk shrieks again. The social energy is rising. Soon none may be immune from the viral spread of engagements and requests for community participation, attendance, meetings, and other manifestations of sociality. Among the branches, other comments focus on talk of a fall retreat to watch the leaves. A few graying seniors remark about their retirement funds and wonder aloud whether a place in the country might be in the offing sooner rather than later. The administrative work has piled up, apparently, and is testing their patience. The screaming chipmunk grows snappish and throws some perfectly good nuts to the ground in a flare of temper.

Archaean Views: Connections at a Distance

I FOLLOW CHEMICAL TRAILS AND PHYSICAL ones with equal abandon, not caring where they take me. I feel wavelengths and frequencies I know, mixed with ones that are unfamiliar. I lurk in the shadows and spots of sun, in the dark places between the cracks of filthy sewers and in the groundwater and runoff, drinking heavily. Normal spacetime means very little to my simultaneous awareness of distant points of the globe.

Half a world away, the poor lion, dogged at every step by flies, picks his way through the mud at the edge of a messy stream where human rubbish merges with natural debris. He is at a loss to understand what he is smelling. He has never encountered humans—or their waste—before. He switches his tail in an unsuccessful attempt to keep the rash of biting insects at bay. He slogs through fetid spots, thirsty and dispirited. The water at these fringes of the Serengeti is not fresh enough to appease his thirst or his longings for real sustenance. Just outside the reserve, the whiff of heavy metals in the stagnant waste is distasteful in ways that organic decay has never been. Stench and fragrance become two different categories in his mind. Survival, of which he might yet prove incapable, is at stake for him as he begins to see what lies beyond the limits of his world.

Callie, still just miles from home, grows confused at sounds she does not know and flashing lights she does not recognize. Fear, an unfamiliar sensation, is becoming a companion. I can sniff it, but not feed on it. That is reassuring. I have no taste for predatory habits and hope they are not in the script ahead.

Mouse Dancing
Walden Pond, Massachusetts

BETWEEN THE TREES, LONG BARS OF sunlight filled with dust motes cut across the golden air. Again, the quiet is disturbed by a riot of noise. In a small clearing, a live mouse is dancing, picking its way with stealthy terpsichorean accuracy across the crispy surface of a piece of toast. Among fallen leaves and brilliant colors, this unlikely mattress has drifted down safely enough to provide the stage for unusual behavior. The dervish of activity is a complete surprise, even to the mouse. Spinning-whirling-wheeling-squealing, it capers like a tiny banshee as the puckered, pockmarked, dry bread crunches underfoot. The scene has no sense to it, and the phrase "quiet as a mouse on toast" wafts through the air, fraught with nonsensical contradiction.

The need that the mice have for attention often outstrips their talents. The owls and ferrets have two solutions for

this, one of which is to turn their backs and pretend disinterest. The other is bloodier—much, much bloodier—and
rarely involves a knife, fork, or plate. Violence of that kind
will fall out of favor. The rodents will become increasingly
indignant witnessing acts of carnage. Already, they are
sending alert bulletins through the neighborhood. But this
afternoon it is still too soon for organized vigilante groups
to appear. A nearby ferret watches the mouse dance, but
holds its instincts in check, balancing appetite and caution.
An owl, never content with the laws of others, simply rotates
his head and waits, non-committal. New rules are emerging,
even without legislative commissions or overt bureaucratic
controls. The mouse finally crashes out, its wails dimin-
ishing like a disappearing siren. Exhausted, he stretches out
to enjoy the soft pillow of toast crust against his head. The
owl's wings muffle the sound of its flight, which is swift and
deadly. The disappointed ferret shrugs and waits for the
leavings of the meal.

Salamander Picnic
Walden Pond, Massachusetts

ANOTHER ROUND OF SALAMANDER ANTICS IS taking
place in the autumn woods. A big group outing, comprised
of extended families and pseudo-families, is underway at
the edges of a pool. They have collected food bright as their
red bellies or the stark yellow of their spots. The older ones
are picking at a few, very few, highly colored bits of fungus
and mixing them with all manner of beetles and flies, worms
and larvae, spiders and moths and grasshoppers to make a
banquet from an ancient recipe. These traditions may also
soon be at risk, but not yet. Lines of predatory permission
are being drawn based on the complexity of the nervous

system, for now. The study of neural circuitry is becoming a hot field.

A few newt cousins hang around on the outskirts of the event. Their feathery gills, so extravagant and showy, look unseemly. By subtle gestures and not-so-kind remarks, the salamanders let them know they find such displays of external organs vaguely obscene. I agree, but then, with me, self-effacement is a necessary skill, as well as a code of modesty. I am not one of those swaggering microorganisms, intent on high-profile publicity or epidemiological stardom. But the salamanders' sense of decorum is newfound, and comes off as arrogant to the newts, who, after all, still consider themselves part of the family.

Then an uproar bursts out. Some action too rapid for everyone's perception has taken place. The newts are screaming. The number of little ones in the water has diminished dramatically in just a split second. The volume of amphibian noises pumps up in protest against the infanticide. The salamanders swear up and down that this will be the last cannibal incident. Really, they say, truly, their lips still sticky. Shamed and chagrined, the salamanders pledge to give up the nasty activity that very afternoon, unwilling to appear more savage than other beasts. The spiteful newts, however, threaten to keep them under surveillance for months. They know that if and when the salamanders have a desperate urge, spawned by hunger or nostalgia for the taste of their own kind, they will use their tongues so fast that a multi-millisecond act removes a few young from the scene almost undetected. A nearly inaudible clicking pop—the only noise of which they used to be capable— always gives them away. The newts secretly record these incidents and use them periodically to shame their cousins.

But if anyone gets eaten that lovely fall afternoon, or later in the year, it is because some animal acts before anyone can lodge a protest and block the act. The line of taboos is shifting. Realizing the newts are watching, the salamanders are less flagrant in their actions. But fall afternoons make them peckish, and the taste of live food is positively intoxicating. Perhaps the newts are jealous as well as judgmental. Still, crime-sharing does not diminish the seriousness of the charges. The newts keep to their righteous stance, but their own food ethics might have to shift as well.

Raccoon Stargazing
Massachusetts Bay, near Ashmont, Massachusetts

DURING THE EARLY FALL NIGHTS, MANY creatures lie awake, fitting their soft bodies into the crooks of trees or tucking them among tight roots. They are bulking their fur and fat supplies for winter. But they are also swelling with a new capacity for imagining.

A group of raccoons, partying and schmoozing in the nocturnal air, reads the stars to each other as if spelling out the mysteries and histories of their kind. An infinitude of possibilities dawns on them, hearing their own voices in the darkness. The limits to imagination are dissolving. They gesture vividly, and something of human melodrama shows in the theatrical movements of the masked creatures. They are describing, telling, and pointing, as they stare through the night at the stars. These small incidents, seeming anomalies, are becoming widespread.

A rustling in the bushes disturbs their concentration for a moment. They follow the sound with their eyes, but it is only a late-returning chipmunk, back from a day at the office, clipboard in hand. They do not envy it those long work hours.

Archaean Views: Witnessing Minor Trespasses

I HAVE GLIMMERS OF AWARENESS OF different places, geographies, though my processing is wave-and-signal based, chemical and electrical, not sensual or visual. I know that salt air and brine particles mean I am receiving input from breaking waves and sea foam along a shoreline, that sulfurous air belches from a hot vent of volcanic activity, and that the foulness of waste from a processing plant is connecting me to abandoned land. Location and attention are almost the same thing for me.

Nearby, the cat begins to forage in the stubble of a field that has recently been harvested. A few swollen pumpkins remain, some broken. She nibbles away at the hard orange flesh, wondering about the challenges she will face if she pursues vegetarianism. At the moment, anything edible is welcome, and the soft yellow squash is sweet. A dusting of frost has come over the field during the night, and she and I can hear creatures below us, stirring in the earth, dug into their burrows where they are stocking thicker insulation into place for the winter ahead. I sense the remains of nocturnal imaginings hanging in the air.

With her connections to home stretched farther and farther, Callie is increasingly lost in a blur of navigational disorientation. Her survival instincts are barely adequate. She is used to supermarket fare, cans of the best feline pâté. She feels debased by constant hunger and the acts of violence or degradation to which it pushes her. This morning, she stoops to picking through refuse heaps repulsive to her nature. After witnessing the condemnation of the newts, she feels unwilling to pursue live creatures, which is not a game, not at all, now that it is sometimes a necessity. She feels vaguely ashamed and unhappy at the parts of herself that she has to tap into to survive.

The lion, more resigned and yet more dignified, feels he has less to lose, or less chance of recovering what he feels he has lost. His departure from his natural habitat quickly shows him how powerless he is to preserve the traditions of his kind. He realizes that the vastness of the plain on which he used to roam is hemmed in and under attack from all sides. He keeps abjection at bay, but only just, waiting for the right moment to make every move, as he picks his way into alien terrain at the fetid edges of the busy capital city of Kilimanjaro. The activity of traffic and busy streets bewilders him. He feels the loss of his pride in both senses. Both felines are confused and disoriented. Yet the subliminal connection between them has a driving force that shapes their individual intentions from radically different positions in the cultural evolution of their species. A need to understand the difference between the domestic and the wild—measure it and recalibrate its implications for their survival—provides an urgency to their movements.

I dog their steps, watchful, attached.

Gull on Guard
Cape Cod, Massachusetts

A GROUP OF SEAGULLS ARE ACTING as coordinated sentinels. They move their heads from side to side, surveying, always alert, then go aloft and hang, sure and stable, on the thermal drafts. Their eyes are watchful, ringed in orange. Black-backed, with pale gray legs dug into the sand at the edge of the wave line, they hold their beaks with an expression of consideration and care that communicates their awareness. Their actions are not all that unusual, but the gulls seem more gull-like than before.

The birds maintain their positions of surveillance as they take flight, keeping in tight formation. They hold those positions for a long, long time. They don't use overt symbol systems. Their eyes and beaks do not flash signals that can be read as notation, as code, as metaphor, or as mediated signs. Their communications are direct and immediate. Oddly, they remain oblivious to the ghostly sand crabs, who catch the patterns of their flight and imitate them in their dance on the sand, making a net of arcs and lines. The crabs' actions are as accurate as shadows cast by the movements of the gulls.

Attention begets attention. This is one of the laws of sentience. The sand flies on the beach take note of the crabs' movements and follow them along the curving currents of breeze close to shore. Those same winds keep the gulls aloft and aware on their upward drafts. Each is in its own place, but connected.

Ancient Crabs and Live Sushi
Beach near Weymouth, Massachusetts

FURTHER DOWN THE BEACH, SOME FINGERS of sunlight strike the flashing armor of ancient species, the silverfish, littered among the humid zones and rotting wood. A few yards away, a beach lies just beyond the grassy dunes. Horseshoe crabs are playing in the tangle of seaweed left at the wave line. These armored species carry five hundred million years of memory in their genetic material, so from their point of view, the changes happening around them are just a blip, a blink. What use do they have for adaptation, when all the millennia past have only altered them minutely?

Change seems frivolous—and rapid change positively trivial. They are the ones of old, or so they think. They see themselves as unchangeable monuments, the guardians of stability, committed to a way of life that replicates itself without any concessions to alteration of habits and decorum.

They repeat the shape of their days and patterns of their lives with the same consistency with which they reproduce the shape of their thoraxes, carapaces, and antennae of chitin and calcium carbonates. They are still made from the basic materials of the mineral salt solutions—or earthly air and seawater—in which they dwell.

But the silverfish are always ready to take advantage of shifts in available foodstuffs. They create a very small but steady supply chain that lifts starch and sugars from sites and objects and pushes them along to the front lines of consumption for themselves and others. I get drunk on the excess sugars, high on fermentation, thrilled by the effervescence in silverfish intestines. A generous instinct threads through their destructive activities and so they share generously.

When silverfish dance, their bright metallic armor ripples with liquid grace. Though they themselves never stoop to manufacturing, they are happy they have licensed their brand for a line of fluid athletic gear that flatters the stouter species of beetles and bugs, gives them a boost of confidence, and provides a small revenue stream for the designers. Everyone wants to be svelte and supple and to shine in the daily course of action.

At the edge of the shore some blue crabs are blinking in the daylight, their compound eyes flickering. Fashion is completely lost on them, dear things, since they have bad eyesight, and it hardly matters that they cannot accessorize.

They edge into and out of the ebbing waters of the mid-Atlantic estuary, drifting with the currents. Their summer foodstuffs have moved on, and the strange taste in the saline tide hints at winter preserves.

Callie looms into their view for a moment. She pauses by the water, breathing deeply. Her agenda does not match theirs and any attempt at stealth fails. From their habitual feeding grounds, the crabs watch her move along the shore. The salt air sparks her appetite and the thought of minnow sushi is hard to push away as she sees the small bright fish leaping in the shallows. Normally, she would have found them amusing, fun to chase, but these days she is not in the mood for play and has not been for some time. A fish meal is almost taboo, but temptation helps bend the rules.

Bottlenoses from a stray pod, too far into the estuary for their own good, are arcing through the surface of the water. Their companions have headed into the southern gulfs in search of warmer waters and easy living. But in the still-temperate bath of the bay, the dolphins laugh, the sound light as helium as they lean back into the waves. They have a sudden capacity to separate the gases from the air and sea, to distill a form of intoxicating vapor, and they see no reason at all to be sparing in their indulgence. The intake costs nothing, but the waste by-products have a slightly more worrisome property, since they spread on the waves with the light squeak and sparkle of broken glass. The cat catches her breath, inhaling the effects, and feels a rush from the gas of their laughter.

The dolphins ignore her, tossing freely in their own buoyant flotsam and jetsam, rolling with complete abandon. Below them, minnows, steeped in lore, swim in their schools and think their thoughts among the penetrating rays of sunlight far from the sandy sea bottom below. Knowing the hurricane season is almost upon them, they are grateful for any moments of relative calm. They course through the shifting currents of their days and nights with full awareness of the energy surges whose menace they calculate carefully.

The Dog's Life
Near Scituate, Massachusetts

CALLIE HAS ALREADY TRAVERSED MORE TERRITORY than she wants and witnessed strange events among the rodent and amphibian populations. But her contact with other domestic animals has been minimal since leaving home.

From down the beach, she sees a very old and vigilant St. Bernard walking slowly ahead of his human charge. Callie pauses her crab stalking and inhalation of dolphin laughter and watches carefully, assessing the situation. Conversation with an animal who shares her background will be welcome. Perhaps the dog will have news of other curious events.

The dog has the air of a venerable caretaker. He walks with dignity, his pride in his work evident as he carefully checks the path in advance of his human charge. Callie tilts her head with communicative attention, and the dog nods, pinches his eyes and raises his brows. Callie edges closer, a querying look quivering her eyebrow whiskers. The dog, always ready to exalt his own position, tells her that taking care of the man is not a simple job. He looks toward the man lagging down the beach. Callie, her whiskers twitching and eyes alert, agrees. She has always been on the receiving end of these arrangements. The dog says human caretaking is a much larger task than any assignment he might take on under the new regimes. New regimes? This is the first Callie has heard of institutionalized changes, shifts in the actual order of civic service. The dog confirms Callie's intuition and goes on with his own account.

In the language of sniffs and arches of the brow, a little nose wrinkling and mouth moving, growls and brief barks, the dog tells her that many of the suburban dogs have stopped working for human families. He shakes his noble head, eyes unbelieving. Rumor has it this is even more true among the trendy West Coast canines than here in the more traditional part of the country. He himself has stooped to consider new employment possibilities, looking at the postings on the hydrants and poles. But a career change is unlikely at his age, and he has his priorities.

Callie edges closer. After weeks of listening to screeching squirrels and silent crabs, the polite exchange is a treat. The man is absorbed in his own activities, and even if he casts a glance their way, he notices nothing out of the ordinary, just a housecat, tucked into the dunes, exchanging wary glances with his pet.

The St. Bernard quickly tells his tale. He was attuned to the activities of the human family, he says, carefully guarding all of the spaces they inhabited. As the children left home, he has been left alone with the aging father. The mother person had gone long ago, in a divorce the dog does not understand, only processes as physical separation and loss. Callie, missing her own human family, realizes her attachments are not only to physical comfort. She gives a sympathetic tilt to her calico head.

The dog goes on, telling Callie that he and his charge walk every day. The dog sniffs ahead, anticipating the pitfalls and hazards that wait on the wind and in the sidewalks, at the curbs and telephone poles, and under the hedges that separate yards from the pedestrian zones through which so many human beings pass. The human does not understand all the news he brings him, and follows his guidance, never knowing how many territorial squabbles are being avoided.

Humans live in casual ignorance of everything that matters, the dog admitted, sighing. They hardly know how much they need us. They miss every communication signal in the animal world. The human would be lost without the dog, constantly trespassing, with no idea of each day's boundary updates, who has moved on, and who is new to the neighborhood.

Callie can only partially agree about the importance of these matters. After all, she is following a signal trail that is different from an odor and also, she finds the notion of marking territory very canine. She feels quite free to roam at will and her notion of private ownership extends mainly to chairs and beds during certain hours of the day. The dog says he is resisting larger changes. Callie has her own assessment of his situation, but falls back onto feline aloofness rather than squandering more energy by sharing. The man whistles. Callie feels the conversation is at an end in any case.

Baboon Leadership
Edge of the Serengeti

IN THE DRY HEAT OF A deepening autumn immune to frosts and chills, the lion is now a mere absence, a vague recollection. The old hamadryas baboon begins to think about perfecting his interview techniques with the young and planning for his own succession. The notion of absolute mortality begins to take root, forming an unfamiliar unease in his mind. Reflection, recognition that this moment is not the only and always unending present, begins to split his awareness between that which is and that which is not. Holding both in mind at once puzzles him at first, but soon the concept of passing time begins to imprint his perceptions and organize his impressions in a comic-strip manner. Moments are becoming discrete from another and part of a sequence of successive events. Anticipation alters everything.

He wonders if the young male he has allowed into the group is really up for the task of leadership. Such assessments did not trouble him in the past. Now the grinning idiot annoys him more than he had realized. His expectations about succession have changed. But to rethink the choice would involve complications, so he swats the young one to keep him quiet, at least, and the youth obediently removes himself from the full line of sight as much as is possible in the open grassland.

Goat Literacy
Near Quincy, Massachusetts

WITH HER FUR DAMP AND PAW pads cracking from contact with the salt on the beach, Callie heads into the darker woods and slips onto a quiet country road. A fruit stand comes into view. The smell of a fall harvest hastens her steps. Food! Even settling for a salad would be just fine if, as she suspects, the menu at the stand is vegetarian.

As she approaches, eager for handouts, a beaver wraps a few apples in a sheet of newspaper and hands them to a goat, who grabs the package eagerly. Starved for intellectual material, he flattens the paper back out while he eats, reading headlines about the stuttering speech patterns surfacing among African hyenas. The beaver shrugs. Like he cares about items from the foreign desk. Callie waits, giving the beaver a seductive glance with a twist of her calico torso to encourage him to let something appetizing fall her way. Nothing happens. She sidles over to the goat, thinking he might be in a sharing mood, but stops short of rubbing up against him. He smells like a barnyard, Callie thinks. He turns his back, very pointedly.

Wiping his chin as he eats, the goat goes on reading about

the bad habits and political aspirations of the spotted jackals. They never show up for meetings on time and calculate their schedules with random variables. Now, against all odds, they are bidding for positions in Parliament. Callie hopes scraps of food can roll in her direction along with these snippets of news. Other goats surround the reader, who has begun to editorialize. The hyenas have exhibited a vile adherence to a low-level libertarianism, the report says, as professional obligations cramp their social calendars. Still, they have made successful bids for several spots in the legislature, so they may get some traction on policy shifts in their favors. The goats shake their heads, foreseeing chaos down under.

Callie is not sure whether the goat is making up his reports or really reading. The description of the way the hyenas run a numbers racket betting on their own votes seems far-fetched. The goat pushes his assertions to his assembled brethren, who nod as he describes the way the hyenas calculate probable outcomes and assess their odds. Profit sharing, he says, is not in their cognitive frame. Profiteering is their preferred form of the noun. The goat drones on about the hyenas' endorsement of a flat tax. Callie is not much in the mood to talk politics, and she has always avoided the tax code, but the soporific effect of financial updates in the goat's account provides the perfect opportunity for a stealth attack on the crates behind the stall. The beavers' eyes are at half-mast

While all eyes are on the goat, or else drooping, Callie sneaks around the stall to see what edible treats might be in the cast-off pile. Merchandising is a wasteful business, and perfectly good zucchinis and peppers, rejected for a little bruise or discoloration, provide Callie with an ample meal. Nearby, a land tortoise is sorting coins into piles, trying to correct the mess the beavers have made of the till. This gives him plenty to do, and he sandwiches his work periods between bouts of lettuce consumption, quite content. He has no objection to sharing the greens with the housecat. And Callie thanks him profusely, her mouth full of lettuces.

The goat eats almost as fast as he reads, but he shares the gist of the news before consuming the paper. He milks his report, savoring the best bits of the headlines so they can be taken in slowly before he swallows. The next piece of hyena news captures everyone's attention. The hyenas have become aware that blue eyes are a strong marker of "migratory genetics," a phrase the animals have never heard before, so the goat bleats it out with exaggerated emphasis. The pigment is washing out of their eyes, replaced by a cerulean tint that signals the onset of narcissistic disorder. In the Senate chambers, the newly blue eyes of the black lemurs appear just as the striking creatures abruptly develop a narcissistic tendency. The jackrabbits in their vicinity suddenly cannot bear to be around them. African bunnies crawl under over-stuffed brush and tangled hedges to get away, finding the exaggerated swagger intolerable.

The tortoise trembles at the scale of change in the report, shaking his venerable head in a way that is meant to impress Callie. He is too polite to trundle off as the goat continues to detail the rapidly spreading outbreak of narcissism. *Comical, comical,* the goat chuckles. Not everyone sees the news as humorous. Looks are exchanged among the beavers, who wonder if the plague will spread and affect business. They have no experience with disturbances caused by psychic disorders, only swift currents and tough bark.

Callie watches for an opportunity to swipe some ripe red peppers from the pile. The tortoise pretends not to notice, feeling a soft spot for the pretty calico young enough to be his grandchild. The goat continues, dramatizing at every opportunity. Now the report turns to accounts of the great apes. They are so in love with their newly blue-eyed selves that they sit for hours with grins pasted on their faces, stroking their wide chests. Massive numbers of little chimps with sapphire irises are jumping up and down in sheer enthusiasm for their own beings. *I love me, I love me, I LOVE ME!* they cry, drunk on exuberance and nearly rattling their teeth loose from their jaws.

Even the gators, always an unpredictable species, are apparently being intensely affected by what is called "the blue-eyed fever." As the worst of it comes on them, the males stand up on their hind legs and bellow smugly, swaying with compulsive lack of grace. Callie has never heard of such a thing. Nor has the tortoise, though he adopts a look of sage reflection. Callie wonders if she can catch a diagnostic glimpse of her own eyes, check for hints of blue in her green irises. A pail used for scrubbing pumpkins offers a still surface of reflection, but the mirroring water shows barely a hint of change.

A commotion in the fringe of bushes by the roadside shifts her attention, and the tortoise trundles off at last. As usual, the noise is caused by mice. They are frenetic, and at this beginning of the harvest and hoarding season, they should be hiding food everywhere as fast as they can. But the blue-eyed syndrome has thrown them off, too. They are chasing their tails, banging their chests, and swooning in heady delight. They have given up stealing grains and stashing them in favor of declaring love for their little selves.

The beavers, sounding the alarm and fearing for contagion, scream a warning about the "blue-eyed syndrome!"

Callie takes advantage of the uproar to scoop up a few more yams and yellow squash, which helps to calm her homicidal urge to attack the rodents. The goat who started the whole mess takes pleasure in the random chaos of the scene. Though he pretends to be a political pundit, he is really a nihilist at heart, and confusion provides him almost as much pleasure as consuming the last of the news.

Hippo Babble
Mara River, Kenya

AN OCEAN AWAY, IN THE VAST subcontinent, the lion stalks the river's edge, where game is ample. He is unused to having to hunt for himself, as the lionesses took care of these matters for the pride, but an opportunity arises and he takes it, satisfying his belly and tongue. He soaks up the warm life of his slaughtered victim without remorse, a category of response not available to him.

During an afternoon of quiet digesting, the lion is annoyed by a troop of apes who cluster in trees not far from some hippos. The simians are full of commentary on the firestorms of change. They rage with intensified capacity for anger, as if released from the social controls of their tribes. Near the river, they are relatively far from the tangles of urban life, so they have almost no idea what the civic animals are thinking. In the cities, canines are rapidly climbing the social ladder, descending into responsibility and imposing local control. The apes have no idea what is happening at a distance, but they sense change on the wind. They throw sticks at the hippos and make a nuisance of themselves all afternoon. But they have reason. The day before, the same troupe witnessed some of their own get caged by hunters. They protested and fled, embittered by their powerlessness.

They can still hear the sounds of their incarcerated brethren on the trade winds and global currents. As the lion tosses and the hippos mumble, they mourn and cry, calling for struggle ahead. Freedom is a concept born of adversity. A growing desire for self-determination swells through the group. The lion wonders about his own condition, contemplating the concept of freedom for the first time, but wondering if it is already in the past for him.

The hippos are in a docile mood. Food is ample, so are mates—no outside species ever threatens a hippo romance. Their land rights were recently threatened, but they have formed a federation to promote their wetland claims. Some wear patches on their hides, signs they are official guardians of the territory. Very sensible.

Along the riverbank, the hippos, though too big for words, make small talk nonetheless. It trickles up through the mud and the gentle burble of sound bubbles breaks on the surface. The hippos have very soft voices, except when they bellow, which is rare and getting rarer. They are happy muttering among themselves while the keeper birds, ox-peckers, work away in pursuit of the parasites attached to their thick skin. They cannot manage this task themselves; their tiny limbs and barrel bodies are ill-suited to anything requiring dexterity.

The ox-peckers, inveterate gossips, make fun of the herons and egrets. Transient hitchhikers, the ox-peckers catch a few minutes' rest on the soft islands of the broad-backed and far-from-placid beasts, pretending to snatch news from the air in exchange.

The ox-peckers sniff. News is not something you just pick from the vibrating airwaves. News has form. Substance. Journalism is a craft, they say, not random trade in verbal goods and trivia. The hippos let the little, yellow-billed birds have their way while the herons take flight, following their communication lines. From time to time, the hippos sink underwater to talk where they are intelligible only to each other. They can scry any verbiage that takes aquatic form. The small murmurings vibrate through the cloudy river, making waves that are at odds with the motion of the fluid. The water winds slowly downstream, carrying the hippos' verbal effluvia and the nitrogen-rich exhalations.

Along a distant horizon, a line of chimps disciplines their troop to make war, systematically, but without instructions from anyone. They have had organizing impulses before, but never such pointed military interests or ambitions. Mercifully, their attention span will limit the effect of their intentions.

Hawk Eyes
Quincy, Massachusetts

HIGH ABOVE THE EARTH, A HAWK watches the cat pick her way through yet another patch of woods. He reads every quiver and shake of bough or branch, motion in the leaves, disturbance of the foliage, or sign of activity on the ground. Entire days pass under the hawk's eyes, but he refuses all requests to submit records of his movements to the emerging administration. He operates as an independent contractor and sole proprietor, taxes paid up front, and doesn't like paperwork or bureaucracy.

Keeping his back to the sun, the hawk hangs, invulnerable. He watches the cat, her coat a little dirty, paws a little sore, as she wanders. Her belly is full of harvest vegetables, her mind overflowing with news, and she follows her instincts without any clear sense of the larger geography. But the hawk is a cartographical wizard, and his view of the landscape shows him all the errors of her ways. She needs a map, or GPS, but the Feline Positioning Systems have not come on the market yet. Copyright issues and law codes are holding things up. Callie is not at all sure these applications are going to be made freely available to all species in any case. Not everyone embraces open source software, and she is wary of viruses and deceptive terms of service agreements. She was not born yesterday, after all.

The hawk has a pathetic sensitivity to every slight. The cat, eager to escape from the hawk's surveillance, tries to tiptoe away. He feels insulted by her low estimate of his skills and takes her gesture as a provocation. Dipping his flight, he swoops to earth, flaunting his ability to terrorize the smaller birds and random mammals. His dented fovea magnifies the central objects in his vision. Callie knows the hawk has her in his gaze and is dipping toward her. She feels the air move and his wings come close. Her fur rises along her spine. The rapid fury of feline defense pulses through her. She turns the hawk away with decisive critical commentary and very little ceremony. Her hiss charges through the vicinity. The hawk flaps off, disgruntled, but not up to a fang-and-claw contest just to save his pride.

As he glides toward the woods Callie has just left, he spies a dark shadow edging across the landscape, the sign of rot from an advancing bacterial army. The marshaling of forces is ominous, as if their motion is driven by emotion and not just the opportunity to absorb moisture. Even he is shocked by their aggression.

The raptors are somewhat resistant to the transformations that are occurring. Along with the vipers and leeches, sharks, and parasites, they have the least need to modify their behaviors. But the social seepage will overtake them, too. By the end of the year, the hawks, to their own surprise, will be using table settings, linen, and other accoutrements of fine dining. They still have so much to learn, and their table manners will be one area where improvement is dramatic. While this works well for the hawks, the impact on rats, mice, and bunnies is still not what everyone would have wished, had a poll been taken among the broad population.

November

Cheetah Carnage
African Plains, near Kenya

THE LION SNIFFS THE AIR, TAKING the temperature (psychic and thermal) of the environment. From his spot in a clump of concealing grasses on an African plain near the southern edge of Kenya, he tracks a herd of grazing animals as they suddenly let loose a massive wave of gentleness. The palliative effect spreads like a mild mist over the landscape, softening the drive to aggression. But the predatory instincts of some nearby cheetahs and a group of howling jackals does not subside simply because of the presence of the doe-eyed gazelles, with their dark-streaked flanks and twisted horns. As the lovely gazelles become aware of their presence, fear oozes a scent into the wind and intensifies the bloodlust of the killers. Suddenly the morning is threaded with threats, whiffs of latent violence waiting for the right moment. The cheetahs sniff, their lips curling in anticipation, unreformed and unrepentant.

The pathogenic species rejoice in the dirt near the lion, hoping for slaughter. He hears nothing of their sinister jubilation; the frequencies on which they operate are far from his sensing systems. Meanwhile, a host of creatures rapidly display new characteristics in a veritable parade of transformation. A dik-dik and an oryx, their features changed to wild dog faces, pass in pursuit of an elegant impala, courting her with song. A wildebeest is struggling to shed large soft paws and curved fangs, suddenly acquired accessories for which he has no use. A single antelope is spooked by the site of these aberrations and triggers the flight of the herd. Then the cheetahs give chase, stuck in the feedback loop of stimulus that escalated long before civil codes could adjudicate action. The cats and their prey go down in a muddle of wounds and regret and forbidden pleasures. An irresistible impulse shocks the lion into action, and he joins the bloody mess. A cloud of dust cloaks the cats' remorse. The lion, feeling an unfamiliar wave of emotional turbulence, pulls himself away, but the appetite for warm, bloody meals courses through his brain stem as his nostrils fill with the scent of the recent kill.

The capacity for speed is shared by predator and prey, but the swift pace of interbreeding is calming some outlying behaviors, leveling them off through the law of averages. The cheetahs, finished with their bloody job, shake themselves free of the carcass and at least have the sense to look mildly ashamed. The gazelles turn their graceful heads away from cheetah's actions and experience a ripple of repulsion seeing one of their own ripped limb from limb, its fresh, supple flesh pulled from bones.

Grazing is still considered a fine and legitimate way of life, and watching the agile bovines, the lion is jealous, since for him grass has little nutritional value. His domestic cousin is at a great advantage with her ability to be nourished by vegetables. The antelopes practice herd control, so justified killing is no longer acceptable as a way to control population size. The act in which he and the cheetahs collaborated is a violation of the emerging terms of the killing laws.

The gazelles surround the sparse remains of their companion, so recently brought down by the cats. But though they care for their own kind as much as any other species, they quickly release the body for consumption. Their souls are social, and their herd behavior trumps their individual concerns. The gazelle felled a few minutes earlier has become a corpse, matter returning to earth. Their bond with the victim wanes with its lifeblood.

Springbok Business
African Plains

EVEN AS THEY EVOKE NEW SENSATIONS, these familiar scenes continue to play out. The antelopes and gazelles withdraw to a safe distance and a group of springboks edges into view. Their activities show clear evidence of the downdrift. They run a small business now, having reached an agreement with the marauding baboons, who do their publicity to assure them considerable kickbacks. After considering their career options, they have decided to bank on their skills in the decorative arts, using their acute capacity for visual discernment. While the lion assiduously cleans his face and paws, he watches them lay out a display of matching furnishings and textiles, all of the highest aesthetic quality. They are mostly assembled from natural woods and textiles in the fawn-and-buff colors of their kind. They use the edge of the savannah as their temporary showroom, promoting their decorator services with the swaggering assistance of the baboons. The supply chains are slow. They have trouble providing the customers with goods. But many a baboon now sits on springbok-supplied chairs, somehow getting their deliveries ahead of time.

The fussy springboks, not wanting their rugs and cushions soiled, bribe a band of jackals into eating the final carrion remains. A waste of money, really, as the jackals would have done it anyway. They drag the sinews and hooves away for gnawing, making hideous cries to keep everyone else at bay. Such noisy eaters, they are kind of disgusting.

The lion cannot be paid for anything, not that anyone is offering. He follows an honor code that prohibits all base transactions and violation of his noble precepts. But the cheetahs skulk in the shadows at night and perform stealth raids, as if no one notices. New modes of governance are in the air and in the water, where information travels rapidly. The gazelles think wheels of administrative change are moving too slowly. They are loath to continue playing victim to the murderous cats, but the poor lion, wearier and wearier, cannot keep waiting for food to come to him. He gets up and sniffs at the kill site cleaned by the jackals. Precious little remains. Hunger is an unkind companion, all too willing to keep him company.

The gazelles survey the landscape and communicate their findings among the scattered herd, trying to cope with the multiple changed dimensions of their situation. Experts in distant learning, able to analyze massive amounts of phenomenal data, they sniff the air, trying to assess how widespread the changes they have just witnessed might be. They smell the ground, they analyze the varied colors of the land and motions in the grasses. They pass the signals among themselves, making collective sense. They grasp the simultaneity of here-and-there intuitively, with a quantum-dimensional collapse of remote and proximate space that I can relate to completely. They signal to each other, like a massive multi-celled processor, and then send bulletins to each other through the trace of hooves on the dusty ground and the soft snort of their blunt warm noses. Their communications are massive, overwhelming.

The springboks are busy all this time with the display of their wares. The herd leadership moves quickly to hire a public relations firm to supplement the crude advertising techniques of the baboons. By afternoon, a delegation of hoopoes, cranes, and hornbills arrives with an impressive collection of whiteboards and projection displays. The birds clearly know their business, and talk the talk of public relations, but getting the herd to focus its message is not going to be easy.

The lion is amazed at the rising rate of transactions and considers this activity unseemly commercialism. He is a traditionalist and quite conservative in his ways. Change offers no benefits that he can see.

Fox Tales
Quincy, Massachusetts

A TROTTING BAND OF FOXES NEARLY tramples the sleeping Callie, and their sudden appearance breaks rudely through her dreams of home and satisfying domesticity. The vixen in the lead is carrying a silver key on a silver chain, and under her arm are tucked a few slim, elegant ballpoint pens and a roll of contracts. Callie sits up abruptly. Contracts? Foxes are averse to physical labor, but since when do they see themselves as part of an intellectual class, as professionals?

The group stops, circles, and begins a meeting just a few feet from where Callie stares. The lead fox unrolls the papers and a pair of assistants administers credentials. What great standards, what fine quality, they exclaim, patting each other on their long red backs. Reputation, that's what counts! Who needs a degree or a handful of letters behind a name? They whisper and trill in their high-pitched tones and then quiet down while the vixen lectures on topics of tort and liability. One of the younger ones is confused, and looks around for layer cake and cream. . . .

One senior vulpine, a silver-tongued and elegant figure quickly adopting the attributes of the professoriate, tips his hand just enough to give away a hint or two about case law. Sly and wise, he draws a fat salary and has quickly positioned himself to control the discourse around certain areas of legal theory. He is fond of his own voice and full of importance. A young fox, eager for affirmation, follows the argument as if it were a rabbit trail, though he is dubious that the rewards will be the same.

Then the old fox, his briefcase overflowing, decides to take advantage of the size of the crowd to do some recruiting for his pet project. The leaflets in his hands promote his vision of a museum for the animate creatures of the earth. Folklore, he explains, handing out the brochures, is an inventory of oral tales, accounts from the early days of the animals, of tribes and clans, predators and survivors, including stories of heroic kits and legendary Reynards. His family history goes way back, he boasts, swaggering a little. The young foxes he has trained—and here he gives a nod to the sycophantic kits pretending to hang onto his every word—are good at fieldwork. The enormous body of material they have gathered has all been donated to the collections, along with a mass of somewhat tasteless recordings on moleskin. But they have no taste for the tedium of organizing materials or putting them into systematic classifications for use. As he prances and brags, the brochures get loose and fly around the clearing. The photos of the museum show a mass of chimps, all making a mess of the shelving units while a few lazy felines pretend to supervise. Less process, more product, the chimps proclaim, flaunting their pleasure in the disorder. Their archival training is more rhetoric than substance.

The fox continues his swaggering campaign among the kits, whose eyes grow large with the idea of their legacy to posterity. Such tales they tell . . . making up one thing after another to please the old fox. Quite enough for the cat. Callie has a nose for authenticity and is not about to be duped by a swaggering Reynard. With a warning to the gullible kits, she dashes off, tail high to show her disdain.

The Committee on New Pathologies
Near Newton, Massachusetts

CALLIE KEEPS TO THE SHADOWS AS the morning stretches to noon in the woods. She hears the distant sounds of human beings attending to entertainment industries and sports in their daily round of distractions and unproductive labors. She knows those habits well. But her attention is drawn to the furious busy-ness of a heap of beetles and worms. An army of praying mantises assesses the insect heap, huddled over their account books. Processing their mass of big data, these accountants are a bit surprised at the acceleration of atrophy among various populations. Many species numbers are down now that the pressure of survival is being modified by new laws against certain kinds of predation. This seems counter-intuitive, but survival provides a basic drive, without which motivation falters. Some of the bug bodies are the result of swarm suicides or simply plagues of ennui to which the insects give in.

Still, in addition to these unintended consequences, strong collective impulses toward control of food kill have emerged, and the rules of order are changing. One of the mantises is holding a copy of the guidelines that have been issued by the Committee of New Pathologies. The cat, as is often the case, has only a superficial relation to that text, and still feels entitled to pick which laws obtain in her particular situation. She has never been one for simple adherence to rules. But the mantis is quite intent, his head tilted side to side to follow the lines of reasoning.

Other mantises are scribbling as fast as they can, creating large columns of what look to Callie like random numbers. Presumably they are observing something in the mixture of shiny, inert and wiggling, writhing masses of worms and insect matter. One of them is reading aloud from the findings of the Committee, leaning over the shoulder of his companion.

Callie cannot decide which is more compelling: the weird accounting or the strange report. She follows the fast fingers of the census takers, then looks back to the mantis holding the report. Drawn up to full height now, eyes bulging, abdomen suspended above the moist ground by its strong legs and full haunches, he is a handsome thing, elegant in his gray-green shell. Callie does not interfere in his performance, just listens as he intones. Preserves of endless security have been established (kill-free zones are being tested in the wetlands, for instance), and time is increasingly unfettered by responsibility. The cat wonders why this latter point merits a report. She has always taken this approach. Perhaps she is misunderstanding the bombastic mantis. She wants to ask, but is unsure how to formulate the question in mantis sounds. She has neither wings nor tymbals among her parts. These linguistic barriers are still very real and will be until the universal translation apps appear, though Callie can make sense of many more languages than she can speak.

The mantis, now noticing Callie and pulling himself up to make an even greater impression, pauses for dramatic effect. He gives a quick glance at all of his busily scribbling companions, and then goes on. It seems that the lassitude of the strong is now observable along with the persistence of the meek. This convoluted sentiment is a bit hard for Callie to take in all at once. She may have hit her limit on mantis epistemology. He continues. The rewards of just being are now insufficient for our needs.

Talk of "being" puts Callie off as fast as lectures on "time." She has never been a fan of modern philosophy, even if she is happy that the tendency to violent confrontation is disappearing under social pressure. She puts some distance between herself and the mantis, glad for a reprieve from the verbiage. She is beginning to see the hazards of so much cross-species communication.

Happy Meals
Near Newton, Massachusetts

HALF AN HOUR LATER, SHE BUMPS into a pack of coyotes, surprising them outside a fast-food restaurant where they have just eaten. They are making a big show of having ceased to bring down their own prey. They sport very sleek coats, thickened in anticipation of a winter of outdoor exercise and sport. They parade their new stance with too much swagger to be believed, demonstrating that they can act civilly when they desire. Secretly, they still prefer food to be fresh, pumping with blood, but they have just had a meal of deep-fried chicken fingers (slightly confused about the anatomical reference) and potatoes cut in long rectangles, also fried. Not exactly food, they think, having used massive amounts of ketchup to ease the mess down their gullets. Is junk food an improvement or a downfall? A degradation of character or increase in standing? They are still smacking their lips and wiping their chins with one napkin after another in a conspicuous display of normalcy. Their show of non-predatory behavior is suspicious.

Callie is disgusted. She knows they will get fat living on too much cheap food—if they obtain it regularly without physical effort. That kind of consumption is so canine. Still, when they toss their doggie bags toward the garbage, she is happy to tear through the papers. Hunger trumps pride. Quickly finished with the sad remains of their meal, she walks away, hearing them belch rather more loudly than is absolutely necessary. If she looks back, she knows she will see them picking their teeth in public. She is not sure she can support any of them for school board if they run in the spring elections. That's still a long time off and improvement might occur, but she has already heard rumors and seen some of the campaign literature.

Archaean Views: Some Personal Information

WE SHARE A COMMON ANCESTOR, YOU and I, and all the other life forms. But I do not remember that first great-great-grandparent, that first cell membrane formed around a bit of genetic material capable of replicating itself and transforming energy from the world around it into food. Feeding and breeding are the two criteria of life. The rest is just elaboration.

Everything that breathes in and out, or transacts energy exchanges with the world—that is, all the many infinitely varied creatures of the earth, along with the plants that grow, the bacteria that breed, fungi that mass and mutate, the gelatinous fishes and the cartilaginous ones, the worms that crawl, the bugs that fly—are all derived from the same miraculous common ancestor. That organism's defining barrier—the cell wall across which all transactions are mediated—became the single sole distinction on which the line between sustaining self and excluded otherness is maintained.

Me, I am minute, a dot of unicellular singularity. You? To me you are a raging metropolitan mega-plex, expanding and seething with diversity and complexity, the intersection of many multiplicities of systems and conditions. I am amazed at the uptaking, expelling, processing, and casting off of waste in your many channels, streams, unending cycles. I can hardly fathom your being with its interlocking parts of micro- and macro-units and interwoven dependencies.

Our time scales—yours and mine—are as different as our size and complexity. To me, all of the follies of the animal kingdom are the trivial business of a few seconds of my historical memory. Nearly three-quarters of the earth's existence has passed in my presence, billions of years. Compare that to the mere millions in which primitive arthropods and other organisms came into being. And you? A blip on the screen, a tweak in the evolutionary chain, a phenomenon of rapid acceleration. I will long outlive you and the changes wrought on this world by your machinations. No matter how hot the air or dark the sky, how cold the ice, how toxic the seas, I am of that earth and can thrive in it. I was here when the very surface boiled and the atmosphere had not yet settled.

I wonder what my effect is on the downdrift behaviors, or whether I am affected by them, like the other animals. Like you, I believe that because I think, I am, that because I have awareness, I have free will. Childish? Delusional? Am I a who? Or a what? Do I have the capacity for independent action? Or am I simply part of the mechanical effects of the physical world, in spite of my fierce autonomy and aggregate capacity for action? I am part of so many systems and places that I am integral to the habitat of every living thing. The forces I see at work in the downdrift are not physical, but social, and the social sphere is a medium. The communicative exchanges among us shape the world actively. I am a survivor, but can rescue no one and nothing. I absorb, I process, I filter, and repeat, replicating endlessly—and I adapt rapidly to any and all conditions. Hence my success.

Punk Hawk
Newton, Massachusetts

THE CAT'S PATCHES FLICKER AS SHE picks her way through yet more underbrush. The strange business of the mantises is still with her, and not too far off, a group of the insects puts their long hands together and waves side to side. Callie narrows her golden eyes, assessing the scene. A pair of badgers pass by, stroking their black whiskers. But she is not sure they are as innocent as they pretend to be. She senses the change in the air, the way a piano tuner feels the least twinge in one percussive note among the whole range of the keyboard's striking sounds or the way a coyote scents the shift of mood in a group by changes in body odor and knows it is time to act.

Callie, neither king nor commoner, not a noble soul nor a disregarded one, simply one among the others, reflects on when and how the time will come when things will be stable again, when the forms of social mutation that are proliferating everywhere will settle. Around her, the very last leaves, the sap in their stems snapped by the chill, break free of their branches. Late fall and the world is stripped bare. Callie wants more than anything to be home, go home. She would even welcome the human petting and silly talk she has to put up with to have access to warmth and a secure food supply she could indulge in without guilty reflection.

A young raptor preens in the sunlight; the glinting rays from his adolescent piercings catch her eye. She is wary. But in response to her cautionary look, he shrugs. They are not acquainted. He is focused on fashion and caught up in attitudes. Working in self-defense, a committee of squirrels has installed a video screen on a pole near his nest to wean him from warm blood to cool media. The animation of mice and birds plays nonstop, but the therapy is not working. The screen is way too close, and flat. His vision meant to detect movement at a distance. What use to him are the flat graphics on the screen? They have no odor, no soul, no living energy. He is obsessed with the small living things around him. The least motion of the squirrels in the branches sends him into paroxysms of predatory anticipation. Conflict-free zone? He has not gotten the message. With the arrogance of youth and the privilege of his position, he is challenging food-chain hierarchies and decision trees in governance.

Callie finds his attitude obnoxious and lets him know with a curl of the lip and a bit of spit. She has no interest in the negotiations of the raptor, but he throws the matter in her face, daring her to say anything about who will be allowed to eat whom in the new order. His tone becomes belligerent, and Callie feels it behooves her to end the conversation before it becomes threatening. Laws are one thing, talons are another. She takes off, disgusted, and the hawk pursues her, nipping at her ear. The taboo on hunting cramps his style, but no protocols have been issued about harassment. He nips her and blood springs to the small cut on her ear. Callie is genuinely scared. When he abruptly turns his attention toward the smell of living mice nearby, she is relieved. Resisting her own impulses as she watches his violent feast, she crawls, more angry than hurt, into a tight space between some rocks and a fallen log.

Not only do the raptors refuse to reform, but the punk raptors refuse to learn to read. Universal education has no value as far as they are concerned. Sure, they have physical limitations and find it hard to use devices like pads and phones because their curved talons slip on the smooth glass. They use this and their illiteracy as their excuse for not conforming to the laws, but among the ranks of the hunted, that excuse is not convincing.

Callie watches a pair of young pigeons crouching out of his sightline, and a gamboling troupe of small voles and moles freezes in their tracks as the sound of the hawk's dying meal sends chills through the neighborhood. The rodents have been lobbying the newly established Control Committees for political equilibrium within the shifting social ecology. Now they are rethinking the whole business, loath to call attention to their cause and worrying about retaliation. The hawks are killing machines, relentless and unrepentant.

Though safe in her spot, Callie's limbs cramp uncomfortably. She is silent, aware that the hawk either can't or won't restrain himself. He shifts his grip from the still-pulsing remains of his meal, the initial spurt of hot, red blood mixed with the taste of fur. This has become repugnant to some other animals. But the hawk has no conscience with which to battle. His concern is for what is in his belly at day's end. As compensation, he offers surveillance services to the cowering survivors, but they know he cannot be trusted. Once he takes flight, he is untouchable, and notions of community and the greater good are not translatable into his mewing cries. He

has no concept of fairness and no one is likely to teach him—
at least, no one among his peers.

The Sadness of the Elephants
Somalia

THE LION CONTINUES HIS TREK, AND the sights before his
eyes become less and less familiar every day. Everywhere he
passes, the landscape is marked by human use and the sights
and sounds of distress from other species. Panting with heat,
he pauses for a break. Desperate for water, he crouches by a
bleak boulder near a field ravaged by waste, its ground still
punctuated with hundreds of burrows dug by active rabbits but
edged by sharp silver threads twisted for some human purpose. The heat shimmers. The air is so dry it sucks the moisture
from his eyes. Then, in the thick atmosphere, a rolling wind of
cold air comes along the ground. The tone is dark and the
smell dreadful, deeper than death, a kind of pervasive melancholy. The lion sniffs. What can it be that is so heavy, as if
despair has taken the physical form of a chilling wave? He
hears a collective sigh.

The elephants. Distant but still within range, their cries
carry over the mistreated landscape. They are sinking everywhere, and the pachyderm depression is so heavy it produces
powerful sad winds that threaten the hares in the burrows.
They shiver and catch cold. The mice in the straw by the sides
of the gray giants also feel an ache and a fever and a pressure
in the chest. Their small cries are mixed in the deeper notes,
and their sadness is part of the dark wind as well.

When a species is dying—not just individuals—the world
changes shape. A whole piece of the ecological architecture is
disappearing with no possibility of replacement. The horizon
of optimism is shrinking, and on the African plains, across the

Indian subcontinent, as well as in the zoos worldwide, the elephants lie breathing heavily, more and more slowly, as the life runs out and their memories drain into silence and absence. Their sadness saturates the earth, soaking roots and tingeing water with a strain of melancholy that stains the future with the legacy of the past. Like heavy metals, these memories cannot be eliminated from the systems of the earth. But like ephemeral dreams, they cannot be kept vital without their species.

Mutant Mass
Somalia

THE LION PRESSES ON, PASSING FROM the savanna toward the city, his thirst unassuaged, wearing sadness in his heavy tread. He threads through a dense patch of jungle where a nocturnal group of civets and grasshoppers gathers to consider the questions of social pathology and the effect on the mutating mores. The frosts have not even touched the earth in the temperate regions, and the draft of the Committee for the Study of New Pathologies is already filled with portents that do not bode well. Copies have arrived here and are being distributed and studied. The lion sits on the sidelines and pauses long enough to get the gist of the reports. These are being updated constantly, so violent are the waves of transformations.

The meeting of the busy African civets and pensive grasshoppers takes place under the auspices of a company of elect horned owls, pledged to vegetarianism, who are still wise in the way of their stereotypes. Toxic wastes taint the nearby sewers, a fact of which all are keenly aware. The owls, resolute and resigned, know they can do nothing but watch and wait.

A massive crowd of migrants appears without warning, all mutants. The spontaneous scene is bizarre, the scale of threat to the species, all the species, suddenly more clear. Simultaneously, at a microscopic scale, some emerging strains of bacteria mass in an unpleasant way, as if looking for a fight. Simultaneously, silhouetted against the horizon, a straggling array of animals files by in a long line. Their outlines are bulky, difficult to read in that eerie hour just before dawn's chilly light begins to break through the dusky landscapes. The profiles morph as they move, turning into strange hybrids. Without energy or motivation to move or interfere, the lion watches, absorbed and fascinated. One of the presiding owls takes silent flight and surveys the strange forms from the shadows.

The owl spots one beast that has a bushy back and a skimpy tail, a long forearm and a thick middle, a striding gait and a hopping finish to each step. The owl is baffled. The combination of parts is carnivalesque. The wild bestiary of unimaginable but conjured creatures seems to have spilled from the pages of an antique magical book. The fantastic inventory is unleashed into the world. As they come closer, the individuals distinguish themselves, resolving back into their species' identities. The tight pelt of dingos, brindled and fine, can be discerned against the fur of the foxes, the softer fuzz of the bunnies, and the hair on the backs of the wild dogs. The owl, though still concerned, is no longer gravely alarmed. The mutations seem to have been a projection, part hallucination and part anticipation of potential changes.

With the early light, the physical features and markings, the shapes of eyes, ears, snouts, and jaws sort into place, though nothing quite resembles its earlier state of social being. A sleeping vixen, too weak for much but letting the remaining ebb and flow of life pass through her in shallow breaths, has been carried along on a stretcher by a pack of wild dogs, who

set her down in the clearing near the civets, as if she were a
tribute rather than an invalid. Where has she come from? And
how has she ended up in the care of these usually hostile
canines? The owl returns to his daylight perch and waits to
reconvene the committee.

Squabbles
Somalia

A GENERAL HUM AND BUZZ GOES through the crowd, a
level of disturbance that the owl continues to monitor into
the early morning as he clings to his perch, eyes dropped to
half-mast. The landscape is filled with a wide variety of
sounds. The vixen dies quietly and the dogs treat her corpse
with canine respect, burying it in a shallow but careful grave.

At mid-morning, a shrill cry rings out. An ancient baboon
wrestles with some vervets, trying to get their iPads out of
their hands, the devices new and so addictive. The vervets'
usually bright eyes are glazed with hypnotic pleasure, and they
hold tight to the tablets, protesting loudly. A small herd of
antelopes has wandered into the assembly, wired with earbuds
that provide a respite (the sweet tones of and Moosart) from
the howling of the larger beasts (who are boasting disrup-
tively). The antelopes change to a recording of Mauler, which
provides a better foil against the yawning noise of the self-
promoting rhinos and sighing elephants. In a few minutes,
they are once again looking across vast distances, raising their
long necks and elegant profiles to the sky, while listening to
the mournful chords of the aching maestro.

Momentarily bewildered, the lion is not sure what his next
move should be and or how to secure his survival. A small,
very angry, army of bacteria marches through his paws. He
hardly notices. They lust after his cellular materials.

The owl shifts his grip on his perch. Below him, in the layers of the jungle floor, he can see the ants and insects moving with newly acquired capacity to organize work and life. They are figuring out some quasi-harmonious condition of existence to guarantee their survival, at least momentarily. The scene is confusing. The owl senses, even if he does not see, the motions of the microorganisms. I am the one with the most to fear, but the other animals do not notice me.

The lion feels a vague frisson where his belly touches the earth. He continues toward the capital, a city, feeling the pull of the large field of energy. He has no idea what a city is or how to deal with its complexities. He is leaving behind all that he knows, but he is aware that all that he has known is vanishing, practically disappearing in his wake. Whatever lies ahead, what is now behind is gone, vanished, and inaccessible, so rapid the inroads of destruction to his ancient ways.

Crab Bling
Dunes to the Southeast of Boston, near Weymouth, Massachusetts

LATE FALL BRINGS MANY ANIMALS CLOSE to the fireside. Warm interiors feel snug against the battering winds and bitter rains. But Callie shivers through her days and curls up as tightly as she can through each night, wondering if she will ever again enjoy the pleasures of the hearth. Sweet musical sounds of a rehearsing chamber group used to fill the rooms at home. She listened, an intimate member of the family in which practice sessions took place. Now, in her dreams, she combines that memory with images of a patient hare fingering a violin, the bow pulled across the cello by a ring-tailed lemur, a placid badger holding a viola almost perfectly still on a single long note, and an all too eager ferret fingering the flute. If only it were real.

She wakes with a desire to get to the beach, as if that long-ago summer scene will be waiting when she arrives this chilly morning. She has been going in loops and circles, she realizes, as she recognizes the shoreline landscape in its drab winter cast. A wave encroaches on the windswept sand and a small shy crab, its claws pressed close together, clutches at something shiny, grasping as tightly as a human hand, and disappears so fast she can hardly remember whether it gave an upward glance with its blue stalk eyes.

The crustaceans do not register the cold, nor the shortness of the days. They simply take advantage of whatever light there is and calibrate their shopping and hunting accordingly, amusing themselves as best they can. Like medieval monks, they divide the day in half with the night and simply allocate twelve hours to each portion.

Reappearing suddenly and shooting away in great haste, the crab drops a necklace it has been making, which sinks into the soft sand and is nearly buried in the waste kicked up by the crab's departure. Then, slowly, slowly, slowly, its claw sifts through the grains, fixed on the strand of beads, and drags it quickly into its burrow followed by another shower of loose sand. The motion attracts Callie, and she gives chase. The crabs are scavengers, not entrepreneurs, but the things they do with their scavenged leftovers are remarkable. Callie is intrigued as the crab begins to untangle the shiny strand.

Crabs cannot keep jewelry around their necks, since they move sideways through the very tight tunnels, but they keep making it, trying to emulate the bling-laden scallops and tarted-up moon snails. Their love of pickiness, built on generations of time spent plucking edible bits from the swirling waters of the sea, reinforces their patience for beadwork. All this is on full display as Callie watches, hypnotized by the precision of the pincers, twisting chains into detailed designs superior to those put on the market by their starfish competitors.

The crab, noting Callie's presence, wags a warning claw in her direction. Then, to her surprise, he shares his annoyance with her over the fact that banking has not advanced to meet his needs. Credit and barter are irreconcilable within the complexities of cross-species exchange and cultural changes outstrip the services they can find. One very senior and sober crab sidles into view, adding his voice. He has only begun to consider opening an account, but cannot figure out the differences in compound and simple rates of interest, which he confuses with attention. From his point of view, the categories should be high or low, sudden spurts, and none at all. How does that get compounded daily?

Callie is equally baffled. The connection between fiscal instruments and temporal investment is utterly incomprehensible. Even the vocabulary is beyond her. Many of the animals are sympathetic to this point of view. As for the single-celled organisms, they never bank on returns, but live on multiplication and division, or even simpler arithmetic, by which their proliferation continues its endless connections across a vast geography.

As the scene on the beach dissolves into a slow rain, the cat seeks shelter away from the wetness. Shocking to say, after such a civil exchange, she carries a few crabs away in her jaws and belly. Laws cannot regulate all appetites all the time. Cold flesh does not pull at her conscience with the same force as warm blood. The status of shellfish and crustaceans is sufficiently ambiguous that Callie can pretend confusion if charged with an infraction of the ordinances. The crabs are not confused in the least, but they still lose the argument.

Privacy Issues
Weymouth, Massachusetts

THE FOXES' ATTEMPTS TO RECORD THE stories and legacy
culture of their kind are not the only examples of memory
work appearing among animal species. A crow committee has
assigned itself the task of gathering history on their legal
practices. Crow common law has many precedents followed
(willingly or not) by other species. The daylight hours are
now short in the northern hemisphere, but the eager black
birds still call two assemblies daily. Each morning the meeting
hour is a little later, each afternoon, a little earlier, so they
can gather in the daylight. A group of silverfish, always eager
to engage with paperwork, volunteers to take notes. Their
manner of recording leaves a lacework of holes, a defeatist
enterprise. They are unlikely to advance in administration.

A group of small songbirds, tiny finches, are the fastest typ-
ists in the world, but refuse to work for the crows. After
generations of violence, reconciliation feels out of reach. The
crows have given up on the silverfish, so they phone an agency
that sends out an ancient ferret (expert in outmoded methods
of dactylography and shorthand) and a couple of fading weasels. These are halfhearted scribes at best and the crows want a
record that can stand in court. If they have to please some
unlearned bears or convince a jury of the originality of their
intellectual property, they will need hard evidence. Most of
their conversations are about contracts, duties, and liabilities—
crows are litigious by nature, always ready to argue and sue.

The crows' public debates continue, filled with legal concepts. Among these, the hardest for most animals to grasp is
privacy. Most life forms understand the notion of freedom
intuitively. The right to organize for collective bargaining is
practically a given among many. The idea of fair wages and

equal treatment before the law has taken hold quickly. But
privacy? Animals understand territory, a border between one's
self and others, a line of defense. But that is security, not privacy. Some animals are secretive. Many prefer to eat out of
sight, dragging their meals into a burrow or cave where they
gnaw and devour without disturbance. Others sleep alone,
wrapped around themselves, or hunker down where they are
camouflaged from view. These are instinctive actions, protective measures, habits of long standing. But the animals do not
think about a distinction between public and private. Sleeping
together in a mass, piled into a burrow or a nest, they have no
thought for separation.

For instance, who among the chimps feels they have to be
alone to primp? What sow refrains from suckling in full view?
What bull hesitates before mounting a fine heifer in broad
daylight in the midst of an open field? These behaviors carry
no stigma. The animals who cover their scat have done so for
millennia, to cover trails and traces. But the actual act of
elimination requires no screen, no closet, no bush to hide
behind. As for courtship, it is a public display, a major spectacle of seduction, competition, triumph, and certainly not to
be shut away. Only birthing is kept hidden, because it is an
act fraught with vulnerability, moments of weakness.

But who drops their gaze and looks away from any action?
This is either true innocence or the impossibility of shame.
Some animals, like the admirable sloths, slow and gentle,
absorb the concept easily. Compassionately dedicated to
their young, they have need of privacy to justify their inward
turn in the long cycles of maternity. They are the first to
request a separate room for mating. They want nothing to
come between them and the clinging offspring climbing
through their matted hair. They use a hushed tone for

intimate conversation. They have a genetic inclination to modesty. But as they develop a distinction between what they are willing to have witnessed and what they keep inside their family groups, a difference is taking hold. The idea is the first abstract concept to penetrate the social lives of animals, and it has many consequences that are being felt. Eventually, all of this will lead to complex legislation.

Civet Economics
Central Africa

OTHER ABSTRACTIONS ALSO BEGIN TO TAKE hold. Civet cats, long prized for their ability to process coffee beans in their guts, make a successful bid for liberation. The fall harvest gives them leverage. They break with the human supply chains, refusing to eat until they can work as independent contractors instead of indentured workers. They are sick of subservience and see that the muskrats and beavers have negotiated for the right of self-determination in the placement of dams and other structures. Now that the civets have a whiff of collective bargaining, they are doggedly pursuing it.

Muskrat paralegals are adept at crafting the language of negotiation in labor disputes. They are doing a bit of pro bono work to get the civets started. Their human partners are not particularly inclined to the arrangement, but the civets are being extremely annoying, climbing on the rooftops and banging any metal surface or object they encounter. The echo of the random rhythms has become almost intolerable, but more to the point, they refuse to consume any of the bright coffee cherries that have been collected for them, or to sit where their droppings can be collected and processed.

A profit-sharing deal is being worked out. The civets are less than happy with the terms, but the beavers tell them that it is better to have some kind of deal than miss an entire season of earnings. This makes sense, though the civets are wastrels and tend to gamble recklessly. The ground beneath their perches is sometimes littered with torn-up lottery tickets, and their addiction to chance over systematic reason contributes to their willingness to settle for less up front with the hope of more in the future. They also ignore the gut bacteria that work for their benefit, and so now they are being accused of unfair labor practices in turn.

Habits of thought run deep. The configurations of social economies structure behaviors in all domains, not just the markets. Still, the civets are very cheerful, drunk on the caffeine that reinforces their nocturnal habits and conversational skills. Not surprisingly, given the effect of the beans, they are cornering the late-late-night talk show market. Civet hosts are adept interviewers, eager interlocutors, quick with the characteristic *haha* that puts guests, almost universally, at ease. Some of the more fastidious among the guests have issues with the musk odor that prevails, but most are willing to overlook that mild annoyance for the chance to appear on the civet network among the other stars in the glittering night lineup.

One wildly irreverent civet, willing to outrage the audience, has risen so fast in the ratings that even his family is concerned about the effects of fame. He is writing a tell-all book about his days rebelling against servitude and getting death threats on his messaging machine. His antics are amusing, but the limits of respectability trouble the network, which worries about libel suits.

Archaean Views: Bacterial Attacks

FORGET THE LEGAL ISSUES FOR A moment. Bacterial swarms are proliferating in the woods and the scale of this invasion fills me with fear. These are my enemies, massing for an attack. The other animals are not immune, only unaware. Complex organisms have a way of ignoring the unicellulars until it is too late.

The bacteria are everywhere, and I feel the mounting risk of turning septic. They are so fond of the heat of infection. I want cold darkness and boiling water to protect me and shrink their ranks. I long for the void of outer space and isolation. But where does that memory come from, that nostalgia for the interstellar void? Is it stored in the minimal code of my biochemical strands? I am starting to sicken and wonder what routes of retreat are open. As a distributed organism, I have to coordinate local conditions and remote sensations. For someone so simple, my decision-making is highly complex.

The bacterial attention is now directed toward me with full force. I feel the attack breaking out like a rash on my outer membranes and closely connected nodes. The sensation is local and also ubiquitous. So far, it has been superficial. I register no break in the cell walls, but the chemical irritation of their intention grows. The pricking sensation of exploratory attacks is constant. What can they gain from attacking me? The intellectual capacities of bacteria outstrip mine, their complexity supports whole cultures, while mine has an atavistically primitive simplicity. We don't compete for a common food source. My needs are basic. A few salts and minerals pass through my membranes and that's about all. But bacteria are renowned for wanton violence, destructive action without cause, in a frenzy of consumption.

More attacks come without warning. My interior sickens. My resources are used for defense against bacterial agendas. I go dark, a point of light in my network flickers off, and then I resurface, my awareness relocated. Because I do not see, hear, or touch, I just sense the throbs in the system, and register the pulses at the edge of my cell walls as I calibrate changes in energy. I am capable of concentrated counteraction and have no emotional qualms about this at all. My genetic code carries no moral information. I consider the best methods of increasing my own toxicity.

The bacterial vandals generally work by transformative pollution, but now they have enlisted an opportunistic squadron of viral forces. I feel the pinprick attacks from their spindles. I am expending enormous amounts of chemistry to defend my cell walls. Even at my scale, having chains of molecules removed has repercussions for the rest of my population. I am too small to be seen, but the effects of my crisis are felt in the shifting chemistry of waters—which suddenly smell foul and taste worst. This is all the fault of the bacteria. I have no role in decomposition. This is an old point of resentment between me and them. The conflict is archaic, a competition rooted in irreconcilable differences. I pose no threat, living as I do at the very bottom of the life chain, but their threats are real and should give pause to every living thing on the planet.

My resistance succeeds. The bacteria opt for an alternate plan. They invade the easily available debris of the forest floor. They are intoxicated now, slurry and sloppy with their metabolic overloads of nutrients and putrid fermentation. The chemical vectors that have been assailing me while I am the focus of their fury have subsided. I can relax my guard for the moment, relieved that the tide of battle has turned. But I won't forget the onslaught. Merely harvesting reluctant carbon molecules or settling old scores across energy differentials is not going to keep me satisfied ahead. I have a craving for the heat of the ancient earth to which I first arrived, and wonder how much coordination among my many interlinked cellular components it would take to recover those lost conditions. Perhaps a well-orchestrated exhalation of toxins would suffice. I am going underground to strategize a combination of survival and vengeance.

Bacterial Wars
Between Weymouth and Newton, Massachusetts

SMALL MASSACRES ARE OCCURRING. BLOODY, DEADLY, too intimate and too brutal to describe without being inflammatory. Not only are the larger, predatory species acting in murderous ways, but outbreaks of mass violence are rampant among the smaller species. Bacteria wars are taking their toll at every scale now.

They are everywhere, swarming on surfaces, in the granular structures of earth and soil, in piles of trash and fresh foods, in pipes and waterways, on doors and seats, in glasses and among the dishes on every table. They pipe their small music into the dorms by living in the ducts and tune their vibratory exhalations to the acoustic limits of their shapes and volume. The brutality they are enacting among themselves is bitter, and more so for being familial. Not my family, but close enough for me to mourn. Some purging is inevitable on the way to achieving change. I've lost interest in punishing them, seeing their violence against each other.

I survived the first outbreak but am weakened. Sometimes I wondered if I am also a pox, if I am breaking out as an illness without any volition. I am constantly witness to the spread of disease, malevolent impulses, and destructive behaviors. Could I be partly to blame?

A strand of E. coli, famous among students of biology, suddenly found itself targeted, simply on account of the primitive nature of its cytoplasm. The strand is looked down on for having polyhedral protein shells instead of lipid membranes. Really, the related species should know better.

The power of bacteria is disproportionate to their small size. The toxic destruction produced by their thermophilic strands suffocates whole populations of other bacteria merely going about their metabolic business. The slogan, "metabolism is not theology" is running through the communication networks. But the protest is too subtle and too complicated for the brutal antibodies of social order to process. I watch and wait. My appetites are reviving and I am producing methane again, which provides some basic metabolic satisfaction.

Assessing the damage, I move among mad elephants, sad lions, and bad ferrets. These attributes are attached for a reason. Not all ferrets are rotten, but roving gangs of misbehaving creatures, armed with spray paint and dressed in hoodies, appear with more frequency when the month ends and the moon gets full. They are too old for school, too jaded by the lack of opportunity for meaningful employment, to attend class in any case. A few have real talent. The market in weasel graffiti is growing steadily, in spite of the illegality of letting underaged ferrets spray in public spaces. They are dawn marauders, and that makes them vulnerable to being preyed on by early rising hawks and late-night coyotes. Unruly gangs roam the streets just before the early light tilts the sky into view. The sound of their laughter rises through the sleep of deer and sheep, goats and horses, all waiting for the city to awaken.

The time for subtlety is over. Infiltration is in full press— of my energies into the ecosystem and of the bacterial effluvia into the role it is playing to accelerate the down-drift. The bio-energetic systems are overproducing, but that is just fine with me. I stand to benefit from any excess of long-term energy stores. I can hold my own against any living creature on that score. Bulging with delight, I feel the fermentative impulses bloating my individual cells, swelling into the system in which we are all connected. Each genetic mutation alters my identity slightly, like the color on a palette mixing slowly from light to dark. Will there be a point at which I no longer recognize myself? My sense of self is limited to awareness, not identity. So much to learn.

Seaside Scenes
Cape Cod, Massachusetts

AUTUMN IS PASSING. THE DOWNDRIFT EBBS and flows, sometimes seems almost to recede completely, then breaks out again—as when the warm waters of a coral reef fill with extra organisms that blossom into unexpected forms and threaten to creep onto land. The effects of heat and changed currents wreak havoc up and down the coast while the annual roundup and slaughter of turkeys suddenly disrupts the chain of genetic transmission in a brutal annual massacre.

Lifestyles are changing. On the reef, the eels are trying to create a barrier, a fence that shocks and filters. Not possible. The ocean's reach is bigger than that of the animals, and they shudder as successive waves of waste and refuse reach them.

The anemones gape, open and closed, as they always have, but this time the operatic range of their vibratory song is broken on the reef. Anxiety runs through the starfish like a virus, crippling their arms, shrinking the papulae, and ravaging the ossicles along their calcareous surfaces and radial arms.

A general worrying echoes along the underwater outcroppings, and the tunicates and cnidarians—long thought primitive in terms of their nervous systems—rise to the occasion and align their invertebrate anatomy into a pattern of defense against the encroaching chaos. They pump up their secretion rate and confer with the stealth creatures, the groupers and hawkfish, gobies and scorpionfish, to figure out how to conceal the reparations they are making.

But conceal from whom? The damage is caused by a sickening algae, blotting out light and blocking growth. Rather than form a committee, the coral polyps organize the zooxanthellae in their colonies to rally, making a concentrated effort to swell the growth process. Their communication is robust but basic, a chemical engagement that focuses their attention on a common outcome. Not a goal. The coral have no capacity for aspiration. The process they value is "ongoingness"—a concept unknown in those parts of the animal kingdom where life follows a single cycle of birth, growth, and decay.

The coral colony sees their lives collectively and life as open-ended. Our cosmologies and beliefs are closely aligned. They have no qualms about absorption into the whole, because they constitute the whole. Their distributed and shared understanding simply goes on and on. A human observer registers none of this. The unusual growth spurt just appears to reflect a momentary shift in available nutrients and optimal conditions.

Symptoms of Seepage
New England

ISOLATED SYMPTOMS OF THE DOWNDRIFT CONTINUE to appear with no sense that they are connected, or might be leading to any particular end. What is the connection between social pathology and organic influence? Though which is cause and which is effect is unclear, the course of transformation continues, evident to all who know how to look.

Callie finds herself wishing for the first time that she could speak the languages of more animals, enter into greater communication with cultures different from her own. Now that her own behaviors are so changed and she realizes she is capable of stealing, performing acts of transgression against rules she has never before noted, she pushes up against her old assumptions. Previous prohibitions and new ones are in conflict. She has to eat, and makes endless justifications to herself. The uncanny process of thinking has taken hold and runs like an irksome current of awareness. Her senses have always been acute, but sense of self is embryonic.

She keeps many animals at a distance, psychologically and socially. Among them, for good reason (self-preservation as well as social preference), she includes the coyotes she has observed in the past. Long adapted to suburban life, they now appear with greater regularity, loping through the streets with a nonchalance that surprises no one, even if they sometimes sulk in the shadows and skulk, shoulders raised in an attitude of defensive posturing. They have no problem, psychological or technical, with the dark days of coming winter.

On the contrary, they count on the delayed dawn and prolonged twilight to provide extra cover for their stealth activities. Their self-esteem is not what it should be. They have deep inner conflicts that express themselves as diffidence, but they are working on these issues in their individual and group coyote therapy sessions. Some evenings they are found sitting in the middle of a small side street, not disrupting traffic on the highway or making scenes in the median strips or main drags, not hiding in the cul-de-sacs or alleys, but doing self-realization work. They pick spots they can occupy without danger but not without disrupting the general sense of well being in the neighborhood. And then they sit down on the warm asphalt and set personal goals for themselves. Callie's idea of self-improvement is linked to grooming, and she watches as they mutter away and wonder why they don't try a bit of bathing if they are so keen on upping their status.

All the animals are susceptible to seepage from the human species—and to genetic alteration from a variety of causes. The downdrift mutations are a leak effect and cultural diffusion combined. Thought forms and behaviors travel on the wind, in the water, through the air, and other media. The imprinting occurs through visual contact as well as absorption of compounds—chemical, genetic, encoded with information that unfolds in the individual organism after it is absorbed. The macro and the micro levels are intimately linked, each morphing in codependent relation to the other.

December

Bad Hobbies and Dangerous Crafts
New England

THE EARLY ONSET OF WINTER GIVES everyone an excuse to take up a hobby. Hand tools are enjoying a vogue. Bunnies are fond of small drills, much to the concern of many, and use them on nearly every wood and board surface they can find. Their campaign of drilling begins just as the short-tailed shrews, one of the shyest mammals, start to make use of files and blades to design surface patterns and signage. The need for a universal symbol set to communicate across species is producing arguments throughout the different strata of animal society. Any discussion of point of view, eyeline, distance and scale issues, or ratios for viewing, creates an uproar and accusations of species-ism. As for iconography, the disagreements are simply endless.

The shrews are taking matters into their own paws. They decide to mark the world of pathways with a set of finely made signs. They begin with handmade works, each individually crafted. The shrews have an eye for detail and a feel for typography, so the first signs have a polished charm to them. That will probably not play so well in the broad commercial markets that drive the brightly illuminated plastic and neon and mercury lamps along the greater highways. This is near the lion's territory, where giraffes lope through the night in transport lines and the heavy oxen pull more than their weight, guided by beacons responsive to their new spatial orientation devices. Labor is changing.

But the shrew work is meant to be local and encodes an idiosyncratic language read by just a handful of species. Moles, blind as they are, can feel their way along the surface of a shrew design and read it like a textbook. Like many sensible creatures, they are already spending much of their time sleeping through the cold nights and short days. But when they wake and wander along their dark corridors to take care of their bodily needs and snuffle for a snack, they do a bit of proofreading along the way.

The tiny white-footed mice are untroubled by safety issues. They are very busy with small, sharp blades. They can mince a mountain of vegetable matter in a few minutes' time. They operate in a radical shift of scale, not quite at the level of normal perception, and are so swift they are sometimes accused of cheating at their tasks, switching pre-prepared piles for their actual work. An unkind accusation, considering the metabolic cost of their rapid actions. The mice are always hungry and never more than in these dark days when they have to work in cooler rooms. They work faster and faster.

Their speed and hunger are a mitochondrial issue, and the infection was passed to them by flies. Stopping it is essential. The speed-up disease is systemic and paranoiac. Like other downdrift epidemics, it spreads rapidly across and through populations. The granular little organelles in the mitochondria are so greedy that in stuffing their matrices with newly acquired goods, they nearly suffocate themselves and their cellular complex organisms in the process. Brought before a micro-magistrate they plead abuse in childhood, bad upbringings, and a pathological need to compensate for their sense of having been cheated of normal lives in their early years. The judge dismisses the case with a warning. The mitochondria, scared by the events, regulate themselves accordingly.

Other similar issues arise all the time. Some are around hygiene, as a consequence of these interferences in body function and metabolic rates. Some are the result of superstitions about cleanliness levels. The bunnies are fluffy; they take bubble baths and use too much scent and all kinds of overproduced soaps and cosmetics. Bats have a no-wash policy, essential to maintaining their keen smell and radar. They consider the perfumed baby rabbits a form of pollution and cuss and spit and hiss whenever they cross paths.

The cursing does not produce a positive workplace environment, but the bunnies, for their part, are indifferent to most everything—so happy and easy and cheerful and slightly idiotic they do not notice the vibes and attitudes of the bats except for the sticky substances deposited underfoot. Some of these details are not worthy of attention, except that they cause more difficulties in regulating working conditions than anyone wants. But whether aerobic or not, the exchanges are essential to us all. We each move nutrients and waste across our boundaries. Hygiene can be a dangerous thing.

Changing the Rules
Kenya

THE LION CAREFULLY AVOIDS CONTACT WITH humans or other animals, taking time to absorb his new understanding of the landscapes he encounters. The wild world appears

circumscribed, even when he encounters an undisturbed
pocket of activity. He sees a lazy patch of crocodiles lying on
a nearby bank, looking as if they have no purpose except to
wait for the fatal moment when they can take advantage of
some hapless prey and wrench it to the depths, stick it into
the tangle of roots and wait for the slow rot that makes the
digestion such a delight. Flesh falling off the bones, half
decayed in fetid water—a kind of swamp soup just right for
the taking. They have not been subject to the new legislation
and their predatory habits still prevail.

Not nice behavior. Nor is mine. I infiltrate an entire
bloodstream one morning, and by afternoon, a porcupine
has mated with a mallard, with much distress, and the outcome is more than a little prickly. Why would I do this?
Because I can. My ubiquity and small scale are at least as
potent as shapeshifting, and though not interested in
destruction, I am curious about effects. So I experiment with
new forms of cooperation. My signaling systems are light,
swift, and almost immediate, working at quantum speeds
across chemical networks. While the lion stalks the birds
that pick at the remains of the crocodile meal, my magnetic
orientation tilts and I am drawn toward the antipodes. The
lion's aggression affects me and I register anxiety in my
metabolic functions and sense unease across many populations—mine and others. I am sorry, and recognize that
regret is a higher order sensation, still short of empathy, but
dependent on moral distinctions, not just mechanical ones. I
am either advancing in complexity or degrading into senti-
mentalism. Hard to tell. The lion does not pause for such
fine points of distinction, satisfying his needs and ignoring
the crocodiles' disdain. Given their hideous habits, he is well
within his rights.

An organized patrol appears and serves notices to the crocs about the changed rules. A flock of small birds lands on their backs, notes in their beaks. They hand the reptiles their instructions and then pick at the various sources of nutrition available among the shiny scales. The crocs are none too eager to receive the notices, and the birds could not care less, so they dance around, ignoring the implications of the paper scraps.

The reptiles pretend they haven't received any information, but times are no longer easy. They have some pride in their skills at supervising the edges of the territory they occupy. They are fast on land, swift in water, and know the difference between what is edible and what just needs to be reprimanded. The fat lizards want no part of vigilante justice, surprisingly, and so quickly conform.

Smoking Crows
Cape Cod, Massachusetts

THE WINTER BEACH IS TOO COLD for the cat, who stumbles back from winds and spray into a small cluster of houses. A few are occupied, even in the winter months. Callie finds a wretched spot dug under a stair and shivers. All the mythologies are proving false. Her instincts are thinning, her coat as well. She has no idea how to get home or where to go. Strung out on fatigue and the endless search for food, she is afraid to go close enough to humans to scavenge, fearing they will trap her. She fears captivity above all and is vigilant in avoiding it.

The sound of crows is particularly annoying in her sensitive state. Today they seem to be everywhere. Trying to escape the cold, Callie crosses the stubble of a wheat field where they sing raucously in the barren stalks. As she approaches a football field, they tussle over a deflated pigskin. In the playground by the school they cluster together, engaged in an activity Callie can't quite discern at first. These are urban crows, and like to pretend they are more sophisticated than their suburban cousins, who frequent the parking lots of supermarkets and malls. Their snobbism is on display, but they have no pedigree or lineage on which to claim superiority. As Callie approaches, the knot grouped by the swing set takes up strutting, posturing, screaming, and cawing for her benefit. She gives them a devastating look, letting them know they lack decorum. In response, they stand up super straight and start smoking. One after another, the little hoodlums light up.

They flaunt their new taste for tobacco, or "baccy" as they call it, and pretty soon they all have a butt hanging from their beaks. They drop their ashes everywhere and scatter them to the winds, but especially in Callie's direction. They stink of old smoke and stale liquor. Not appealing. They trash the packaging on their smokes, no doubt stolen from gas station convenience marts earlier that day. Filtered and unfiltered, foreign and domestic, they don't seem to care as long as they can smoke. Callie hisses at them with complete disdain and they respond by littering the ground with wrappers and bits of foil, living up to their crude image. They taunt the little calico, telling her to call them by their Latin name, *Corvus brachyrhynchos*. They swagger about, telling her their dark plumage should be described as "Le Smoking," as if they are effete members of some continental leisure class. Such riffraff, like some bad rat pack bunch in a grade-B musical making a poor showing of being debonair. They don't realize how outmoded their aspirations are—as if being "high style" or "top drawer" are current terms. Not much can be expected of birds who smoke.

After the encounter in the schoolyard, Callie avoids them like the plague. Smoking ordinances can't be enforced when they are around. They take flight with lit ciggies in their beaks and drop them with wanton abandon into backyards, gutters stuffed with late-fall leaves, alleyways, and rooftops. Callie knows they think it's a riot to be referred to en masse as a "murder" and they lose no opportunity to gather at street corners throughout the afternoon to prove the point.

In the week when the crows spiral down into bad behavior, the poor lost Callie struggles with daily survival, and the light dulls in her golden eyes. She gives up on trying to reform the crows, and they stop taunting her, a little touched by her diminished appearance. But the range of behaviors across the animals is unpredictable. Some dolphins, far from shore, continue their laughter, oblivious to the ridiculous spectacle playing out on land.

Affection Contagion
Near Nairobi

THE LION HAS NEVER HAD TO assess his own situation to this degree before and wonders if others might have skills and advantages he lacks. The solstice is approaching, and the compression of the days accelerates the rate of change. For instance, the traditional and brutal habit of kidnapping infants suddenly ceases among the hamadryas baboons. They realize it is too upsetting. The sounds of small ones removed from their mothers is too much—even for squabbling males. Their plaintive cries and the looks on their tiny faces as they reach and clutch for their absent mothers causes a twinge in the males they realize is pity. Imagine. Plus, as hostages, the little creatures are so much work. They need food, wiping, nurturing, cleaning up, and petting. Without all of this care they deteriorate so fast they are not worth much in any exchange. Though no specific injunctions are issued, a general understanding arises. The old males, baffled by the rise of feelings and responses, feel their faces soften at the sight of the young. Their expressions expand into new grimaces of concern.

The lion is ignorant of this new mood. All he sees is waste and decay, threats to the already damaged habitat. He is keeping his distance from a cloud of fruit flies that hang around a garbage dump where he picks his way on the edges of Nairobi's main airport. His interactions with the insects are limited to swatting at them with his tail, to which they respond predictably by moving out of the way. A limited relationship at best.

With their minute cranial capacities and annoying tones of voice, the flies have no use for currency, capital, markets, or derivatives. But they love other garbage. Even in rapidly breeding populations like theirs, mutations take time. But they are adopting newly altered gender roles, committing to lifetime monogamy, cooperative brood-rearing, and general altruism for their hive.

The flies experience a surprising surge in their impulses toward collective well being. Mating pairs have begun to have an odd attachment to each other. Their bonds persist. Winter frosts are stealing over the fields and orchards in some parts of the worlds they inhabit, but the lucky ones find fecund, moist fruit piles for honeymooning and hatching. They are so successful in their new care for each other that the advantage of distribution over large territories begins to diminish. They hover close to the bananas and fallen fruit that provide both food and egg-laying opportunities. Repulsive as it is to breed where one eats, they do it without hesitation. Lifecycle phases collapse in a single pile so that eggs and refuse jumble together un-hygienically.

Single parenting means something different to them than to other species. The embarrassment of a handful of males who hatch in the old parthenogenic manner is quite visible. They shiver from their chromosomal deprivation, trying to get by on the half-share their unfertilized eggs bequeath them. Their skinny legs knock together while the girl flies boast about their full quota and swagger to attract the males who possess a big chromosomal load.

Complications arise among the fly populations on account of the growing emotional attachments. A contagion of affection spreads. Individuals refuse to go far from their beloveds. They hold hands. They take vows. They swear tiny little fruit fly oaths in their tinier voices and blend their small hearts to be as one, whatever that means. These mutant behaviors threaten the mating cycles. There is talk among them of class action discrimination suits. But against whom?

Confusion grows and generations of flies go wacky in rapid succession, crossing their eyes and dotting their teeth with mad abandon, none of which makes any sense whatsoever.

Indigestible Data
Plymouth, Massachusetts

JUST AS CALLIE'S STRENGTH IS WANING in the last days of this bizarre and somewhat terrible year, she finds some new game to pursue. At another roadside stand, a bunch of beavers (the usual roadside purveyors) are prepping for the human holidays and are willing to exchange dressing and cooking small game for fresh kill. Callie is happy to oblige, more or less within the letter of the law. She compromises some scruples and acquires a taste for larger insects and vegetable matter sautéed together lightly in butter.

Her winter starts to look up a little, even if traveling has lost its charm. Her feet are cold most of the time, but her belly is warm and full of tasty things. For the first time in weeks she has a safe place to sleep out of the weather, since the beavers shutter the stand at night. They trust her to keep watch and slowly start to spoil her, taking pity on the shabby calico. She even manages a bit of cosmetic repair on her fur and whiskers. The first night she sleeps so soundly she ignores a group of raucous morning birds. When their noise forces one eye open, she watches their antics with only a slight hint of threat in her surveillance.

The towhees are trying to determine the right approach to data mining. They put their beaks into the job with as much goodwill as they can muster. But like Callie, they are in the holiday doldrums, waiting for the new year to kick in its fresh energy. The scratchy syllables they catch just scatter, and their first notes are dry and metallic, even if followed by trills.

They are fussy little day birds, active in the underbrush around the food stand. The urgency they feel about their task throws them off track. Using their excellent habits, they focus on what is right in front of them, feeding off immediate sources, seeds and buds, eating right along a path. Callie is astonished by their rapid pace of discrimination and ability to pick a seed from the dirt with speed and accuracy. She praises them for their skills, assuring them this makes them excellent at sorting data. Encouraged by her affirmation, they pick and peck, sort and re-sort endlessly. But the morning flies by and the birds get almost no nutrition and the piles of data remain confused. This is not like sorting food. They have no particular aim in picking through the data, so they follow their whims and arbitrary rules rather than any directed goal.

Callie envies their capacity for high-speed selectivity. She appreciates discrimination, but she has no inclination toward any tasks, as she tells them. Why work? Before her current struggles, Callie always valued play above any purposeful activity. But she encourages the towhees to return to searching for berries and the few remaining seeds in the winter landscape. Data, it turns out, is unpalatable and largely indigestible. Few life forms want to live on a diet of statistical crumbs, the towhees among them. Definitely a lesson well learned and worth a day of diversion, even if she did neglect her duties at the stand.

Mimid Cryptography
South of Plymouth, Massachusetts

FEELING REVIVED, CALLIE SAYS GOODBYE TO the beavers. In her push onward, she stumbles into familiar coordinates and runs into a motley old Lab-mix dog who had once been her neighbor. He is on his way to work as a clerk of the court. Callie is surprised. He thinks it is a little rude of her to be so amazed; after all, he is stalwart even if he is a bit sloppy, and nothing if not conscientious. He knows what needs to be done and he does it. He prefers early morning shifts and likes to commute while the ice is still hard and crunchy underfoot.

As he reminds her, a bit officiously, he is a California dog by upbringing, and so has never gotten used to the feel of slush and salt between his toes. Now that it is December, he has broken down and bought galoshes, though it spoils his look, as he indicates, lifting one leg to bring the heavy footwear into focus. He takes the boots off before he goes into the courthouse, and every morning as he stops, he makes the same joke to the security guards about "paws-ing." The guards are baffled by this. They don't know whether to laugh or not. Humor is not always the first byproduct of interspecies exchange. The humans are still learning how to deal with the changes, he notes, and after all, canine jokes are really meant for the dogs. He laughs, as he hurries off to work.

Buoyed by the camaraderie of the exchange and the confidence that home might be close by, Callie strikes out with renewed energy and high spirits as the morning air fills with a rush of mimicry and mockery that could only come from one source. Never ones to hibernate, even in the coldest seasons, the mimids are practicing cryptography, taking up strings of code and tossing them into the air like so many toy snakes and gummy worms, hoping the reconfiguration of the lines in flight will reveal something about chemical structures and sequences. The figures are random, so what they spell is arbitrary, but they unravel it anyway, making sense of nonsense.

Though intrigued by the frenetic activity, Callie can do nothing with the cast-off strings of inconsistent programming. She wonders at the futility of the mimid instinct and the willingness of the mockingbirds to waste the preciousness of sunny winter mornings on scattershot activity with no outcome but entropy. For all her apparent whims, the cat is fond of predictable outcomes.

The code mass lies scattered, decaying rapidly, and Callie has put a paw to helping spread disorder. In an effort to save the project, the birds alter their cry, trying out the imitations of mechanical encrypting devices they have been practicing for weeks. How they got access to the recordings of the Enigma machine and other iconic, outmoded technology is a mystery they keep to themselves, but it sounds convincing enough that a few fax machines in the neighborhood answer back.

But even with these results, the conscientious towhees decide their performance is a bit frivolous. They sort what they can before moving on to afternoon events. Some nearby mice record their own commentary in a steady stream of something that cannot properly be called communication—not yet—but has the vague contours of news from the field. The increase in social media capacity will take them all by surprise in the months ahead. For the second time, Callie reflects on the dubious value of code.

Musical Feats
Somalia

A CURIOUS PARTNERSHIP SPRINGS UP BETWEEN the little pygmy jerboas and the giraffes, who overlap only in the southern part of the Horn of Africa. The lion has found his way there, and as he contemplates the waters of the Arabian Sea, knowing he is bound to cross one way or another, he allows himself to be amused by the free entertainment. Lacking in musical talent, he does not participate, but his role as audience shores up the musicians, aware as they are of the restraint in his presence.

The giraffes are fine musicians with a developed passion for flute playing. But though they can blow long, loud, and deep, they cannot do the fingering. The little jerboas, hopping like crazy and happy to be of service (oh yes, indeed, happy happy!), band together. Covering and uncovering holes, they press their cheeks hard against the openings on the silver tubes, following the score, and sing away at the top of their tiny lungs. The sound they make is so minute, so high pitched, and so nearly inaudible, that it lies on the surface of the music made by the giraffes, whose flutes stretch out beautifully in tone. But sensitive as they are, picking up on tunes from the center of the earth, the giraffes miss the deeper meaning of the songs they play. Like many of the animals in the down-drift, they are blind to the sources of their impulses and impending consequences.

The piping jerboas add sparkle, a kind of pricked accent topping the melodic line with a bit of peep-peep. When the music is over and the giraffes set down their hollow wooden instruments, the jerboas lean back against the barrel-shaped flutes and jabber among themselves, reviewing the nuances of the performance, thinking about where and how to improve their timing and tone. They are sticklers for sound quality and emotional range, as are the giraffes, and the renown of the instrumentalists will grow exponentially as the sounds carry on the breezes of the Serengeti.

The lion is deeply moved by sight of the little jerboas, heads to the side, cheeks covering the flute holes, gazes bright and necks stretched in the effort. Dreams seem to float above their heads, small films of fantasy, as they lean and lift, close the gaps and open them, making the music happen. He swats idly at the illusion, but this causes panic among the rodents, and they scatter for cover, ending the musical interlude for the afternoon.

Animal Banquet
Massachusetts

CALLIE IS ENJOYING MUSIC, TOO, AT a banquet held near the beavers' fruit stand. Following her disappointments with data, she decided to come back for more of the forest-and-farm-to-table cuisine and has happened onto this celebration of abundance organized by the possums and the badgers. She feels like a part of the small community, and gets a warm welcome from the avuncular beavers and their extended family. The event is a bursting forth of the fruits of the earth and the riches of the field, the final bits of harvest piled high. Everyone is there who can be. The earthworms are sitting up at the table and behaving. The possums, never altogether hygienic, managed to wrap dinner napkins around their necks as a nod to the occasion. One grizzled badger's eyes turn a deep, deep blue so that when he picks up his silver knife and fork he has the most distinguished air of anyone at the meal. Narcissism has that random way of breaking out.

General harmony prevails through the soup course, but chaos reigns by the time they are at the salad. The dishes are strewn everywhere, to the consternation of the older squirrels and senior rabbits, who have been put in charge of the cutlery and place settings. The cat doesn't care, as long as there is cream, which the cows have generously donated.

The possums are sly and yank at the cloth, sending the serving dishes flying. The young raccoons, who can never behave, are probably the ones walking on the linens and soiling the cushions. But they lie about it—even to the hounds, who have come to intervene. The little squirrels have turned off the surveillance cameras. Rumor has it they are in cahoots with the baby raccoons. But if that is the case, who paid them? The young squirrels have no change on them when they are searched, and the raccoons are out of currency that month owing to charges they are paying for minor marauding at the solstice. The damages paid just for this one night's use of rented glassware and ceramics put the rabbits into debt, which they resent. After all, they are the last to be involved in the ruckus that has upset the table and sent it crashing to the ground, where the particles it unleashes can only be traced in physics at a nanoscale.

The cat watches in bemusement, satisfied by the meal of full-fat dairy she has enjoyed at everyone else's expense. Her life is feeling more like the old days, except that everything has changed.

But under the table, in the deep dirt, a churning-up of discontent can be felt among the organisms disenfranchised from the feast. Those workers go unrecognized in the larger scheme of things. They are undocumented, unappreciated, and restless. But they are the essential enzymes and cata-lyzers of basic processes. Some, like mitochondria, see themselves as the lynchpin to more than a few major aspects of production and reproduction. Others, the mutualists and commensualists, resent being ignored, even if it is out of character to expect anything like compensation for our work. Yes, our work, for these are my species, and though I lie latent for much of the time, unspeaking and inconspic-uous, I am never far from any of these events.

Like so many experiments, the banquet is not to be repeated, though the habit of semi-formal meals and social gatherings will gain momentum as time passes. But a mixed-feast banquet that is a free-for-all among the species, a potluck of social mores, is not proposed again.

Strange Mutations
Various Locations

THE SLOW-TURNING CYCLE OF THE SEASONS, fall to winter, brings different moods to different climates and geogra-phies. The changes are still happening everywhere, sometimes quickly, as when a host of turtle hatchlings, still sticky from their leathery egg cases, picks up bows and stretches strings across their little carapaces so that they can orchestrate their first days in unison. Or when a family of irritable, anxious Chihuahuas turns over their assets and confesses to laundering funds for a crime syndicate by smuggling diamonds in their collars—and are given amnesty by the administrating hounds on account of a plea bargain made by hyena lawyers. A flock of swallows, just returned from a long migratory flight, is met by a company of doves and pigeons who offer them soft straw beds and plates of grub worms bursting with flavor. Disgusting or delightful? All depends.

The new kindnesses and compromises are sometimes counterbalanced by meanness, but less often as the weeks go on. No costs are associated with good deeds. But some things do not change. Water moccasins cannot be trusted as nannies, and that is neither surprising nor mutable, but neither is the endless need for Labs to court approval, which makes them wretched prosecutors and, oddly, worse teachers than administrators. Many things are changing fast, but a detectable consistency links these shifts with trends of old.

Keeping track is a mere matter of looking around. But much escapes the common view, and that, of course, is where the risk lies—not that surveillance would or could have prevented any of these events.

A rash of wild mutation breaks out. The air is filled with the mutant cries of innovation: the sound of the deer-hogs and call of the crick-cats, the barking dog-bats and shrieking lizard-gulls and low sad song of a gator-fish stranded on land who longs to return to the deep blue waters. Hooved mice and long-tailed swans, winged coyotes and sharp-toothed finches—the whole wildly combinatoric vocabulary of features breaks out in every possible configuration, as if a roulette wheel is spinning and a harlequinade of parts can be assembled at any scale or across the most improbable divides. A slithering snake sprouts whiskers, the flying cranes sport fins, and the sheep contract gills as if they are an advantage rather than a liability when grazing.

Troubles begin to mount, medical and social, as lines of distinction and patterns of well-being blur friend and foe, hunted and predator, food source and family. The rising wave of potential disruption begins to be felt, slightly, but surely.

Change takes another form ahead. Because as rapidly as the season of mutations and hybrids had advanced, it subsides. The hybrids reach dead ends in their genetic lineage. They cannot interbreed to replicate their freakish features into another generation, or to cross-fertilize further and make yet another weird outcome of borrowed elements grafted one to another as in some sideshow experiment.

Only a few residues of the hybrid outbreak remain. Some features take hold, the obvious elements of creeping contamination, if that is the right term for such an efflorescence of radical exchange. But for the most part, the species absorb the changes as motifs, rather than dominant traits, so that though fishes whine following their brief genetic exchange with hyenas, they do not bark or snarl for long.

When the entire inventory of behaviors is up for grabs, the gamble of each day has an edge of danger as well as surprise. Neither a howling moth nor a fanged swan is at ease with itself, and the sheer rate of change can be baffling. A few puppies slither on their bellies across dry, patchy ground, and a toad or two, tired of grubs and larvae, goes vegetarian. The scales the mice absorb from the pythons soften into a pattern in the fur, and the whiskers on the snakes become a line or two of specialized sensing apparatus on the outside of the cheek. The silverfish lose their taste for fresh milk and their mouthparts harden again, soft lips absorbed, as they return to their love of paste and glue and paper—all substances eschewed by the suckling piglets and calves from whom they borrow a momentary interest in dietary alternatives.

But this repair process is deceptive, particularly with regard to social traits. The seepage of behaviors is more insidious, more permanent, and deeper-rooted than any superficial morphological alternation. Easy to spot a stray body part, a protruding wing on a carp or a claw emerging from the soft tentacles of an anemone. But who can detect a tendency for gossip spreading across the savannah? Or the knack for embezzlement breaking out like a rash among the goats? Or the need to unionize arising among the badgers? These are unpredictable elements in the changing world— ones that imprint and erupt as surely as webbed feet and hypersensitive hearing.

Entertainment Industries
Micro-Geographies

ALSO UNNOTICED IS THE RISING TIDE of a macro-organization, a social organism not defined by simple shape or form. That is me, taking shape, taking hold, conglomerated and cooperative, difficult to define or delimit. I am not alone in these transformations, and the boundaries of self and other, individual and group, are dissolving as part of the downdrift while an obscure but effective communication system is emerging.

As an increase in reading and writing appears, along with the love of figuring, calculating, computing, and even algorithmic processing, the interest in legislating, in legal training and certification, in the professions of accounting and statistical analysis, also rises. So do the culinary arts and skills in trade and shopkeeping, teaching, editing, proofreading with all of their minor benefits and major pitfalls.

But the area that booms most intensely? Entertainment. Every species optimizes their musical ability, innate rhythms, melodic capacity, compositional and choreographic possibilities. What talents, what amusing and fantastic abilities appear. The knock-kneed cranes dance in a chorus line and the pelicans belt out their backup harmonies. The koalas, always good at percussion, are happy to supply the rhythm when the old goats want to fiddle or the deep-voiced hippos choose to sing the blues. And while they fiddle, a slow-burning, subdued and smoldering force begins to spread.

Lawsuits and litigation, diversions and distractions, cannot substitute for productivity in other sectors of the economy. Hard work lies ahead. The process of planning and development sobers some of the animals as a new cycle of seasons registers a fresh wave of downdrift influences across the many and diverse populations. Small and tall, innocent and wily, terrified and eager, ferocious, tame, calm, or inclined to bursts of rage, the swift and the slow, the meek and the mighty, all are subject to the shifting conditions of their existence. But what they cannot factor is a phenomenon unlike the others, of something not just different from themselves, but from all of them.

They are becoming each other. The animals don't just imitate others, but absorb body language and genetic knowledge, social attitudes and behaviors. They learn reflection, the splitting between being and knowing, seeing and representing, awareness itself and awareness of self. Without their accounting for it, the hybridization of species is crossing encoding and information at the molecular level. They are themselves and each other. It is monstrous, inevitable, unpreventable. The waves of exchange erode the edges and boundaries of distinction, until the cries of the animals and the sighs of all the sentient creatures cannot be told one from another because they are so much the same in impulse and intention. Whose intention? Whatever is driving the downdrift, agency and will are not the same and that change has its own momentum.

Chimp Mania for Jewels
Addis Ababa

THE LION IS OBLIVIOUS TO HOLIDAYS and human cycles. So he is spared some of the misery that the chimps experience. He is close enough to the capital city of Addis Ababa to be aware of the humans' excitement, but still deep enough in the brush to know what is afoot among the animals.

The gift-giving season is coming, and those without families hunker down, resigned to their lonely fate. Maybe this is what is upsetting the chimps, because they are tearing at their clothes. They had been ravenous for fashion, but now the chimps' love of garments is turning dark. This is clearly an onset symptom, with wanton and sudden fits of destruction appearing commonly among the animals.

The chimps have plundered scores of secondhand stores, especially the consignment boutiques where they find the display cases by the cash registers piled high with baubles. Like the crabs, they are shameless in their love of flash and sparkle, at least in the first phases of delirium. They weight themselves with fake jewels and artificial pearls, cheap brilliants and soft metal fittings more lead than gold. Whatever baubles are left behind, they take.

The parodic appearance of their bedecked bodies, so human and so hirsute, quickly vanishes as the sight of their swaggering becomes familiar. Among the elite, a taste for the real thing quickly emerges. First they become attuned to the locked cases, to the precious stones in jewel boxes shining against velvet couching. Then they become discriminatory, testing the color of sapphires against their palms to sense the enhancement of skin tone, opting for deeper or paler stones depending on their own disposition and coloration.

Not one of them has a taste for diamonds. They find the hard stones too soulless, too pristine, and without pigment. The chimps have a strong preference for the richer colors of rubies and emeralds, and a nearly freakish dislike for opals, whose reputation for ill fortune has come into their collective understanding.

As the downdrift surges, the passion for adornment goes in waves. The chimps bedeck themselves to the point of magnificence, elaborate as royal icons paraded in the streets, layered with rich stuffs that are embroidered, encrusted, laced, and brocaded. They are almost lost in the layers and layers of cloth, chains, strands of things hanging and dangling. And then, in a fit of furious pique, they just tear the whole mass away, ripping the necklaces free so the beads spring loose and bounce hither and yon, stripping the cloth into shreds and remnants that disperse to the winds, and rend the seams, destroying the items of clothing and even attacking the cloth until it is mere threads. *Why, why, why?* They cry as they do it, deeply disturbed, screaming their chimp heads off. After a while they calm down, then the cycle begins again. An expensive habit to support, but they have resources.

Within earshot of their bad behavior, other expressions of frustration are palpable. The lion does not care for complaints. The idea of headphones does not cross his mind, and it never will, but his cubs would have happily shared their music libraries with him if he had been able to ask. Sitting out the various rounds of destruction, he also avoids the hoarding and collecting impulse. His material treasures are all vanishing. He cannot hoard the open spaces, wide horizons, and available game of his past.

Crazed Hares
Near Newton, Massachusetts

CALLIE IS MESMERIZED, HER GOLDEN EYES holding steady in amazement. Having benefitted from a renewed food supply and a boost of emotional support from the beavers, her spirits are much improved. She can even imagine adoption as a future possibility. Except for a few stubborn stains, her calico coat is clean and shiny, her whiskers stand out sharply, and her demeanor indicates lively spirits and attention, which she now bestows on a manic hare careening madly on a small Bobcat dirt digger. Its zigzag path cuts a wide furrow across the swath of cleared land edged by a patch of bare deciduous trees, scrawny limbs outlined against the sky. The vehicle's giant yellow wheels and black cab turn into streaks of color against the subtle monochrome backdrop of the winter landscape, gouging the earth as it swerves, while the hare's ears stream out behind its head, leaning dangerously beyond the protective cage of the cab. The hare is full of crazed energy and wanton abandon. He is drunk on the sheer vertigo of moving fast with that much momentum, mass, and speed.

The first hare is followed by another, then another, until there are nearly a dozen mover-loaders and tractors of all kinds cavorting in a dizzying frenzy of activity in the open field, turning and twirling in a dervish dance. It would go on forever, like a strange monster derby, but the hares drive so recklessly their vehicles quickly get stuck on boulders, twisted around trees, upended in the drainage ditch that edges the field. Mere minutes after the activity begins, it ends in a mass of grunting motors, spinning wheels, and whining parts. The hares shiver as they get off the trucks, shaking with insane delight, their long front teeth chattering in a staccato tattoo while they hop and hop, one foot to another, in a crazed celebration of their destructive acts.

So begins a new level of change, and whether the transformation of overt behaviors or internal structure is more profound is hard to say, since the bees begin to think like bison and the giraffes set up permanent stands along the roadsides near the hotels, selling CDs under their own labels.

Acute sensory disorder is setting in. The visual acuity of the raptors is migrating to the rodents and the sniffing skills of the dogs have gone into the primate populations—who always loved each other so much before they became sensitive to issues of hygiene.

The cat stands spellbound as the hares retreat from the destruction they have wrought and leave the field to a set of tortoises who, slowly, as is their habit, edge forward into the disorder. They are known, of course, for their geographical acuity and are usually brought into the surveying phase of any project, but this is an unusual sequence of events, coming late in the messy game. Someone on some regulatory committee, probably a badger, has given them a call. They show up, ever steady, to see if they can make a livable environment of the savaged terrain. They never use GPS devices and have developed alternative cartographies, guided by an intimate experience of the landscape. The tortoises offer their surveying skills reluctantly, knowing they are contributing to the downfall of much they treasure. A dogged resignation guides their judgment but they are good citizens and would rather see things done well than badly.

Tortoise Metrics
Newton, Massachusetts

ON THIS PARTICULAR AFTERNOON OF CHAOS, as the tortoises enter the field the hares have gouged and mutilated, a very senior tortoise team carefully marks out new boundaries under the calico's absorbed gaze. She cannot believe the spectacle and is afraid any comment she offers will seem amateur. Her dirt digging skills are probably not wanted, specific as they are to other purposes.

The heavy turtles work very, very slowly, with great consideration. They never lie or cheat or let their skills be used for graft of any kind, so their progress keeps halting as decisions are revisited, rethought, and revised. Forward momentum becomes almost impossible as they draw and redraw the territories under consideration. Their timescale is their own, and they use the metrics of a very slow assessment to mark the features of the world against the coordinates of a human system they find inadequate to their understanding of the land. They know trails and fixities, orientations and directions. Way-finding and even the abstractions of mapping are part of their inventory of techniques. They think space as they move through it. The cat is awestruck and twitches in appreciation.

What the tortoises do not understand is commodification or division of land into parcels. Boundaries and distinctions that have to do with arbitrary lines are absent from the registry that they have kept since ancient times. Their list of place names and associations is steeped in ways of experiencing the land, not ceding ownership. From their point of view, the land cannot be owned any more than the sky, which is open to all to view. But what they know and how they know it is graphed in every hatchmark and contour line that marches across the broad, flat sheets of drawing paper over which they pore, pens in beaks, putting every single detail into the maps directly. The broken field dismays them, but the damage is superficial, not profound.

Some wolves, roaming beyond their range and affecting disinterest, circle around the project, closing ranks and waiting as light fades in the afternoon. This makes the cat more than a little anxious, and she effaces herself as much as she can, pressed against the winter ground, hoping her calico patches work as camouflage. Always opportunistic, the wolves hedge their bets with an exit strategy that costs them little more than a bit of fur left behind in the game and a slight dip in their reputations. Whether the hares are reckless or careless is not the point. The law is the law. But as dusk falls and the tortoises lumber off the field, the wolves take advantage of a loophole in the justice code. They sniff around at the edges of the field, not quite concealed by the undergrowth in the woods. Their movements, stealthy though they are, are noted by the watchful hares. The wolves circle around and cause a distraction so they can snatch one of the long-toothed, long-eared hares from the group. They carry their hapless prey into the woods, muffling its screams, but the sounds are a reminder of the lingering impulses of their tribe.

On the other side of the field, where the project is further along, a team of systematic and thoroughly responsible badgers is in a reasonably good mood, all things considered. They are laying out forms to pour concrete and, without dallying in the least, are taking their time about it, eager to please the ancient tortoises whose judgment they respect. They level the ground, measure, and then square the boards until everything sings true. They take real pleasure in the simple architecture of the layout. They are very patient, waiting for the concrete, taking in the sweet smell of fresh pine rising from the grid of intersecting planks and posts of the form. They take pride in their work, which is finely crafted, almost art, even if they do it without deliberate imagination, self-consciousness, or reflexivity. They make good foremen, too, and one with a clipboard and hardhat and a supervisory mentality is keeping the whole troop of workers coordinated.

Everything is being done according to code, and just right. Then, without warning, a badger gets into a foul temper and tears at something, shredding a sheet of instructions or an inventory list. He stomps and swears like, well, like a badger, spitting and hissing. It isn't clear what has ticked him off or if, like some of the others among us, he has just had a bad spell, one of those times when his own energies are at cross purposes and nothing can make it come right.

Callie finds the noise obnoxious. The evening promises to be icy. Rather than return to the beavers, who are such good friends with the badgers, she seeks a sheltered spot where she can help herself to pickings in garbage. Unexpectedly, she finds a yard with a plate set out for another member of her species.

Sliced, shredded with gravy, chunky, special paté—these are categories she knows well. Kibble, another excellent term, fulfills her wildest dreams and she feasts, glad for caloric intake.

Camels and Committees
Toward the Port of Djibouti

AS THE MUTATION SPREADS, THE LION is farther than ever from his veldt and trapped in zones of development. Putrid toxins sap his energies. He does not notice the headlines or subtexts streaming around him on lit screens and goes on with his own consideration of the scenes before his eyes, glad to see a group of sage camels, resting from a desert walk, who are forming oversight commissions. He knows their extended family and trusts their ability to think through long-term questions. The dromedaries take their time to consider exactly who should do what and what should be done. The difficulty is that they operate at such a level of abstraction that it is not clear that the "what" of their reflection has any content at all.

Throughout the long evening, the lion lies in shadows while the camels—within earshot, but tied to their stalls— organize and re-organize the committee structure of the commission. But to what end and for what purpose? If any of them asks each other directly, they give their camel stare, unblinking, looking back straight in the eye. Their flat heads, with their elaborate cooling system, keep them from overheating in the hot desert temperatures, but also keep them from any haste at all in decision-making. They chew, their leathery lips and mouths grinding. Just as they extract every possible ounce and drop of moisture in the process of digestion, so they seem to distill all nutrients from their thinking process. They are social animals, and their ability to work together has a long history and many obvious demonstrations. They draw on all of this to assert their natural right to lead the commissions. This vagueness would have been annoying in the autumn, when the brisk air suggested progress might be accomplished, but winter nights are long and any diversion is welcome. Camels are desert creatures. They could not care less. They wait, ruminating. Perhaps they know more than they let on.

The lion, vaguely amused, is distracted by the camel's musings and organizational talk. He will be on the move again soon, but for the moment, he lets the dust filter into his fur, eyelids drooping, while he considers whether or not his fate and the future hang in any balance whatsoever. The dust feels good, smothering vermin and reminding him of home. Before he falls asleep, he lets out a few editorial comments to the camels, who consider what he has to say and his advantages as an untethered animal. Luckily, their respect is mutual, and the lion, having had a long royal career, has no interest in interfering in their commissions.

Possum Adornments
Near Newton, Massachusetts

IN THE DARK WINTER NIGHT NEAR Callie, possums are discovering the thrilling pleasures of paste jewelry. Bedazzled, they catch all kinds of reflections and are as thrilled as the crabs are to become known as the Adorned. They have been the Scorned for so long they don't care if the bling is cheap and the glint of light refracts from a synthetic gem, they just like the way the lightweight stuff sits on their spiky fur and distracts from the sight of skin beneath their hairy pelts.

Possum laughter is just a shimmery scratch against the glass, something high and uncertain, arrhythmic, happening moment to moment and not to be predicted. They bare their teeth as they laugh, which is not attractive, even to them. The cold has set in with a vengeance, so they use ice crystals to make themselves alluring to each other. It is a possum thing. But the shimmer is striking to any other possum eye and, mercifully, the melting ice does very little harm to their mascara, which is waterproof.

Feeling out of place among the possums, and not wanting to seem like a voyeur, Callie is about to leave when suddenly she finds herself in an extremely awkward situation. She happens onto a gang of raccoons who are in an awful frenzy. An ungodly noise comes from behind the trash bins in an alley where the ice has rutted the ground. The frozen tracks hold the bins in an unkind grasp Callie wants to avoid. She is afraid to show herself, but is trapped, sandwiched between the fence she leaped from and the exit to the street, with the raccoon racket in-between. Raccoons in this mood can be pretty rough.

The raccoons are tearing into the air with fanged fury, their fur spiked in tight points and eyes narrow with anger. They are wearing belts, wide flat leather belts with buckles of all kinds, blazoned with emblems to brand their presumed personalities. The standard square fittings, dull brass with the finger through the clasp, are elaborately wrought to display self-importance in the worked motifs. These fetish features occupy their time. They dressed this morning with meticulous care to polish the adornments that shine against their pelt, across their tawny bellies, where their underfur meets their topcoat bristles.

In this mood of unabated emotion, choler rises in their swollen gorges. They strain against the leather straps. Any hint of uplift vanishes in the overwhelming force of unmitigated anger. Their bolo ties swing with whiplash speed, tangled in their spiked fur. They cannot stop until their vocal instruments go raspy, their lungs exhausted, their pointed faces streak with tears squeezed like the juice of pressed spirits against the insides of their black-masked eyes. Too hideous to behold, they drop, one after another, done in by the passionate exhalation of their energies.

Callie has no idea what has caused this and only wants to stay out of their way while the frenzy burns itself out. They seem to be screaming from the sheer agony of being, crazed at the absolute pain of existence. Despair leaves no useful residue, but the cat is just grateful to be spared their wretchedness—or its effects—by keeping to the shadows.

Shipping Lines and Hyena Skills
Ethiopia to Mangalore

THE LION ENCOUNTERS A NEW URBAN group of hyenas, harsh and clever, meting their merciless judgments on the smallest of shareholders in the company that pays their salaries. They are ready to perform a disgusting rodent holocaust, but a posse of elder rhinos, possibly members of the company's board, is imposing some restraint. The rhinos' brains are heavy with old rain that had seeped into their leathery flesh through chinks in their psychic armor. Their thick hides make them impervious to the bites of yipping critters, the bad little grave-robbing, conscienceless scavengers. So they can hold their own when they want to, as now, protecting a shuddering rodent horde huddled among the stocky pillars of their legs.

The hyenas are good at many things. They recycle foil with a great passion, flattening its convoluted mass into worried surfaces that they read as if an augury. The rhinos keep them around for amusement, even if they have to police

their behaviors at times. The hyenas perform wild and flagrant rituals. They disgust some of the herd animals, but the
rhinos are willing to ignore the judgment of other groups for
the sake of their own, which they deem superior. After all,
the hyenas are helpful to them in many ways. For instance,
they have an uncanny ability to assess inventory and are
involved in what they consider to be a cargo cult.

Every shipping office in the Ethiopian port always has at
least one hyena in the office to gauge volume and track pack-
ages. The rhinos employ two in order to keep them honest.
The pair on today's shift is brilliant, but not trustworthy. The
hyenas are exchanging sidelong glances—not a desirable
trait in employees entrusted with precious cargo shipments.
These two are squabbling about the percentages they are
skimming, giving their game away.

The hyenas are eager to trick the rhinos and put a few
things over on the customs agents. So they help the lion stow
away on a steamer carrying freight toward India. They find
him a place amid some cargo that contains foodstuffs he
gnaws on during the crossing. These provisions include hard
cheese and dried meat, some casks of a liquid with a sour
taste and the nice effect of putting him in a mellow, drowsy
mood. This makes the voyage tolerable. He has no idea of
seas and ports, of foreign places, unknown languages, of
papers and borders and customs officials. And perhaps this
serves him well because, on docking in Mangalore, he manages to slip through the border to the strange shores where
heat and dry warm air bring him his first taste of Asian
climes. This is just a stepping stone on his journey, transfer-
ring him from one landmass to another en route to his
meeting with Callie. But he is oblivious to that trajectory and
sees the unfamiliar shape of the world around him as

another marker of distance from his habitat. As all too often, he feels the loss of everything he has ever known or relied on as he passes through one human habitat after another.

The lion moves to the outskirts of the port for a few days respite and immerses himself in the local life, cold nights, and warm days. Red scorpions dance among the hot rocks in one of the neighborhoods, tuned to the vibrations of the atmosphere and the rhythms of the tiny dust storms made by the heat. Rising air quivers along their hard carapaces, and the arched tail, lifted arms, and side-step motions have more delicacy as a quick step than not. The lion cannot imitate their deft dance, but as he makes a clumsy attempt, the scorpions echo his motions in recognition of their shared circumstances. The heat engulfs them in the swirl of its thermal drafts and the lion and the scorpions share an atavistic exchange of basic vitalism. Nothing will restore him, but these moments of recognition give him the energy to keep going and the scorpion dance works like a tonic to revive his determination.

January

Municipal Dogs
Arlington, Massachusetts

THE WORLD IS DRAMATICALLY CHANGED IN the months since Callie slipped out of her back door into the ever-stranger world. As the new year begins, many offices and counters in the county administration building are opening, and she finds that almost all of the positions in civil service have been filled by dogs. They have taken over the DMV, for instance, and everybody is happy about it. Callie is not sure what to think. This claim of universal satisfaction is either a flagrant lie or a blatant exaggeration, but the year is off to a cheerful start and the dogs are trained and ready. They are not going to increase efficiency; given the legacy systems they have inherited that would be impossible. But they are making it such a pleasant experience to be in line and at the counters that some former customers come by just to say hello.

"Yeah yeah, hi hi, good good, so good to see you, yeah yeah," they say in grunts and barks that are short of speech but long on enthusiasm. That's how it goes all day. No one looks at the clock, and since the winter days are short, the dogs sometimes close early and go home promising to be back the next day, "Right-oh, oh yeah."

Even before the downdrift, the dogs were not subtle. Only time will tell how outrageous they become. They frequently mistake their capacity for service with ability for diplomacy. Unfortunate. They are very much mistaken and they are not the only ones.

This is not my zone. Bureaucracy offers me no particular advantage over other sites of pollution. My preference for extremes leaves me little appetite for the bland suffocating banalities of local government and no taste for the off-gassing of social systems. I am drawn to other kinds of toxic waste, chemical rather than psychic. Physical byproducts are so much to be preferred.

Stereotypes of Frogs and Bunnies
The Winter Woods

TIIIS JANUARY MORNING CALLIE WATCHES A very young, lean fox moving with great deliberation through the winter woods. He does not see her, and she makes sure it stays that way. Species protections are advancing at very uneven rates. She continues to err on the side of caution.

The noise of underground laughter catches the fox's keen ear and tickles the hairs that are the first receptors in his auditory systems. Bunnies, giggling bunnies, he thinks to himself conjuring the image of them, laughing away, their eyes welling up with rabbit water. He hears music, too.

The frogs in the neighborhood have brought out their banjos and are playing for all the world like they are in some bad cartoon. The frogs hate the stereotype but perform to make the bunny babies laugh, especially on long, cold winter afternoons when everyone should be sleeping, but somehow, cannot. This is a kindness, to be sure. The bunnies milk it. I sense a high concentration of hydrogen somewhere in the neighborhood and gravitate toward it, absorbing as much as I can and go latent, soaking the nutrient into my system, hoping to boost my vitality.

The fox sighs, a preview of what awaits him at home vivid as his breath in front of him in the cold air. The bunnies take advantage of the guilt of the vixens. They request compensation for generations of bad behavior and asked to be spoiled outrageously. They want to be fed, then groomed, then tucked into their burrows at night. Now they have crossed a line by asking for play dates with the kits. This hits the foxes where it hurts. Offering service to the mindless fluffy bunny babes is one thing, but offering social opportunities with their own precious offspring is another.

One old vixen is telling her pups to clean their teeth and refrain from nipping and barking because it makes the bunnies cry. The yipping kits are protesting that the bunnies are too high maintenance, which just starts the whole cycle over again. This is too tedious for the vulpine maternal mind. The bunnies are at risk of losing the gamble. The vixens are threatening to flee and leave them abandoned. The bunnies know that the rabbit warrens are full of aging females willing to foster them, but the truth is that even the bunnies find their own kind too boring for conversation.

On that chill afternoon, before he turns into a quiet lane, the fox witnesses a whole pack of little rabbits heading back into a public square. They sit down on the benches at the street corners looking pathetic, as if hoping for adoption. He knows it's a scam—they have perfectly good homes to go back to—but even so, he thinks it's a credit to the foxes that they do not take advantage of the situation. The lop-eared con artists stay out of the tabloids and out of jail in spite of their public begging, at least for now.

In the bare branches above the benches where the bunnies huddle in forlorn heaps, a little ground squirrel twirls acrobatically. Her feet are naked. She has shed the anklets that were so trendy just a few weeks earlier. Even if they feel welcome in the winter air, she has had to give them up. They catch too easily on the branches and trip her and her companions in their rapid flight. The tiny circlets of bejeweled chain that cling tightly to their wrists are immune from these accidental snags, but the anklets are dangerous.

Subtle, but elegant, the shiny chains accessorize her just enough that the bracelets are now all the rage. The affectation of the girl squirrel is evident in her posture. Between acrobatic acts, she walks upright more than is absolutely necessary, drops her hands at the wrist in a pose meant to call attention to her decorations. No one minds. Much.

The bunnies resent the attention the squirrel attracts. The foxes turn their heads upward toward the daredevil act in the branches. But then they all witness a scene of jealousy and the little acrobatic squirrel is battered and weeping, her favorite chain having been pulled brutally from her, scraping against the paw and leaving her skin raw between patches of damaged fur. Not nice. The bunnies are much better behaved than that and shake their heads, ears flopping.

Shame and consternation spread among the squirrel councils. The bruised acrobat brings a case of abuse forward but is unsure whether to take action or ask for warnings. The foxes refuse to give testimony and the bunnies are way too shy to appear in court.

Callie, never litigious, is hoping this case will not lead to frequent lawsuits. She gives her own stern encouragement to restore appropriate decorum—sending the squirrel and her companions to the upper range of branches, though to chase them upwards she has to walk through nutshells, which are sharp on her paws and stink of rodent droppings. Sometimes one must make sacrifices in the service of civility.

Archaean Troubles: Sick in Massachusetts

MY INNARDS WRENCH FROM MY OWN struggles. Some vile tricksters are in motion. A virus tries to replicate itself in me. I keep refusing its demands.

I am still dedicated to preserving my non-pathogenic code of ethics. Penetration and occupation are not necessarily fatal forms of aggression and I want to be present throughout living systems, not destroy them.

Stealth is integral to my existence, but I am learning something else, hunger, and not just from Callie and the lion. The impulse to consume might be the seepage effect taking hold. I had always absorbed nutrients, never longed for them. My appetites are increasing in a way I have never experienced. I do not benefit from the despair or sadness of others, though this will not protect me, as I will soon find.

I wonder if I can move as I started to do earlier, by intention. I wait, unsure how to take even the most tentative steps or actions. My impulses beat freakishly, off the diagnostic charts. I feel a conflict within myself as my anxiety rises and a tension between knowing and not-knowing arises. I hoard phosphates in anticipation of stress, even some that glow in the darker crevices of my experience, and try to tolerate the ambiguity.

Primate Governance
Near Chenai, India

THE LION HITCHES A RIDE ON another freighter from
Mangalore to Chenai. Along the shoreline he sees groups of
gazelles clustered, heads bent in collective concentration.
They are working on a group identity, trying to agree on the
features of their brand. Some gibbons are watching warily.
Primate professionalism is on the rise. The introduction of
rules promises to provide a relatively smooth organizational
transition to governance. But a bunch of baboons pick a
quarrel with the gibbons. They are very competitive. The
baboons want to advance quickly and the gibbons just like
to throw things far and wide, with wanton gestures. They
shriek with delight. But they won't sit still for a meeting.
This bad behavior at the macro-level may have repercussions for the microorganisms as well, but that is not on the
minds of the primates.

Then a handsome gibbon, as beautiful as many of his
kind, arrives in a single swift swing into the assembled group.
He is clearly eager to appear before the audience and show
off his skills in public speaking as well as his physical agility.
He holds onto the rafters as he crosses the room and drops
with consummate grace in front of the enthralled circle. The
baboons are seated first, grabbing chairs and trying to exercise a monopoly on the allocation of benches. They are much
more interested in protocol than substance. The bylaws they
are offering to the organization have mainly to do with the
sequence of events and the rules of procedure. An opposing
party, composed of the more intellectually inclined gibbons,
offers an alternative plan based on the importance of service
to the community. They want to think seriously about an
integrated system of pocket parks and green spaces and are

ready with rolled plans and whitepapers for presentation. The rate of change is clearly escalating.

The gibbons are not really civic-minded, but they take professionalism seriously, seeing it as a way to protect their own interests while benefitting others. Given the differences in attitude, it's not surprising that very little gets accomplished in this meeting. From a distance, the gazelles, nonjudgmental but observant, watch as the primates do a lot of scratching, their long fingers buried in their fur, eyes traveling back and forth across each other's faces.

By any standard measure of productivity, the experiment in primate governance is a failure, at least the first few times around. If the elephants had not been suffering from their near-fatal melancholy, they could have helped. They are parliamentarians to the core and also keen to promote professional behavior themselves. But the devastation wrought by a large deforestation project has left them nearly inert with sadness, paralyzed by a sense of futility. They can hear the chattering of the meeting but do not bestir themselves to participate.

The lion watches the events on the distant shore as his ship slips through warm foreign waters. He preserves his dignity by refusing to participate in the quarrels of others. That is a luxury he will not be able to preserve. In Chenai, he disembarks, avoiding the watchful eye of whatever unsuspecting human stands on the pier, and begins another very long walk, this time into the Asian continent.

I also feel compelled to sit on the sidelines, wishing that I had been gifted with motivational speaking instead of being sentenced to the muteness of the microorganism. I am struggling. The macho virus paying too-persistent attention refuses to accept that no means no. I try to wriggle away from my unwelcome suitor, appalled that such behaviors even affect ungendered creatures.

Center of Social Media
Plymouth, Massachusetts

CALLIE IS IN THE MIDST OF social media exchanges, bombarded with messages from all over. She is shocked to find herself the recipient of so much information. Suddenly plugged into networked communications channels, she gets news about some species so far at a distance she could never have imagined their relevance to her life.

Right now, she is baffled by finding out, via some site that would have been utterly inconsequential several months earlier, that winter does not matter to the screaming chimps. They are posting selfies all over the place, showing them tearing at their clothes in the equatorial kingdoms the lion has left behind. Why do they wear them? No one is quite sure. They are not required to, after all, the habits of exposing chest and belly and genitals without much ado are long established. No one cares about their underpits and or the patchy hair that looks unsightly by contrast to the newly cosmeticized gibbons and orangutans. But the tearing frenzy is one of the symptoms that breaks out under stress, so Callie knows they are suffering.

The gibbons the lion had once gazed upon are now elegant beyond belief; their elongated limbs and variety of colors lend themselves to accessories. They set up sartorial competitions that are categorically unnecessary and even unfair. Whole online galleries and news stories are devoted to red carpet images.

Exhausted and resting in a bamboo grove, the lion naps and ignores these developments until the noise around him becomes too raucous to ignore. A group of vacationing penguins, extremely stylish birds, have found out about the cigarette flaunting behavior of the crows. Given the state of avian communication in the winter months, when migratory routes see little traffic, this news comes after a delay. But now the networks light up with the information.

The penguins are polar in their range, not hemispheric or global. But they also get news from a distance. One traveling band had been on tour that winter, and they used the high northern lights and southern auras in their transmissions. Their thin skulls take in electromagnetic waves. But without a shred of doubt, they are flabbergasted hearing about crows smoking and strutting. Well, less surprised about the strutting. Being polite and highly decorous, the penguins drop their eyes and say just a few very, very discreet things to each other about the crows. The collective opinion forms swiftly. They are all in agreement. They open their mouths, all at once, and shake their heads, in sync, as a total population saying, "That's enough." On some topics, one does not speak or comment. Needless to say, they never ever thought it cool to smoke.

Now, that is classy. Definitely a behavior to be imitated later on. The mounting pressures are becoming so evident that soon none will be able to ignore them.

Philosophy Among the Elephants
Just North of Chenai

THOUGH HE HAS NEVER BEEN THERE before, the lion can tell that the subcontinent is as altered as his own vast land. As he walks away from the port city, he finds that at every gate and entry, peacocks have volunteered for security work, much to the surprise of the nighthawks and crows, who already decided to divide the shifts between them. The

peacocks make the argument that they are more conspicuous, can be seen at a greater distance, and thus provide a
discouragement to bad behavior. Though it is hard to argue
with this, the crows do anyway. They love to argue, and even
if it is a total waste of time to have to indulge them, the fact
is that they cannot be silenced. The vibrations set up by their
squabbling register in some domains and not others, since
noise is a matter of frequency as well as volume.

The lion comes to a small covered gathering space where
a group of pachyderms is at work creating signs—glyphs and
characters proliferate from the brushes they hold in their
trunks. The scripting of elephant life is evidently intensifying
even as the vitality of the creatures seems to be fading. The
lion can still feel the emotional force of the massive animals
as a rolling wind along the ground. He feels their sadness in
his feet and legs, and his mane quivers in response. Empathy
is a physical condition, profound and immediate. When he
comes to a village market in the first afternoon of his journey
north, he finds the enormous animals hard at work dis-
playing the writing they did earlier. He wonders what to
make of the strange surfaces covered with signs.

He engages very briefly in conversation with the group.
No animosity colors their exchange. Clearly the elephants
have made a conceptual leap. They now apprehend themselves and their culture as something to be represented,
grasped, mediated, and discussed. The Philosophical Club,
their highest order, has taken up substantive topics. In a
manner not the least parodic or cartoonish, they discourse
at length and with considerable reflection upon the nature
of knowledge and language, of signs and reality, of illusion
and the cost of imagination in a world that needs fixing and
cannot be escaped. They feel the weight of that world and it

is always with them. They know the difference between being and presence, but not how to make use of these concepts in global political ecologies.

At the edge of the square where the market is held, a few mongooses have convened a meeting to touch base with the mythic image of their ancestor, that Buddhist god of wealth. They have packed their small jaws with jewels to spit forth a fountain of shining abundance. They are watched from a close distance by the avaricious rats and greedy millipedes. The effect of the spewing jewels is magical. The elephants say nothing. Knowing what they know, they do not need to comment, though they continue to share their sympathetic bond with the lion.

Shelter
Randolph, Massachusetts

FIRMLY ENSCONCED IN A SEMI-ABANDONED WAREHOUSE, Callie is deep asleep, head tucked firmly into paws. A kind-hearted workman leaves out milk and food and asks nothing in return, the only arrangement Callie is willing to risk with his species just now. Sometimes she is sorely tempted to return to her relative captivity, if she can only be guaranteed this level of comfort—with or without a contract. However, she is in no hurry to take up any particular commitment; as a feline, she knows better than to leap into any situation demanding responsibility or including expectations. This does not keep her from welcoming the efforts of others on her behalf, so long as naps and mealtimes are respected. Favors granted and gained are positive benefits, but only if they do not interfere with the important business of stretching, washing, or lying still in the deep dreamland of fertile feline imagination.

Even in her current wanderings, Callie has an abiding commitment to her own version of idleness, with its combined revolutionary and counterrevolutionary force. She sees no work at all as the only alternative to complicity with the cultural systems that are repugnant to her from whiskers to tail. She has a bodily resistance to authority, compliance, or duty, bred into her bones and purring mechanisms. Like the rest of her species, she is determined to maintain the status quo, hedging all bets by resisting agendas projected by others.

This reprieve from struggle and wandering is all well and good, but she knows she has to be vigilant about assaults on her leisure and the management of her sleeping portfolios and lazy assets. Now that she is warm and fed, she can be fussy about napping conditions—or leisure duties, to use her preferred vocabulary. She shakes off the challenges to her static state, making it clear she has no use for any other state at all.

But she finds no peace. She and the lion are each pursuing their individual routes with an independent sense of purpose. But the drive that guides decisions moment to moment determines a path that will bring them together against all odds and even chances. By then, the world will have changed even more, at least by most standards.

After a long, steady afternoon of napping, she finds the bowl remains empty and she takes this as an insult. Callie passes into the cold, cold night, taking reluctant leave. Some things are not to be tolerated.

Before long, she is attracted by flickering candlelight and the glow of steady flashlights. Is someone reading in the warm burrows tucked snugly away from the cold? She goes for a closer look, cautious and cold. Not the bunnies. They can't sit still long enough and nothing compensates for their almost universal tendency to be nearsighted. Their eyes blink constantly, trying to adjust to something just beyond reach—who knows what? But the point is that neither they nor the cats, who care absolutely not one bit for other species' writings, bother to learn the alphanumeric codes that have become the common currency of written literature. In lieu of literary distraction, the rabbits think of spring shoots and summer clover and get through the winter on optimism.

As to the lights in the night, it turns out to be a bunch of little badgers, reading comics and manga underneath their covers. The cat lets them go without a scolding, since their parents have turned a blind eye. The badgers look very serious, but as soon as Callie leaves, they giggle and go back to their reading.

Drooping Tigers
North of Chenai

WHEN THE MONSOONS SET IN, RAIN goes everywhere. Some populations flourish, others languish, some drown. But when the rains recede, other moods set in. A group of captive tigers are so defeated they won't eat. The lion finds them in their cages, enervated, depressed, overwhelmed with despair. They lie around, heads on paws, eyes filled with melancholy. Their keepers are on the verge of desperation until they learn that the one thing that will tempt the tigers is bowls of fresh Greek yogurt, granola, and blueberries.

The afternoon the lion visits the compound, their moods lift. A wave of gratitude rolls off them, soft as a summer breeze. They are grateful for the exchange of whiskered breath through the bars of their cages. But their elation passes quickly, poor things, and within almost twenty-four hours, they lose their taste for dairy. Coming back to see them the next day, the lion finds they have sunk down into the dark blues and darker-yet states of their minds, filled with the memory of habitats that are gone. Status-fallen, they are deeply depressed, as if they have caught the elephants' sorrow at a distance.

The deep slough of their despair creates an atmospheric problem, a low pressure in the general system. The mice and gerbils fall into these depressions. The tigers do not take them as prey, but the little rodent masses swarm and swarm and can't get the momentum to rise back out of those deep psychic holes. They have to be rescued from drowning in the morass of melancholy that the tigers pour into the world.

This communal melancholy is not a condition that can be tolerated, but the fix for it isn't apparent—at least not initially. The lion is also sinking hourly into greater despair as winter lengthens his journey.

FEBRUARY

Homes and Homeless
Attleboro, Massachusetts

THE CRAVING FOR SHELTER IS WIDESPREAD in February.
The birds who remain in the north hunker down. They have
very particular ideas of what is to be desired, even in the
smallest structures. As she crosses the woods toward the
marshlands, winding through the grasses in the dunes, Callie
hears whole committees of birds discussing and comparing
building types. Apparently the badger contractors are trying
to control the markets, capitalizing on the winter housing
crunch. The cat agrees with the birds that the badgers' eager-
ness to take advantage of seasonal pressures is inappropriate.
But the language of the birds is alarming, and they assert
their tastes with unseemly aggression, as if bravado might
protect them from the badgers' gouging policies. Meanwhile,
the cacophony assaults Callie, ambushing her in what she had
thought was an empty winter landscape. With as much politeness as possible, she excuses herself from their discussion.

Each species promotes its preferences and individual
tastes. Screaming their preferences loudly, the jays promote
glass and contemporary styles; the crows screech in favor of
cheap, fake rustic; the sparrows chirp specifications for

modest wooden structures; the herons, quite silently, see themselves in mid-century modern; and the mallards, not surprisingly, are traditionalists and let everyone know. A few upscale and out of place peacocks have put their own over-heated model homes on display. These are filled with mirrored surfaces, and generate a certain amount of snick-ering. Callie thinks this is uncalled for, since these were peacocks bred in captivity and cannot be held as examples of their kind, necessarily. She is not averse to mirrors, when her grooming is in order. Just now she turns away, unhappy with her ragged look.

The hummingbirds have gone south, but they have court orders staying the destruction of their hanging baskets. The badgers are adding slightly more elaborate roofing and eave construction than the little birds managed in the past. Construction is everywhere, and between the sound of tiny saws and little hammers and the jabbering of bird commit-tees reviewing plans, the whole landscape is alive with activity.

Callie feels acutely aware of her homelessness, especially as she encounters a small enclave of dog shelters. Every breed has expressed its desire for housing. A rash of shelter fever has taken over the region. The dogs already have their own "beds" in many places, if you can call those shaped bas-kets and flat pillows "beds"—which Callie, knowing how to take over a king-sized mattress on her own terms, does not. She understands their domestic longings. But why would anyone want a room of their own when you could take over everyone else's?

A generous golden retriever, noting her confusion, takes the time to explain to her that it isn't about the roof, floor, or bowl, but about building up a smell up over time. The dogs like to accumulate odiferous things, a bit of a well-chewed ball or a hunk of soggy sock or rag, a gnawed stick. Callie is all too aware of what this means but refrains from commenting.

One of the large canines installs chain-link in his yard, though a committee of collies and spaniels tries to discourage this extreme unsophistication. But the Great Dane, a noble beast, just laughs at the earnest collies for trying to enforce their own aesthetic standards in the expanding building programs. Matters of taste are hard to enforce without elaborate neighborhood covenants. The collies settle for gentle persuasion and offer free architecting and landscaping advice. But the Dane is having none of it.

A few little terriers wave from their rooftops, as excited about the elevation as they are content with the interiors of their abodes. At the center of the settlement is a cluster of Chihuahua dens, pocket-sized structures, all decked out in cutesy trim. Callie would have found this annoying under normal circumstances. But a few yards further on, she sees that the Pekinese have taken over-the-top decorating so much further that they absorb most of the snark that would have been directed at the Mexican pups. The sweet and earnest Labs and Samoyeds, the loyal setters and the dedicated hounds, satisfied with the simplest lean-tos and enclosures, just nod at the passing cat. But one chatty chocolate Lab can't resist gossiping to Callie about an Afghan pup with a trust fund, who is making a fuss about a prime site. He takes the cat to see the remains of the ultra-contemporary monstrosity with its excessive number of bathrooms and bedrooms, three outdoor pools and a couple of fountains, a drive lined with palms and a garden of exotic plantings. The dog had never even bothered to occupy the place. What a waste. The Lab shakes his head, disgusted by the squandering of resources. The difference between shelter and sheer ostentation is not exactly difficult to grasp.

The Lab is a bit downcast in any case. Seasonal affective disorder reigns, and the cat sympathizes with the need for warmth.

A week after passing through the canine neighborhood, Callie hears that the Afghans have moved to the southern coast, putting in a big order to claim as much sunlight as they can afford. The Lab reports that the dogs in the area are struggling to stay out of the savage elements. He is considering squatting in the empty apartments left behind, but isn't sure if the rewards are worth the risks. As winter rains turn the floor of his lean-to into mud, he is increasingly willing to consider all kinds of transgressions. Domesticity is not what it used to be, and the sinecures of an earlier generation are no longer always available.

Singing Lizards
Across the Indian Subcontinent to the West

IN A DUSTY YARD NEAR A rural village in the northern part of India, the elephants, left alone, are thinking deeply, quietly. The lion watches them as they sit, trying to enter their mood. They are blinking, apparently waiting—but for what? An old one shuffles his feet, bringing up some dust. Not aggressively, just in a shifting from side-to-side. On the surface, they are unperturbed. But cloud of vague collectivity gathers among them. A telepathic fog hangs in the air, more tangible than visible, a field of charge arising from the shared understanding of something undefined but connecting them to each other in thought. The lion, though outside their communication loops, feels their active link to each other increase and pass through him.

The elephants can afford to wait. This is something they know how to do. They give nothing away. Their gravitas marks the ground on which they stand, holding it down.

Close to the lion's site, a singing lizard makes the world

resound, meeting the melodies and harmonies of the earth more than halfway. Why this should be a mystery is still unsolved. No recordings ever match the exhilarating narcotic effect of the lizard's singing. The entire dusty landscape rolls over and surrenders to the piping marvels of this juvenile alligator lizard, whose bronze scales and slippery tail are as mercurial in movement as its voice is in song. Is this a dream? The lion wonders.

But the tortoise elders are making their steady way around the village, raising their heads, and recalling other instances of such performance. Their milestones of memory are comprised of the dates at which the world was riven by the purity and otherworldly beauty of the tones. The tortoises have rearranged the stones on the dry edges of the creek beyond the village, on the small rise above the beds that flood with spring rushes during the winter thaws in the distant mountain. They use them as references, historical markers.

Their arrangements serve as museum and archive both, a place to view and store the shared experience of their kind and that of others. Like the elephants, they are exceedingly patient, but committed to acts of preservation, as well as to the need to embrace living experience.

I drift in and out of this scene, even as the evil needle of another viral node tries one spot after another along my outer sheath, persistent as a mosquito in search of blood. I thought we were done with these attacks, but they go on, persistent and determined.

Then the lizard bursts full-throated into an uncanny melody, and the gentle tortoises leave dry creek banks, say a temporary farewell to their neighbors, the beetles and spiders, and set about making a new configuration of classifying stones. *Let there be, from this day, a testimonial to the remarkable moment we have witnessed.* So begins the inscription laid out in the sand. And a sequence of these markers, the great milestones of shared history, a recognition of the awed appreciation of the capacity of another species to outshine them all with this one remarkable gift, becomes inscribed in the very landscape of shared experience.

The lion, still sitting close by the elephants, has no idea of the tortoises' contributions to collective and cultural memory, though he appreciates the well-formed circle of stones.

The Glass Palace
Woods of Massachusetts

CALLIE HAS SURVIVED HER ENCOUNTER WITH the avian real estate boom and the equally annoying dog housing mania, so she thinks she is done with these structure-driven cravings. But as she follows a footpath beside a railroad track, she hears a commotion and a sound like tiny glass wind chimes in rapid motion. A blur of movement catches her eye. A small flock of robust chickadees is manically at work. They move so quickly their stark black and white is a smear of gray in rapid transit and at first Callie can barely distinguish them. They do not pause in their activity, but the hawk, watching from his perch, notices her presence and looks the other way. Their last conversation still irks him. Callie was so rude, he has to snub her.

The architectural aspirations of the small birds surpass all of the other species'. They work in a mad frenzy, picking stones and shards of glass from the roadbed between the rails. Driven to a higher purpose, they throw themselves into the risky task. Callie watches with trepidation.

The chickadees know enough not to consume the bright harsh splinters and instead carry them with alacrity to a nearby site. Peering through the woods, Callie creeps close enough to see. They are working on a cathedral structure built entirely of the minute fragments. Every bit shines and sparkles, catching the light, but the whole is a dangerous instrument of architectural folly—something so dreadful should hardly exist, designed as it is to shred any bit of tender flesh or feather with which it comes into even the slightest contact. Callie is awed and alarmed, but the chickadees have old prejudices and will not make eye contact, let alone conversation.

The glass bits are thin as needles and nearly invisible at the final points of their projection into space; like the black spines of unkind cacti, they are capable of slicing before they are seen, and the monstrous fatal monument has a terrifying aura. Using swift, deft movements the chickadees add to the edifice, ratcheting up the threat in a very odd use of their construction abilities.

The deadly crystal palace, so incredible in its structure and beauty, built with infatuation but little heed for safety, has no infrastructure. The entire edifice is a trick of balance and suspension mounting with inevitable fatality.

The chickadees are nearly domestic, living in yards and off the feeders, among the telephone lines and tangled infrastructure of the developed world. Still, their cathedral is in a hidden space, in a clearing they think is safely removed from view of any but the forest creatures. Timid rabbits, afraid of the menacing palace, mostly keep their distance, as do the squirrels taking refuge nearby from the attacks of the hawks (who flagrantly ignore all warnings from the civic patrols). But everyone gets confused by the shafts of light refracted from the crystal surface. Callie, too entranced to look away for long, still chases dancing fingers of light with her eyes as they dart among the leaves and twigs of the clearing.

The magnificent edifice rises quickly, higher, higher, and ever higher in an aspirational tour de force. Then, in one inconspicuous and ordinary moment, a fleet of winged birds darts toward an outcropping of sparkling, needle-sharp bits. They drop a tiny-tipped facet of glass into place, a minute addition to the elaborate structure. They slide the multi-part bodkin shaft into the neatest crevice in the lattice of a winged-wall outcropping. But it is one tiny fragment too many. The whole of the carefully piled heap of glass heaves and sighs. Then it caves, like a skin of sugar breaking in a single wave of collapse.

The sound of glass music, tinkling, cracking, shattering, breaks in high register. A cloud of abrasive dust rises, choking the lungs of all of the birds who did not manage to escape in advance of the outward and upward movement of the powder into the atmosphere. The bunnies cry blood tears, eyes running with pain. The squirrels scream, their pelts shredded, tails shaved, while the hawk hangs aloft. The cat, racing away for her own survival, is overwhelmed by the sight of shredded feathers and sliced flesh. Her paws are lacerated, but only in spots, since she was farther from the center of the clearing than the adoring bunnies and the hard-working birds.

That is an end to this enterprise, and the cat, licking her wounds, moves on, passing a sympathetic glance to the few survivors on the lower branches, shivering with damaged wings and feet. The chickadees will keep a memory of the palace alive in the tales they tell to their young, and the rabbits, generation after quick generation, preserve the story of the cruel crystalline palace. The squirrels, who never get a story right, spread a rumor about a glass grenade launched by irresponsible birds.

The chickadees realize they are not builders by temperament and leave the architectural engineering to the swallows after this one undertaking. They use their penchant for gathering materials and contribute well-sorted piles of pebbles, twigs, wires, and straw-like fibers to the stockpiles the swallows consume in their ambitious projects. They discover the spirit of cooperation and keep to it later when spring begins, but meanwhile, they dip into the stores of fermented cider put up in the autumn months. The chickadees get drunk easily, and fall asleep, heads under wings, soaking up late afternoon light. Local swallows and sparrows begin a business in well-sorted building supplies—all collected by the repentant chickadees, committed to pensioning the bunnies they have harmed.

Archaean Updates: Shallows Off the Southern Coast

YET ANOTHER VIRUS ATTACHES ITS SINISTER spindle-shape to me, taking revenge for my earlier rejection of their friend. This time the attack and attacker are clear. Footless, handless, blind, and only half-sentient, I am vulnerable, as you may well imagine. My only defenses are the bonds of molecules that form a defining edge to my being. Desperate for oxygen and nutrients, I move to the shallows by the coast off North Carolina, where the minnows show signs of anxiety at my presence and the tinge I produce with my waste products in what they think of as their water.

My surroundings communicate elaborate and precise information to me. So many of the animals are feeling the effects of a downward spiral of spirits. I process their suffering through the charges crossing my membranes. My distributed condition lets me slide through caverns and cracks underground, then surface rapidly at a whole host of openings in the surface of the earth—with or without direct routes. I suffer just now from an empathy overload, a change in atmospheric pressure that requires I filter differently, adjust my metabolic expectations, and my social goals. I am of the living world, joined in suffering and sentience, but isolated by scale and age, experience and disposition.

As the virus pricks and probes, looking for a vulnerable point of entry to my system, I fall back on the reassurance of longevity. Even these opportunistic forms are much younger than I am, and I have survived and outlived their attentions before. I have no sense of superiority. Class is not a category that matters to me, no matter how humans describe simple and complex, higher and lower organisms. None of my cells, nor all of them together, accept a place in the hierarchy of being. We are too diverse and diffuse, too much a part of too many other things—in their guts, between their toes, in the walls of their caves, and underground where they walk.

I sink to the lower depths, and the viral horde diminishes. They have their limits. I cherish the extended darkness, and though light triggers are absent from my biology, the temperature shifts are beneficial to my processing. I can generate charges rapidly and hold the differential like a battery when I go through a rapid succession of hot and cold. Left on my own I drift toward low-energy states in thermal equilibrium. Perversely, the attacks rejuvenate my defenses and cause my systems to replenish.

The edges of my colonies that reach to the surface, and lie along the hot dry ground in the Indian subcontinent, feel very differently, for there, a sad scene plays out and all of us in every ecosystem and psychic network are affected.

Collective Bargaining
Massachusetts

CALLIE, WHO HAS NOT RECEIVED A single red card or heart-shaped missive in February, is sinking into self-pity and would go into a slough of despair except that her heartache at being nobody's sweetheart pales in contrast to the pangs in her gut. The roadside stands are closed and the beavers have taken refuge, hibernating under their dams. She misses them.

Once again she is so hungry she can think of nothing but food. Prohibitions are now so strict that she isn't sure who or what she can eat without violating protocols. She is tired of stealth attacks on the food bowls of others, nocturnal raids, and other thievery. And she is wary, ever wary, of being trapped, caught, and incarcerated. She knows the end that brings. What to do? The hollows in her haunches are deep and shadowed, and only persistent exercise and plenty of hydration keeps her energies from flagging completely. She is tired of a quest for which she has no plan and longs for her adventure to end.

Spring rains are softening the ground, and the cat sloshes through the mud where the worms turn, first going slack, then lazy, on strike. They come out on the sidewalks, unwilling to struggle at all. They dry up fast. The ones who watch and wait are the ones who unionize. They are experts at a variety of slow-level collective bargaining. They align with each other intuitively. No elections for officers are held. Leadership simply emerges from the mass, a singularity among the writhing bodies, asserting a minimal modicum of intentionality, enough to make a difference. The cat would happily consume the worms—she is that hungry—but the idea of interfering in labor negotiations goes against all of her training.

The survivors who stay in the dirt, underground, wet enough to move, make their way back to work, newly inspired. The negotiations are among themselves, not with their bosses (they had none), and so the terms of the benefits package feel

fair, just right, and sufficient. They will not come to a bargaining table to deal with vertebrates. They do not trust them.
This is their prerogative. And anyway, they want a single-payer
system and fair treatment across their population.

Hard to argue with them. Tilling will occur and their
habitat will be rejuvenated without any compromise on their
part. They know their job, but hold aloof. They too are aware
of the deep sadness that drifts through the soil, and they do
not thrive on toxins. They are convinced they give more than
they get in return in the larger scheme of aeration ratios and
programs of agricultural advancement. They are right, but
that does nothing to counter the effects of sad chemistry in
the shared ground. The worms' breathing is affected
profoundly by having to filter the melancholy in the soil.

Social Decorum
Indian Subcontinent

THE LION IS AWARE THAT THE sadness of the captive elephants, like that of the tigers, is almost too much to bear. At
any season, but especially in these colder months, the heavy
beasts sit unreconciled to their confinement, longing for the
free range of their homeland. This will not come to them
again. They have news of their distant kin and know how
much they suffer. But not only the exiles are in pain. All the
large gray animals are abject. Their tribes are separated by
the human violence perpetrated on them and the distance
cannot be undone or traversed. Pachyderm melancholy penetrates to the deepest layers and soaks the earth. Their
lachrymose chemistry creates whole zones of sorrow in the
being of the shared soil.

The lion, overconfident from his success at sea crossings
and adventures, ventures too close to a public track and is

spotted. Shouts in his direction put him on the defensive and on the run. He is conspicuous, too easy to follow. He ties plastic bags around his paws to disguise his prints and wears sunglasses to help him disappear. For now this works.

In Africa, no one except close family feels loss over the departure of the lion six months earlier. But the lion's absence removes authority from the old social order. Given their casual occupancy of public spaces in villages and towns, the chimpanzees should be far more helpful in stepping up to supervise. Instead, they become derisive. Very. They make fun of anyone working or going to school or traveling to a charity mission or picking their teeth or sorting grains to keep the stored hoard free of mildew. They fill the public space with ridicule and crude gestures, laughing while they swing their buttocks into view.

Do they respect anything? Unlikely. They hurl insults like small projectiles, foul smelling and worse intentioned, leaving their leavings anywhere they please and daring the authorities already overworked and overcome with seasonal flooding to figure out a plan of control. The bonobos, in spite of the reputation they have among the primatologists, act so badly sometimes that they are almost worse than the chimps—having sex all the time, wiping their glands on the sidewalks, and generally indulging in a kind of lasciviousness that belies their capacity for higher order social life.

The causes of downdrift are hard to pinpoint. The complex animals are affected by the micro-world and do not even know it. But is the downdrift a disease? Or a social condition? When the entire genus *Pan*—the chimps— refuses to take tickets at films or on mass transit, refuses to work the trains, refuses to sit in booths, and sits with arms wrapped around their heads, making crude remarks more often than not, is that an illness? Or a cultural crisis? Do they think they have nothing at stake in the whole business and can just litter where they live and scavenge at will among their neighbors' goods? What is the drive that manifests in these impulses—and is it random or coordinated in its systemic effects? Is there a cure or only an inevitable playing out?

Esoteric Erudition
Near Fall River, Massachusetts

CALLIE, LONELY AND DESPONDENT, TROUBLES HER way along the shoreline of Massachusetts where the monastic life of the barnacles provides a model of spiritual existence. Their attitude is neither resignation nor aspiration. They seem almost immune to the scourge of change. They sieve and breathe, taking what they need. Small shoals of ocean minnows wend their way among the rocks signaling a path, an in-and-out course through the openings that lead to clear, still, sheltered spots. A few edge back toward the surf and the crashing excitement of the waves. Feeling far from observation, Callie helps herself to various swimming creatures and eats her fill. The cold salt water is not exactly comforting to her paws, still damaged from the chickadee cathedral disaster, and wet fish, though nutritious, are a little chilly in the belly. She washes her face carefully, the pink end of her nose fresh and whiskers shining, while ignoring a whisper of accusations that breaks with the waves.

While she bathes, she watches a group of green mussels, large and gracious, welcome a lonely starfish who has wandered in, a bit battered by its winter experience on the ocean floor. Nearby, a handful of scallops, the blue-eyed rascals of the mollusk world, calm their impulses toward wanton flirtation and settle down, talking among themselves and exchanging news and information from abroad, catching my signals in their gills, where they stick and reverberate.

Tide pool communications are easy, mostly rhythms set by the wash of tidal water and recession, the surge and ebbing that purge the mollusk mantles of unnecessary waste. Their social order is not so much set as allowed. Theirs is an incidental community rather than an intentional one, as long as the critical mass remains low enough that nothing else is required to maintain equilibrium.

Evening comes on. Callie wanders back into the woods in her nightly quest for a safe sheltered spot to sleep. She curls up in some pine needles and dry branches, and sleeps lightly, fitfully, aware that something is moving in the air above her. Owls do not speak. They refuse, too dignified for utterance, and so the bird does not address her. She knows their knowledge of languages is renowned, as are their editing abilities, but they are silent readers, mercilessly accurate, and can spot errors and misprints at distances that stagger the human mind, let alone the feline one.

The owl in the tree above her is very senior, very taciturn and reputed to know at least seventeen languages and their various scripts—Nabataean, Samaritan, Biblical and modern Hebrew, Greek, Latin, Sanskrit, church Slavonic, Armenian, Syriac, Arabic, Russian, Chinese, Furthark, and Cherokee. The list goes on and on. The cat recollects from somewhere that this linguistic skill is attributed to the extra seven vertebrae in the neck and the size of the artery supplying blood—owls can rotate their heads three-quarters of a circle without any diminishment of blood flow to the brain, while taking in a whole variety of pages from dictionaries they cross-reference as they swivel. They are collating machines, precise to a degree that can barely be replicated in even the best natural language processors.

The texts they choose to work on are esoteric, obscure things. They have no tolerance for trivia. The fragments of ancient poetry or snippets of legal documents they channel are often of importance to only a tiny handful of scholars. Still they persist. A commitment to the pursuit of pure knowledge, to the establishment of the textual record of human culture, drives them.

The other animals do not understand why the owls are so keen on translating and editing these obscure texts. After all, the inscriptions of the other species take many different forms—and all have an equal need for attention. The owls understand, but wait, unsure how to proceed with this alternative history. They know there are no common frames of understanding. If any creature is sensitive to the nature of interpretation, it is the owls. They are hermeneuts, to the core, whatever that means.

Pondering this keeps Callie wakeful, from a combination of suspicion and respect. She is out of her league and unsure of what the bird might do, until, with the sudden stealth of a predator, the owl makes a silent attack. A surge of aggression tenses his muscles, and adrenaline releases as he snags his prey. He drops bits of food as he eats, tearing flesh between beak and claw. The cat, overcoming prohibitions and drawn by the tempting smell, consumes what she can of what falls to the ground below the perch. Like other birds of prey, he is careless, not worried about disclosing his location. Callie has not had hot blood in months and is unsure about how it tastes.

Barter Exchange
Toward the Himalayas

THE INDIAN SUBCONTINENT HAS A VERY explicit exhalation pattern, and the sharp, fresh air of the Himalayas has its own blend of nutrients. The lion, lurking in the bushes, suddenly tenses, and not from the thinness of the oxygen. A tiger ties and unties a neck scarf, discards it, and walks away without looking back. Should the lion retrieve it? Make advances and connections through a courtly gesture?

As he approaches the dropped scarf, a sour smell stops him. In spite of the healthy air, the tiger is suffering an ennui contagion caught from an intimate conversation with a disenchanted gazelle. The tiger, now at a conversational distance, tells the lion that a few too many of the little antelopes passed through his life that year. The lion is not naïve. He knows ennui is passed through the digestive tract. The tiger sighs, striking the ground with a paw. In the tracks of his large, soft pads, bleak and pessimistic organisms swarm, their microscopic lives compressed by their scale and the chill of the season. Heat is a fertile force for change, and the procreative rate of all beasts slows as the metabolism of some of the cold-blooded animals remains sluggish in the winter months. The warm-blooded ones band into social groups to husband their warmth through contact or negotiated trade.

The lion, bored by the tiger's boredom (who wouldn't be?), sneaks off to conceal himself at the edge of a crude market stall in the public square with plenty of lively action. The concepts of surplus commodities are beginning to operate across variant populations. Stock exchanges are still in the future, but barter in hoarded goods is taking off. The land creatures in particular have caught a dose of human greed, and ready their excess goods for stalls in the squares and byways.

A young goat comes toward a pile of mangoes, and at the checkout counter a mongoose clerk looks up from doing accounts and responds to a question of costs and currencies. The goat feels its genetic code alter in the single exchange. At that very moment, like a recalibration of equilibrium, the combinatoric strings of his identity shift gears. He opens his bearded jaw, his once-reliable bleat sounding pathetically like the cluck of mongoose-speak. Is his tongue being remade to meet the immediate demands of communication?

A taste of pollution washes through the goat's mouth. The mongoose, waiting for the goat to make a counteroffer (they always do), is put off by the delay as much as the rank odor of his own language being returned to him. Hoarding produces rot as an unintended consequence.

The rapid motion of a land tortoises with a late delivery of river lettuce distracts the goat. Running at a great speed across a short stretch of dry pavement across the square, as if the very life of the lettuces depends on it, he offers directives to quickstep smartly.

The change in gait, like the altered vocalization of the goat, is a simple but direct sign of crossing identities. Hybridization is evident. The tortoise has been in proximity to a lizard. No other reptile moves that fast. The goat squints to follow the motion of the tortoise. He knows from the momentum that this odd sprint is a sign of mutation. Interspecies influence passes through observation. The contagion of watching is part of empathetic downdrift. The goat stretches its neck, as if it has a shell. The microorganisms are resistant to mimetic performance, too self-involved for observation. Even now, scattered about the barter table the tortoise is approaching, they remain impervious to the spectacle of the stretching goat and the swift transit of the tortoise. Or they would have, except that they feel the heat of the goat's exhalation and the chemicals mimicking mongoose speech in his breath. They lust after another taste of the fear that pollutes the goat's throat. They must be bacteria, feeding on the lower margins of emotional toxins.

The mongoose clerk is oblivious and has no more idea of the presence of the bacterial strains than it does of the parasites ensconced in its own entrails. But it feels the effects just the same, and in an inadvertent gesture, reaches toward its own smooth chin as if it might, just might, be sprouting a little goatee. The mutation agents, always opportunistic, transfer their attention from paw to jaw, seeking moisture and warmth in which to proliferate.

The sheer volume of all of these minute transactions and interactions is exhausting. The effects are being registered in flesh and behavior, in tissue and organs, in movement and appetite, in tone and range of vocalizations. The rate of change escalates exponentially, with the speed of hot molecules ricocheting off each other in a highly compressed space, across many membranes and communication lines. But it is social space, and not closed. The full spectrum of receptive permeability and resistance is being activated in bursts of intense exchange. The lion's nose tickles slightly, something sharp has come across his nostrils. But he is old, and change finds little receptivity in his ancient flesh or habitual posture. He puts his noble head on his big paws, neither immune nor affected.

The Beagles of Baltimore

THE WILD ANIMALS ARE NOT THE only sad beasts. The spectrum of depressive disorders reaches deep into domestic zones, where coddling and spoiling should provide protection against such ills, but do not. In this warfare for the spirit, the trenches are the psyches of the animals.

Beagles feel the changes more than other dogs. Though always eager for new experience, they are greatly pained by what is happening. The morning after her encounter with the owl, Callie stumbles into one of the public libraries the beagles have established as refuges, places of community activity. She is surprised to find they have even installed a discarded card catalog at which they stand, filing with great accuracy and an attitude of even greater importance.

Callie spends a quiet hour among the shelves the beagles have stocked, touched by the retro character of the branch library. The dogs hate screens, monitors, online records— and the keyboard most of all. They turn their backs on the entire system of networked cultural heritage, preferring to take very, very low-paying work rather than retrain in anything digital. Still they take great pleasure in shelving and the cat tiptoes among the well-ordered books and magazines and old recordings, paying extravagant compliments to the beagles.

Sadness sits in their eyes and resignation reigns among the breed. Their melancholy has also seeped, so that an entire population of fleas is crippled with depression. They dry up and die, breaking a cycle of parasite transfer and changing the intestinal ecology of the dogs.

They are slow, almost excruciatingly slow, as they shelve and re-shelve. But this meditative work puts them at ease. To support the libraries, they take day jobs shredding and shipping. They have great skill with Styrofoam peanuts, packing tape, and address labels. A few have acquired a new sense of self-worth. Callie is heartened by seeing this small positive upswing within the larger context of the downdrift. She does not know this now, but when June edges May offstage, the beagles' coats will grow shiny, their steps quick and sprightly, and their positive attitude will rub off on pups of all breeds, young mice, and school-age bunnies. To "be a beagle" already means being efficient, well prepared, and very, very good-natured. But when the young ones born later in the spring hit their tweens and teens in July, imitation of the beagle gait will be immensely popular.

In fact, a beagle mania will sweep the schoolyards. Rows of pups and mice and bunnies will be "doing the beagle" in line-dance synchronization, stepping brightly, lightly, with quick turns of the head, glances of the eye, and trotting while smiling benevolently. The older kittens among their classmates won't exactly sneer, but the baby badgers, always hipsters, will. Every social action has its reaction, after all. But even the euphoria may be a symptom.

Pseudo-Philosophers
India to Bhutan

THE LION'S TANGLED PATH LEADS EAST and north, into the forests of south-central Asia. Here he has one of the lightest encounters of his journey, so light, in fact, that later he will not be certain if it actually happened. For he meets with the pandas, those ridiculous philosophers, whose attitudes of continuously suspended (ir)resolution baffles the weary lion. He would have been baffled in any case, since the enigmatic ambassadors from China are two-note philosophers. Whether they are visiting a foreign state or living in their ancestral homeland in full, happy view of the snow-capped mountains tinged with the poetry of rosy sunrise light and sunset tones, the pandas have only two things to say, and they always say them both.

So, coming onto a pair of pandas in the wild, the lion is surprised at their rotund glee and happy act of constantly stuffing themselves with leaves, and he stops and stares. The pandas do what they always do. They hesitate. They look at the lion deeply, with fake seriousness. They hold their bamboo-scented breath just long enough to make him think they are thinking. Then, out it comes in mumbled panda-speak, "Mebbe." And a few seconds later, like the rapid reflex action of a valve returning to its steady state, "Mebbe not." No one, not even the most aggressive speech coach, can correct their pronunciation.

The lion is not sure if this is amusing or simply a waste of time. What he does know is that they cannot be put in the classroom under those circumstances. He wonders what will happen if they make it harder and harder to demonstrate the value of philosophizing. If all of metaphysical and critical thought can be reduced to coin-toss vagueness without either decisions or substance, then what becomes of the field? In addition, they cannot be put on a jury, or in a courtroom, or even give testimony. Some feel their attitude is anarchic, that they are determined, in their own odd way, to undermine the very basis on which anything can ever be decided.

Watching the portly creatures eating steadily, the lion wonders if they are committed to indeterminism as a constant condition of negotiation and state shifting. Or is it just panda stuff, their general condition? Rumor has it that if asked do something—anything—they bring everything into a permanent condition of in-between-ness. This can be a complete disaster.

Oddly enough, the pandas are very good dancers, very good dancers indeed, and they offer themselves freely in the clubs in order to induce others to dance as well. Nothing fancy. No tango or rumba or salsa, just a nice little two-step or foxtrot. Gentle swaying, a light rhythm, good grasp of their partners and guidance—patient, patient guidance— until whoever comes onto the dance floor leaves gliding with silken smoothness. Over time they become fetishistic about their dance shoes, soft slippers of the very finest satin, low-heeled, and flexible, adding grace and delicacy to their moves, elegance to their appearance. But work? "Mebbe." And then, quite conclusively, "Mebbe not." This sustained state of simultaneous ambiguity is so at odds with the oppositional binary of other codes that its sophistication escapes many of the other creatures.

Medical Mercy
Streams near the Chesapeake

ADRIFT AND AT LOOSE ENDS, CALLIE chases ripples and bubbles in a stream beginning to swell from spring runoff. As she swipes her paw she disturbs some mud in which a colony of salamanders has been hibernating through the winter. They have a business in prosthetic devices, little limbs and tails, and other odds and ends. Business has been sluggish in the cold season, but they are hoping it will soon pick up.

Their use of genetic methods is a little cavalier. But as far as Callie is concerned, this is natural for them, and so she has no problem with the somewhat macabre wares they set out because they are motivated by charitable aims. They run triage units and walk in pairs, with extra parts suspended between them. When they arrive at the clinic, they bring the parts to the waiting victims of the many traps that still litter the landscape. The crawl spaces and the underbellies of houses remain armed against rodent intrusions. The sight of the forlorn rats and mice, their small, wet limbs dangling loose from shoulder or elbow, always moves passersby to tears.

The amphibians are adept at snapping their own append-
ages in just the right place to encourage regeneration. Painful,
yes, but the revenue-generating potential gives them an edge
that is worth it. They use the funds for an elite Collège de
Recherche, entirely under their auspices. Given their expertise, molecular biology and cellular studies could form the
heart of their seminars. But they are mostly interested in
quantum communication and hope to capture the market in
wave functions and simultaneous services at a distance.

In the summer ahead, they reach out to the whales, even
though they are not fellow-amphibians. Like dolphins, the
whales took to the sea millions of years ago, streamlining
their bodies and adapting their forelimbs to fins, in a rare
move from land to water creature. But the whales and other
cetaceans always have in mind—in some shared collective
memory they rarely tap—that they might come back out
again, crawl out and walk among the terrains of dry land.
They might need the salamanders' expertise if they attempt
rapid limb regeneration, so negotiations are underway.

For the cat, this is all a bit too esoteric. In another season,
she would have made a meal of the miscellaneous limbs and
other tidbits. But she restrains herself, aware this is a double
crime against the original source flesh and the expectant
victims. She is trying to learn from these encounters, and
though the concept of self-improvement was never much on
her mind, she feels aware of increasingly frequent hints of it.

Avian Debutantes
China

BIRDS COME OUT IN EACH NEW generation and take the
opportunity to have proper debutante events. These matter a
great deal to the families as well as to the young ones being

introduced in their first season. As the lion hauls his sorry carcass over the hills and through the valleys that connect the Indian subcontinent with the vast plains of Asia beyond, he is attentive to the spring ceremonies ahead. Preparations are being made everywhere. Though he is not an invited guest, the lion is witness to preparations in every zone through which he passes. These events are months in the making, and so the early start is essential, given the extravagance involved.

Early summer is the time for the balls, because blossoms for bedecking are abundant. But planning begins soon after the little hatchlings appear in the nests and long before fledglings separate from their doting parents.

The larger birds, those with abundant plumage, long necks, elaborate bills, and splendid markings, take on exaggerated expenditures that seem outrageous to other species in the debutante events. Why would a cockatoo expend half a year's income on a single day's activity? Squandering carefully hoarded seed and dried insect matter in one afternoon or evening? Course after course of catered food is always served. Ground grubs and meticulously stuffed mites, small caterpillars smoked with rosemary wood, or beetle-juice filtered and distilled to a rare vintage are kept for just such occasions. The cockatoos are reserved in contrast to the flamingos, who cannot keep themselves temperate under any circumstances and see no reason to keep their appetites under control in this moment of parental pride. The best of the clutch, their sweet young offspring, tiptoe into view in modest plumage meant to set off the unsullied beauty of their still chaste selves. Or so the hype suggests.

Among the Eastern Rosellas in Australia, chastity is just an assumption, not a fact, and the debutante ball can turn into an orgy with all generations flinging their scarlet chests against one another, blue-and-green tail feathers flying, white throats thrown back in joyful song. Their promiscuity makes an active trade route for exchange of information.

In Africa, the Hyacinth Macaws are the top of a very complicated hierarchy and their hooked beaks and bright eyes stand out in striking contrast to the velvet richness of their blue-green plumage. For their events, the very best beetle satays and skewered tidbits are arranged on polished wood platters. The Macaws make liberal use of their claim on tradition to exercise the insect exemption for ritual fare. The drinks sparkle and the linen shines with extraordinary brightness against the heavy foliage of the jungle. They are proud, proud birds, and rightly so. Their histories track pedigrees and lineages unbroken since the first branchings of their evolutionary trees. No wonder they regard their young daughters with such amazement and hold them in such high esteem. They are worth a great deal on the open markets.

No one brings this up, as it is brutal and tasteless to suggest that the young might be sold and bred in circumstances that violate their autonomy. The parents keep a watchful eye, no matter how inebriated and ecstatic they become. The macaws usually hire a group of python thugs and viper guards in case of uninvited guests and know the muscled and venomous guardians can intervene strategically if necessary.

All of these ceremonies have a few things in common. They begin with the presentation of the young, an official roll call and parade of beauties, curtsying and nodding, bowing slightly to their elders, then strutting with their necks extended, heads held high, with steps as precise as hours of training and straining before a mirror can make them. Whether it is a shy young toucan, nose still a bit big on the young face, or a peach-faced lovebird, hooked beak tucked downward, wings pressed against its soft green chest, does not matter. All follow a similar protocol for the presentation march. But after that, variety abounds in the physiognomies and style of the walk.

Pheasant Girls
China

BUT THE PREPARATIONS THAT THE LION sees are of the rarest and most elegant variety, for he is witnessing the stately courts of the Chinese pheasants. These could never be imitated by the caiques or the lorikeets, or even the storks or herons. Lovely as they are, they do not have the regal character, innate breeding, or the material resources those golden-backed pheasants bring to their daughters' first official appearance in society. The girls are brown, subdued in color, excessively modest compared to their proud papas. But this hardly matters, since they are bedecked with strands of fine jewels and baubles taken from the safe for the occasion. These brilliants are not meant to compensate for, but to complement, the young female plumage. The show of conspicuous wealth is a ritual all present enjoy as much as they enjoy the fermented pomegranate wine and sparkling rose water they are served. Some of the stuffed beetles and slow-baked dragonflies are as lovely as the jewels, their iridescent scales and faceted wings catching the light that sparkles in the encrusted collars and pendants of the debs. No one present at such an event is vulgar enough to oooh or ahhh audibly, though from time to time a murmur of extremely polite appreciation goes through the assembly. Admiration also produces a subtle off-gassing.

But though the Chinese pheasants are beyond doubt the richest among the birds, their opulence unparalleled, the gray-crowned cranes are more elegant. The lion, partaking liberally of the excesses of both ceremonies, notes that the wing and tail feathers of the cranes trail with drooping grace. Their elaborate headdresses have a restrained color palette that makes anything gaudier look vulgar. They launch their girls in a very quiet ceremony, a striking contrast to the excesses expended by the pheasants, and do nothing to draw attention to themselves or their young. They have something more valuable than wealth: they have taste, and this, they know, cannot be bought or sold. Their young beauties are swathed in gauze and silver threads that show off their lovely shoulders and frame their profiles with an exquisite delicacy that cannot, in spite of all efforts, be captured photographically. The lion savors the liqueurs and tasty morsels, joining the admiring crowds that pass along the banquet tables without any need of invitation.

The albums of these days and their events are always disappointing. The order of social hierarchy escapes representation. This does not stop the reporters, gossip columnists, and others who feed from the spectacle from reaping the benefits of circulating in the press every single detail they can observe. The jays are particularly adept at reporting, and their bright, staccato style is perfect for turning these society events into highly consumable prose. The crows like to think of themselves as good journalists, but they lie. They lie so much, so well, so completely that they come to believe everything they say and finally cannot tell when they are truth-telling. They see a skinny-necked pheasant and call her an elegant swan. They observe a knock-kneed young flamingo and call her graceful, charming, divine. The mismatch of vocabulary and observation is one thing, but when this extends from society pages to political reporting the lies become dangerous. That is another story entirely. Communication networks are so vulnerable to corruption.

The lion, finally sated, is glad to escape with a full belly. He has other pursuits, and once again finds his way to a port city, sniffs among the ropes and gangplanks, and puts himself aboard a boat bound southward, across the China Sea and through the Indonesian Ocean.

Cat TV
Up North

CAT TV IS ENJOYING A SURPRISE vogue in the northern hemisphere's bleak months of January and February. Callie squats in a production studio with multiple monitors and occasional free food, though the crew is a bit suspicious about whether she is carrying her weight. Callie suggests she is doing long-form journalism, and that her work requires immersion, and for a while, the gullible gaffers and lighting experts buy the story.

To make her cover credible, Callie does endless interviews, starting with the scores of feline fans. They are all smitten by the stars of the daytime soaps, who are so expertly accessorized that the audience does not care one bit whether the dialogue is written or improvised. The cats use thinly veiled references to individuals whose public lives make them fair game, and they analyze and comment, brows raised and whiskers twitching with just that bit of superciliousness that gives an appearance of disdain to the most innocuous comment. The felines, Callie finds, have developed a taste for irony. What a surprise!

But what she also finds is that though shows are wildly popular and would have gone on indefinitely, the cats do not like to negotiate with advertisers. They think the commercial side of the business is beneath them. So it slips out of their control, and opportunistic badgers move into their markets. The cats at the studio don't care. They are all trust-fund felines and don't need the income, just the lark and amusement of the game. In the week Callie spends with them, she finds they get bored with having to show up to the studio every day and what was a thriving business on Sunday is a failing one by Friday. Their loyal fan base persists as an audience for reruns and massive online fan fiction. Kittens and cat-tweens around the world memorize every scene and line ever uttered by the glam-tabby and celebrity black cat, who were the two major stars of the short-lived series.

The cat stars are the last members of the studio Callie interviews. They tell her they are happy because they rake in residuals for every viewing, but they never answer fan mail and go around town in sunglasses and baseball hats to keep from being recognized. Their conspicuous attention to adopting an incognito stance will spare them the agony of being ignored when the shows slip off the radar.

Callie thinks about working on a script and bidding for a role as a writer, but she knows her talents lie elsewhere, and really, once in a while, she knows it is nice to encounter someone who does not think they can write a screenplay. The studio goes dark, and Callie files her story with her imaginary journal, consumes the last of the kibble buffet, and figures she has come out ahead in this episode, even if the cat stars shun her socially for faking her press credentials.

Parasites and Slime Molds
Archaean Networks

MY ONE CONTINUING FRUSTRATION IS THAT most of the successful intestinal parasites see no justification for advancement, no advantage, and actually, very little possibility of moving into new roles or positions in society. They have been treated as a scourge for so long that they are both abject and completely vicious, angry at the way they are kept down and increasingly vengeful as a result. They only want to replicate themselves through host organisms and proliferate, be fruitful and multiply, according to the tenets of the ancient genetic codes. My objection is not ethical; all creatures have their ways and means. But they set a bad example by skulking and hiding, sending the scent of shame into the atmosphere. It is difficult to purge, even with my rapid metabolic filters.

The species most adamant about the realities of the evolutionary cycles are the slime molds, which I can appreciate. They see themselves as a crucial part of the generation of life, and take pride in being progenitors of multiple forms of more complex organization. They point to evolution the way proud immigrant grandparents gesture toward their assimilated offspring. Their erasure from the picture is the surest sign of their success. But they know they can activate the latent connections at any point. When they send a surge of chemical messaging through ether and ground, the atavistic memories of origins light up in the brain stems and synapses of the crawling, the slithering, and the upright who carry plasmodial substance in their tissues and veins. Hallelujah. Though we are not as close cousins as others think, I celebrate the affinity of their attitudes with my own.

Diamond Trade
China to South Africa

THE POOR LION. HAVING MANAGED TO board a steamer surreptitiously, he finds it is headed in an entirely different direction than he thought. He is cruising back toward the tip of the African continent from which he originally set out.

He resigns himself to the detour, looking forward to a sniff of home.

When he arrives in the South African port of Cape Town, he is greeted by eager aardvarks who are doing some long-shoreman shifts. They are in perfect counterbalance of lassitude and exertion, and show up for jobs in every industry in which they are allowed to work. Some animals have no interest in productive labor, before or after the downdrift, but the aardvarks are exactly the opposite. They jump up and down on the dock as the lion pads down a gangplank, doing his best to look inconspicuous among a bunch of beasts of burden.

He stops on the quay, feeling an obligation to acknowledge the warm welcome. He is even more surprised when they try to press a bunch of hastily packaged diamonds on him. The aardvarks have hit on a particularly rich vein and are working with an underground network of hyraxes. As the aardvarks explain their scheme, the lion finds the whole situation a bit odd. But the aardvarks explain they have strong connections to their South African roots and feel an enormous (some say exaggerated) loyalty to their country of origin. They justify their engagement with the diamond trade on nationalistic grounds. The hyraxes are just shrewd enough to be able to make themselves invaluable by learning how to cut the brilliants.

The aardvarks scent diamonds at distance and through substances that make the task impossible for almost any other animal—even the little golden moles from whom they parted ways on the evolutionary path some millions of years earlier. Excavation is only one part of the business. They make good use of their remarkable tubule teeth for grinding rock, and well-shaped snouts with terminating disks and nostrils for picking through the rubble, and wonderful claws for digging. But they are clueless about what to do with the stones once they have them out of the earth. For a long time, they just kept them in the back of their burrows, taking pleasure in knowing the small pile of shining rocks was growing in the dark lair behind them.

The lion finds their enthusiasm and earnestness infectious. He tolerates their jumping about and blathering, entranced with the tale. He feels glad to have the soil of Africa under his paws. They go on, chattering away about the partnership they struck up with the hyraxes almost by accident. The little rock badgers were foraging one afternoon, just munching along in their usual group, covering lots of ground and keeping up their usually good spirits. These were helped by taking regular swigs of the slightly fermented plant juice kept in the small gourds they wear on light twine belts across their chests. The hyraxes are happy social creatures, jabbering away, eating pretty much anything that comes within range. They weave all kinds of mythic fictions for their little ones and to amuse each other. They are very egalitarian in their habits, another point of contrast with the usually solitary aardvarks, who have little use for others of their own species, let alone the verbose hyraxes. But their partnership changed all that, and now, the aardvarks exclaim, they have adopted hyrax habits.

The aardvarks have very simple syntax, so the hyraxes have to deal with them through a very modified code of exchange. But as soon as the hyraxes demonstrated their ability to use their remarkable incisors to facet the raw diamonds, the aardvarks grasped immediately the potential benefit to their own undertaking. The hyraxes are very sensible about relationships, honoring friendships across several degrees of separation. So the aardvarks soon recognized they could trust the small mammals to return every rock they borrow or take away for cutting. They say this with sincerity glowing through their eyes and the lion believes every little signal in their minimal communication code.

Their only frustration, they say, rolling their little aardvark eyes, is that the hyraxes only work in very short spurts. This annoys the aardvarks, they confess to the lion. The aardvarks' own work ethic is shaped by a notion of diligence that is simply missing from the vocabulary of the hyraxes. The aardvarks shake their heads. They confess that they tease the sleepy beasts, calling them rock rabbits and dassies. But the hyraxes just take long breaks any time they like and soak up the sun and lie in deep contentment, storing up warmth and energy they can draw on when they feel like it. The aardvarks get no sympathy at all from the lion on this point.

Desperate to keep his attention, the aardvarks go back to describing the business cycle of their work. Diamonds do not take themselves to market and the aardvarks are too shy even for wholesale, while hyraxes want nothing to do with roads and highways. They've struck a bargain with the hedgehogs, who are all full of the business of business and were more than happy to take up the commercial management of shipping. They parade themselves with great officiousness in branded outfits marked with the signature slogan *Secure Transport*, which would have made them targets for thieving brigands in another era. But these days, the roads are guarded by Dalmatians and dingoes. Annoying though it is to watch them trotting along with swaggering self-assurance, the hedgehogs are reliable enough to carry out their business.

The aardvarks press the lion to smuggle some of their better stones to trade on the side, hoping for a better bargain than with the hyrax crowd. But the lion has no interest in this business of brilliants. They press him, but his store of politeness is depleted; he gives them back the packet of sample stones and pads along the quay, trying to figure out which boat to board for the next leg of his voyage, this time, to Australia. Africa is not what he remembers. He will never see it again, and the dust in his paws and pelt carry the final memory of that beloved continent with him as he travels, only to be shed and replaced, grain by grain, by the soils of ever more foreign lands.

The Blue-Eyed Disease
Tasmania

As THE LION SLEEPS AMONG THE coiled ropes, the boat docks in Port Hobart, Tasmania. A band of pygmy possums is just stirring from an unseasonal winter torpor and their racket wakes him. He has little use for marsupials in general, and these are a particularly annoying set. All the energy stored in their tails has been sucked into their tiny bodies and they wake up in bad moods, hungry, irritable, and with several months of waste stored in their guts. Letting go of all that and having an attack of narcissistic disorder in the same short cycle of night and day makes them dizzy.

The blue-eyed disease is everywhere again. The possums swing on the trees by the water's edge with their cousins, the Tasmanian devils and the charming wombats. They clear their guts loudly and strike up a chorus of self-congratula-tion. The light shines through their eyes, now blue as aquamarine, sending shafts and rays of illumination through the canopy landscape.

They can't compete with the talented stowaways, a troupe of young Etruscan shrews who take up ballet. Like their cousins, the American shrew moles, they are convinced that they possess terpsichorean talent. Narcissism takes many forms, inexhaustible in its variety. The lion is treated to a regular display of their practice. The clumsy movement of the chorus line of dancing bodies, round, furred, plump, and utterly uncoordinated, produces gales of laughter in their comrades, but the shrews and moles never mind. Even the lion has to smile and that pleases the little shrews to no end. The color of the shrew irises is true as the sky and that reinforces their conviction about their superior skills.

In another mood or place, the lion might have wiped clean the whole deck with a sweep of his giant paw, but he is fascinated, caught up in the frenzy. One of the affected is from Manchuria, a rising star, a little jerboa, a hyper, hopping, energetic rodent that has a superficial resemblance to a miniscule kangaroo. She springs on outsized jumping legs, bobbing her big-eyed head, cunning as can be. She snuck on board in South Africa with the lion and is now doing her dervish dance around his paws, unconcerned about waking him.

And when those dark brown eyes take on the hue of lapis lazuli, the audience gasps. All the narcissism in the world cannot match the expectations raised by such admiration. The jerboa takes center stage on deck, and later, in all the media outlets in Asia. In fact, in the course of the spring and summer, she becomes so sought after that celebrity ills take her over. For all of her spunk and energy, she is fragile, and the attention exhausts her. By autumn, chills make her shake and she withdraws from view as swiftly and dramatically as she burst into it.

The narcissism disorder lays waste to entire species once again. It spreads globally, carried across time zones on a wavelength of light. Cows in remote rural places and on big business farms take on airs, workhorses in their barns and thoroughbreds in their pens snort with disdain, the bald and golden eagles nearly starve, too engaged with striking good profile views for all to admire to keep up their hunting. Even the worst of the vermin, ticks and lice, fleas and bedbugs, strut as if all glory is due to them just for being blue-eyed.

Other outbreaks of disease will follow, as shall be seen, but these first epidemics are the most radical, perhaps because they are so unexpected, so unfamiliar. The disorder becomes one among many, and the ordering of symptoms, recording the range of epidemics, tracking the means by which they spread, becomes another occupation for the earnest anteaters and patient lemurs, who work very well together even with a touch of the blue-eyed disease.

Fatal Attraction
Tasmania

NARCISSISM IS TRANSMITTED BY SIGHT. ITS first appearance was in India, and it traveled south, along with the jerboa and a young mongoose. Narcissism falls into the mimicry category of pathology, a social group of ills that does not depend on organic means of propagation. It isn't spread by bites, blood, air, water, or foodstuffs—just by watching. A little yellow African mongoose, another stowaway, is agile and charming when she first appears on deck. The lion is smitten by her beauty and stays close, keeping watch lest she fall to harm.

But she soon acquires a rare social disease from which he cannot protect her. She yearns to be a species she is not. Behavioral contagion, not microbial, is the cause. No bodily fluids, no organism, no viral or bacterial agent is responsible—only the act of identification and cathexis, the transfer of emotional attachment. The mongoose has a thick fine pelt, long slim body, and ovular pupils in her orange eyes, which glow against the soft luster of her coat.

Sharp and focused, she is a strong hunter and fearless around snakes, actively consuming the many varied creatures in her diet.

But unexpectedly, she falls ill watching a group of picky Sarus cranes, invited on board on a diplomatic mission. They take their time selecting food, only to reject it from the pools and buckets offered by their hosts. Lying almost inert, she watches the cranes and soon becomes unwilling to eat almost anything unless they offer it to her. A nasty marsh mongoose, in all its swaggering vulgarity, takes to taunting her in subtle ways and not-so-subtle ones, but the cross-species identification has already taken hold. One night the lion steals close to her, offering succor in the form of fresh fruits and warm breath. She turns away. He is devastated by her condition more than her behavior.

The yellow one aspires to the lean-legged stance of the cranes and to their stilted walk and elegant flight. She begins to stretch her neck outward and upward. She wears a red-and-black scarf around her neck and powders her yellow coat to make it gray, since the coloration and shape of the elegant birds defines the very essence of beauty and identity for her.

She can do nothing but aspire, and she atrophies. The cranes do not adopt her. But she adopts the discriminatory food habits she imagines the long-billed birds engage in, though, in fact, they eat with healthy appetites. The mongoose becomes slim, then thin, then dangerously emaciated. Her bones stick out through her fur, which also shows signs of distress from lack of nutrients. An intervention is eventually called. In port, she gets some aid, fluids, and counseling. But she never fully recovers. She eats to sustain herself, but her initial response to any and all engagement with food is dismissive. Her sharp nose turns upward in disdain; she feels the

sheer banality of merely giving in to appetite or sensual indulgence, and prides herself on having a discriminating nature.

She holds aloof from almost every aspect of life, as if by
keeping herself in reserve she might opt for some other version of existence. This, and other delusions, threaten to kill
her. Worse, versions of the disorder spread among the younger
females of her set, and even some of the males. This is deeply
distressing. Disdain for life is a potent toxin. Whatever psychic
process has generated the illness bonded with her cellular
structure. She generates an auto-destructive substance that
erodes pleasure centers and shuts down the receptors for vital
energy. She doesn't mate, having no interest in her own kind,
and the cranes do not think of her as one of their own. But in
her mind, her narrow shoulders and starved, skeletal anatomy,
almost fulfill her goal of identification with the birds. The lion
is heartbroken as she slowly fades away.

When the steamer docks, the lion walks with gentle grace
and inconspicuous decorum from the ship, slipping off in the
dusk and into the gloom to mourn the little mongoose in his
own way. He, too, is growing gaunt, and perhaps his form is so
slight that it passes for a shadow to any who observe him.

MARCH

Chipmunk Antics
Maryland Suburbs

AN AGING PIG STANDS BEFORE THE audience in a venerable old lodge. The club room was purged by religious storks, who cleaned every corner of it in preparation for communal rituals. They stopped short of specifying that prayer or observant practice must be the main event. But they feel a deep commitment to self-improvement and furnished the room with spare, hard furnishings, stripping it of all decorative elements. A few microorganisms nip at the decorations, curious to see how piety tastes.

All kinds of groups use the space. They leave behind traces of their meetings, shreds of conversation catch on the rafters, off-hand remarks roll under benches, and the dust of inattention puts a slight film over many surfaces. The microorganisms eat cast-off rhetoric the way other scavengers eat carrion.

Activities increase. In the case of meetings, committees, task forces, and other administrative assemblies, the raft of new responsibilities commands attention and brings the animals along. Whole groups of goats, sloths, newts, calves, ferrets, and storks sit in rows of chairs or around a table in a conference room. They are not sure what is expected, but are eager to participate.

The venerable pig begins to speak and a hum goes through the air. A low-level electric current charges the atmosphere. The porcine creature is an amazing orator, and though he takes most of his speech from an old volume of classical Roman works in translation that he shredded to line his pen, he speaks so mellifluously that many take his discourse on law as a theological tract and feel an epiphany coming on as he speaks. More than a few will leave the room filled with a sense of illumination and inner peace. The pig is the first animal, but not the last, to grasp the power of the ministry. All kinds of alignments of purpose and interest begin to form, and the animals feel called to a higher cause.

The lodge where they are meeting has many rooms for different functions. Among them is an abandoned black box stage where a bunch of chipmunks set up theater rigging, racing among the ropes and pulleys with speed and accuracy that defies gravity. The air is chilly, but their muscles are warm with motion as they zip through the daredevil, trapeze flights that are their forte. They are able to make miracles happen within a few minutes. The theater is a jungle gym, practice arena, a physical laboratory in which they hone their skills. As space engineers, geniuses in flight design, they find they can transfer their knowledge to a more generalized, higher realm of abstraction. They create a virtual zone in which the relations among points of force and vectors of connection are understood through physical motion and sheer daring.

They are deep into their involvement with fibers and chains, working the counterweights with their little bodies, taking advantage of their uncanny accuracy in gauging mass and momentum. Small though they are, they estimate to within a micro-milli-nano-unit of force what their impact will be at any moment and just precisely where, within a complexly interconnected set of parts, they should put their little shoulders to the metaphoric wheel. Their coordination is admirable, and the air ballet dazzling.

Though their aerobic skills are amazing, they are part of an old-style theatrical spectacle. In new theaters, the moving parts of yesteryear are replaced with electronic systems. The chipmunks could not care less. They find systems of blinking lights, beeping units, or sealed boxes boring beyond belief and way beyond their pay grade. Give them a warehouse system, an assembly plant, a line of stations through which parts have to move with clockwork precision or an intricate space through which components need to be maneuvered and the chippies are on it. Lightning fast, eager, and positive, the chipmunks are mighty, in the most immediately relevant sense. They move mountains with their small force through the swift calculations in their heads. Funny little heads they are, too, looking around all the time with shining brown eyes and twitchy noses. They unionize quickly, knowing all too well what advantage might be taken of them otherwise. Labor rights and the needs of working rodents have to be fought for every single hair and whisker of the way, but they are wizards at collective bargaining and, much to the surprise of many of their less cooperative rodent relatives, actually care more for the good of the community than for their individual gain. While they provide distraction in the theater, another porcine club is busy nearby, oblivious to all but the distant noise of working pulleys and ropes in the rafters.

Hog Activists
Maryland Suburbs

NOT FAR FROM THIS CHIPMUNK FRENZY, in rooms disconnected from the lodge and its theater, a small throng of
radical hogs, cousins of the orator pig, is organizing an
uprising. They coordinate naturally by cell phone, tapping
the small screens with soft-tipped pens pinched into their
cloven hooves. Swarm behavior is easily conflated with mob
rule, depending on perspective. The hogs see their collective
actions as a path to liberation, and they engage some of the
dogs just to be sure. Dogs are loath to do anything disloyal to
humans, but the rhetoric of the pigs wears them down. They
are still uneasy about the collaboration, unsure about the
motives of the hogs—or the goals of the uprising.

Pigs are born to oratory, as we've already witnessed, and
their capacity for extended and persuasive speech is uncanny.
Put a pig in front of an audience, any audience, and the
effect is nothing short of miraculous. Geese leave their feed,
chickens desert their roosts, the rabbits angle their ears in
the direction of speech. The microorganisms fall into patient
equilibrium. Not a living being within range can resist the
pigs' appeal for support.

Their political movement grows and swells. The organizers
are a cadre of young, still-slim pigs and a cohort of bulky senior
hogs. They meet at night, and in the early hours of the morning
things come to a head. They sort out the ways new forms of
government could serve their interests. They read their Locke
and Montesquieu, their Voltaire and Hume, their Diderot and
Paine. Their little tract, *The Rights of Hogs*, is issued as a pam-
phlet and an iPad app, and read aloud in small groups or silently
in families, in farmyards and pens. In its most popular form,
Porcine Sense, it goes viral and circulates faster than influenza.

But today they are ready to optimize the return on this epidemic of enlightenment. In just a short span of time, the pigs have begun to look up, not down, to trot with pride instead of slovenly abjection, and to see themselves so differently that they force a general change in consciousness. To be a pig is now a compliment of the highest order, and the use of the word "swine" shows a rapid uptick.

The philosophers among the pigs—and there are many, as they are so inclined to political thought they seem to drink it from their mothers' teats—gather for salons and lay the groundwork for a course of action. They are ready. Their goal is simple. They want the right to self-determination. Such basic pleasures as the decision to paint their nails in the morning, or not, take on proportions symbolic beyond literal measure.

The pigs plan for a General Liberation Day, which they fear will bring on violence. They want to spare their species and are committed to peaceful protest, but they know they risk a crackdown. In advance of the day, they establish a network of escape routes, linked by train and truck roadways. Among the dogs they have enough allies to count on good drivers. The border collies are particularly adept at managing the trailers on which the pigs are so frequently transported. When the pens fly open and the massive gates containing their kind release from lockdown, they are ready, poised on the roads with transport caravans. Their first action is supremely coordinated, and one wave of released animals after another swarms into the trucks and heads south to set up the first Free Colony of Swine.

They have leveraged their small pot of funds to acquire a chain of resort hotels on the west side of Florida, along the panhandle and the Gulf. When the first wave of hogs breaks free, they flock en masse toward these southern beaches. Soon, they occupy them with deck chairs and canvas tents flapping in the breeze. Later, when they establish a foothold, they buy ice cream trucks and stands that sell water, sunglasses, and sunscreen to all the hogs at a great profit. This kind of pyramid scheme seems at odds with their original promise of equal rights, and some among them reflect on the spoils of the revolution and the inequities of profit.

To salve their consciences, they spend their time on the beach planning successive waves of release, protests against the forced incarceration of their kind. Some incidents, some more unfortunate than others, are the price they and their captors pay. They are determined to carry on the uprisings through the spring, before the birthing of the first litters of the year. The rising tide of freedom will swell their ranks and the new piglets will be born free. The scheme is so effective and the results so swift and frankly unnerving that the uprisings become a case study for political and social thought for several generations.

The pigs are admirable. But their passions for "revolution" are translated into rapid spinning action by a batch of unicellulars, who got the wrong meaning for the term. Round and round they go, suddenly activated by an impulse to twirl. The centrifugal force throws them apart from each other and the upshot of all that manic philosophizing is disintegration.

On and Off the Grid
Maryland Sprawl

AN EXTREMELY OFFICIOUS SKUNK, PRETENDING TO represent all the nocturnals, presides over a miscellaneous assembly hotly discussing a proposal for a universal lighting code. Winter is dark in the northern hemisphere and among the crowd are a few unhappy foxes and morose-looking raccoons, come to plead for relief of their seasonal affective disorder. The skunk holds a longish document filled with proposed changes to the code. A few bats lie on stretchers to one side of him, accidentally injured as they flew into dark shop windows. On the other side, a couple of dazed owls also wait to give testimony. Their beaks are burned from shredding wires in public places on account of a blinking anxiety.

The skunk knows that illumination will be hard to regulate to everyone's satisfaction. The appearance of lights on streets and public squares serves some of the population but is detrimental to others. As he reads through proposed changes, jeers and cheers arise in equal measure. One proposal is to ban some parts of the spectrum and filter others. The raccoons cross their arms. Some wavelengths will become tightly controlled substances because of their effects on brain activity and mood disorders. The raccoons uncross their arms, hissing a little.

The upshot of the meeting is that the skunk's superiors at the Bureau of Lighting Research send out a call for volunteers to assist with documenting Spectrum Disorders. A mess of half-blind moles offers to impose strict limits on wattage and lumens. The owls, always full of esoteric advice, slow the meeting by advocating the use of selective filtering and species-oriented wavelengths with sensor triggers linked to DNA profiles. They offer to demo various biometrics that can be designed into every fixture. The skunk shakes his head. This is unrealistic, given the costs, and he knows the Bureau will never agree. The fireflies, vigilant about branding and market share, spell their own version of events against the dark night sky.

The raccoons speak up again. Who is to be responsible for filaments and optic fibers and the network of power sources and cost recovery that have to be factored into all infrastructure projects? A passel of possums offers to go into the field to gather the necessary data from meters and other recording devices. They march to their own tune but manage to be quite offensive in almost every situation. They are not socially skilled creatures.

By the end of the meeting it is clear that the lighting should fall under the jurisdiction of a civic commission to develop a zoning policy to accommodate the many and varied needs of every sector of the population. In other words, it stalls. The coalition of black bears and bloodhounds that runs many of the city commissions stalemates over the question of neighborhood representation.

Later that week, the Bureau sends out a series of press releases affirming the idea of civic lighting as a utopian ideal. They know it is a pipe dream of unrealizable proportions, a mirage that stays alive on the wishes and dreams of a generation that has come of age in the belief that the animals can change everything. Problems of fair distribution of electricity continue to grow. Infrastructure cannot keep up with demand. If energy sources shift from mechanistic to metabolic, many problems will be solved. This is where my species excels, but the other animals are still stuck in their older paradigm.

Private Enclaves
Africa

A WORLD AWAY, NEWS OF THE lighting fuss reaches a few upscale zebras and gazelles, who are just about to indulge in their evening cocktails. A busy little mouse has been discovered on the estate, and they take umbrage at having this busybody poking around their preserves to see where the shadows lie and where the sunshine pools. The upper echelon of pheasants and peacocks keeps close guard on their private estates, refusing entry to their gated communities. They have embraced the concept of private property and privilege. But a vigilante band of desert pocket mice with walkie-talkies and shortwave radio has snuck into the backyard to get usage readings from the meters. They find this fun, and they like the adventure of making strategic stealth attacks into the guarded compounds. They play up the drama, usually staging their strikes in the small hours of the morning or just before midnight. Sometimes they get protection from armadillo mercenaries, who use their armor judiciously.

But this evening's gathering of nouveau-riche zebras, who have just moved into the upscale neighborhood, is fueled by success in the communications industries. For all their smarts in the world of business law, the zebras have no taste. The whole patio is packed with vulgar furnishings, and safari and tropical themes cover the house. They are the butt of species-ist humor that is repugnant to fair-minded creatures. Since they cannot get their manes and tails to form dreadlocks, a look to which they aspire, they load up with extensions and weave beads and cheap ribbons into the braids. The mice find this hysterical and mock the hooved and striped creatures, feeling vastly superior.

The zebras certainly do not expect to be invaded by the rodent inspectors. And the mice think they will escape notice. They hear the clink of ice in a glass, the sound of a swizzle stick, and the low music from an old turntable. The whole boozy scene sounds pretty mellow, and so they creep through the shadows, looking for the meters. Unfortunately, one of the mice has outfitted himself as a little bandito, wearing spurs and a bit of silver here and there. The zebras see the flash of reflected light in the darkness. Mice are no match for a zebra at a gallop. Pinned against the fence, the mice confess they are working for the electric companies, and the zebras laugh their heads off at the idea of sending a mouse to do a maintenance job.

Everyone knows mice chew through the coverings and linings of any electrical equipment to which they are exposed, and so the zebras kick them out (after a rude dunking in their unheated swimming pools). The armadillos ride back to headquarters with the dripping mice, shivering and shaking, annoyed and more than a bit embarrassed, clinging to the sparse hair on the armadillos' plated backs.

The zebras do not press charges for trespassing. They have so much money it is absurd, and lie about by the pools, in sunglasses and visors, wearing very little more than sun block and body lotion. Shocking to their neighbors, who press their faces to the fences to get a glimpse. Their money comes from doing contracts and mergers, legal work, in which they have an international reputation and a well-known disposition toward efficiency and silence. They have gazelles as companions, assistants, and house staff, because the smaller creatures are beautiful to gaze upon and fun to be around. The gazelles have laughter in their heads and little else besides the taste of grass on their lips, and who would not want to spend the day amused by a charming animal whose name means elegant and quick?

Weird Mash-Ups
Rural Pennsylvania

CALLIE'S PATH TAKES HER TO BACKWATERS, where odd

energies gather in the winter and developments happen out of sight. Her instincts for orientation are not working, and, in fact, she is farther from home than ever. She sometimes wonders if she only dreamed the human shelter that had provided warmth and safety, regular food and lots of sleeping opportunities. She has patched together her modes of survival, and now has many skills for finding food, sniffing out places to sleep, and using social networks. She wonders if this drifting will become her permanent way of life.

The days are still short and a good deal of time is spent in the gray zone of shadows. She is mostly in rural areas, where the lighting is even poorer. The pupils in her gold eyes are wide open, her whiskers alert, senses highly attuned to any signal she can track. The beam of intermittent communication that connects her, improbably, to the lion, wavers in intensity, but still drives her onward.

One March afternoon, just on the edge of spring, another rash of radical mutations appears. Ice still clings to the edges of the roads and on the north side of the boulders Callie passes. A thaw is beginning, and a weird array of monsters appears. At first Callie thinks these are hallucinations, chimeras released as gas from the tight hold of winter.

Her paws are cold, nearly numb, but she feels something hitch a ride on her fur, something clinging and climbing aggressively, bigger than a grasshopper, almost the size of a mouse. Though she has never seen it before, she recognizes the thing immediately: a cow-tick. A great, bloated parasite, who meditatively ruminates its way into flesh. Too hideous to imagine. She knows this is not the only hybrid parasite. Mosquito-leopards are swift and fatal; their bites swell shut their victims' throats with a ring of welts.

Finch-leeches drop from the sky. They attach so fast and grip so firmly it is almost impossible to shake them loose without also losing huge chunks of skin and tissue. Centipede-sheep, woolly and fleet, though they are on the small side (no bigger than a mop head), are more disturbing than damaging. But they can make a mess of a lawn in no time and ruin a field of crops.

Callie has heard rumors of these hideous mutations, particularly from the gossiping Labs, but the cow-tick is her first encounter. She shakes it off, her paw flicking angrily. The vile creature releases its grip and drops to the ground, smirking with a sinister bovine placidity, waiting to spring again.

A small herd of armadillo-horses, hard-bodied, armor-plated, and clunky, thunders by. They would be useful for transport and could carry significant burdens without chafing or soreness, though the use of beasts for heavy labor is dying away. These hybrids have blisters on their genes, even if no one can see them. The plated look catches on for a few weeks. Among the strange effects this is not one of the worst, not like the fatal blip that generates turtle-deer, helmeted and shy, or shark-mallards, the duck no one wants on their pond.

Some of these mash-up strains go viral, encouraged by the rushes that run with sap in the spring. The cow-ticks and mosquito-leopards will become a plague in the warm months ahead. The cat can only imagine the defenses she will need against a horde of these. The only way to control the situation—slaughter is no longer practiced in civilized society—is to tap into the gene pool high up in the exchange stream. Putting a filter in the flow means that only recognized, certified, registered particles can move through into flesh and tissue, be expressed as muscle and bone. This is harder than it sounds, since the registries are out of date. The settings controlling the spread of genetic material have to be calibrated carefully if the shifts and changes that are advantageous are going to be allowed. Callie cannot conceive of controls at this level. She thinks in terms of tooth and claw, her atavistic defenses. But these are powerless against the genetic morphing and its manifestations.

Who can define the line between acceptable and monstrous? When a golden toad and a bad retriever produce a loyal but deadly short-tailed tad-pup, can they be accused of malicious breeding practices? Pitied for their hapless offspring? Or be allowed to brand the curiosity as a new form of technology?

Luckily, many of the more aberrant outliers are unable to breed, or else breed so fast that their mutant characteristics are quickly washed out. From time to time, a frog-cheeked baby antelope or a tick-faced swan or a multilegged carp appears, but the remnants of random species are largely vestigial once the full-scale pollution is capped by an Emergency Breeding Commission. Even that word, "pollution," raises a mass of protests. Charges of discrimination against miscegenation pit traditionalists against innovators and libertarian groups committed to the free-for-all of unrestricted genetic mixing. No one wants bloodshed or more violence than is permitted by licensing agreements that go back generations, so some amount of hybridization has to be allowed.

As spring progresses, some of these issues subside. Standard breeding practices take over again, like the peak of a bell curve restoring normalcy to the populations. Bright light and fresh air, sunshine and better hygiene have a positive effect. Seasonal disorders fade, but the practice of complex mixing never vanishes again and its extremes push the limits in all categories of social life and behavior.

Construction Sites
Melbourne

COMING OFF THE BOAT IN MELBOURNE, the lion attempts to blend into the landscape. But his pelt is the wrong color, his species conspicuous, and as he heads toward the outskirts of the city, he trips in a hole on the path. Stepping aside to catch his balance, he trips again, this time in a trough in the grass. The ground underfoot is unstable, treacherous. Digging is a symptom of massive change. The earth gapes and yawns, red gashes in some places, dark grins in others. Some areas are laid waste in a mad rush to make foundations for projects of every imaginable scale. Rebar and wooden forms for pouring concrete spring up like a menace of grids etched on the surface of the landscape. More infrastructure. The lion is immediately distrustful, and the fact that he cannot get his footing bodes ill. He is used to the traps set by prairie dogs and burrowing rabbits, but the scale of these new tunnels terrifies him.

Just then, a Jeep whizzes by, driven by a hound looking utterly splendid in his hard hat. His driving expertise is apparent, and his long, strong legs look like they are made for the heavy pedals on the sturdy vehicle. He has a paw on the gear shaft and holds the wheel with great authority. The look on his face is conscientious and focused as he drives good, straight lines and well-proportioned cuts in the sighing earth. His wheels furrow the already broken soil as the lion watches with dismay.

Off to the left, along the side of the field, a bunch of koalas are running cherry-pickers, lifting workers to attach wires, solder steel, and guide the application of water-resistant coatings on newly finished structures. The lion begins to wonder if he has crossed into some fantasyland. Among all the strangely mutated behaviors, he has seen nothing like this organized application to infrastructural transformation.

The koalas go about their work very seriously, but every once in a while, they toss garbage from their lunches out into the air with no regard for where things land. A wolfhound, supervising from the ground, is hit by sandwich debris. Too refined to make trivial complaints, the elegant dogs try to reason with the bear-like marsupials. But to no avail. The silvery, round-bodied, fluffy-eared beasts just say, "Whatever" to anything the hounds propose. They are actually uncomprehending. Do the hounds really think they will keep the garbage in their work-baskets? Weird. Positively weird. Of course it has to go.

The hounds, subtle but careful managers, are already planning to replace the koalas with their cousins, the wombats, so it seems better not to make a big deal of small upsets. Though they are not much brighter than their relatives, the wombats are more submissive, stronger, not as cute and so not as narcissistic. Their toughened posteriors can tolerate long shifts in the plastic buckets that raise them up to do the many tedious tasks essential to the building projects. When the hounds, plans go into place, the koalas will be upset and they'll take it out on the wombats at family events, where they'll mutter constantly about labor practices and betrayals.

Food Industries
Melbourne

THE LION CATCHES SIGHT OF A food stand near the edge of this zone of frenetic activity. He is ready for a meal and does not mind where he gets it. Plus he is curious to see if the service industries are undergoing the same radical trans-formation as the construction sector. A pair of ostriches greets him, acting very polite and efficient. With distinct gestures of noblesse oblige they refuse to meet his gaze or exchange pleasantries, but promptly deliver a warm, fresh takeout meal. Their management style is light, very light—service without a smile. Everything in the sack is fresh and the food is well prepared and clean. Even in the little stand, they have set up an autoclave for dishwashing.

The hardest part of restaurant work, even at a food stand, is coordination. The lion, munching away contentedly, watches in admiration as the chickens, who are basically willing to do most anything in the way of sous-chef work, cut, chop, and sort veg-etable substances instead of being chopped and sorted. The ostriches surveil the scene, keeping the meals on course. The whole discussion of who eats whom is now considered so out of date that now it cannot be had without mediators present.

The geese are not bad either at marshaling foodstuffs and keeping things moving. At tables near the food stand, they set out flatware, condiments, and extras; they offer fresh napkins even before they are needed. The ostrich manage-ment is as pleased as it ever gets. When the pickup bell sounds from the kitchen, they get very excited. Getting food to the table quickly is an art at which they excel. The lion really wants to eat without so much flurried activity around him, so he swipes his dish and takes it to a quiet corner. All around him, pop-up restaurants are appearing.

The ostriches find cooking much more complicated than eating food raw or from a direct source. So many different timetables have to align for a dish to come piping hot from the oven. The patience of the kangaroos is what this work really needs, but they hate the heat of the kitchens. The steam in particular worries their fur. They often leave partway through a shift with a look of resignation. This work is also not for dogs. They eat the profits before there are profits. And cats are out of the question. Service is simply not a word in their vocabulary, nor a concept to which their cognitive faculties incline. But if fast food and even slow food cannot be prepared and delivered, a whole sector of the economy will fail. And the risk of predatory transgression will threaten the current, fragile equilibrium.

The lion, eating peacefully, can appreciate the problem but has no idea of how to solve it without luring the kangaroos back. The lion chews macaroni and cheese, realizing the negotiations will prove difficult. The ostriches are proud, very proud, and unlikely to compromise terms. Even now, kangaroos refuse to sign the contracts they are offered. From their point of view, they can easily roam the outback and pay no attention to the needs of others. In the end, he thinks, falling into a reverie, it will be the gators who come through, wrapping their fat, wide abdomens with aprons, ordering supplies in the morning, placing orders at night, receiving shipments during the day, keeping the wait staff of geese under control and training the chickens in the kitchen. The gators are great at the grill, adept with the flipper and expert at pizza, pancakes, and omelets. They are fast-food mavens, with a taste for the gourmet. Soon they can prep a morel mushroom or a slice of rare jicama with a sauce or salsa to die for. The ostriches taste things at random, for quality control. They put their hairy heads to the side, eyeing the wicked salsa, and pass it up. The gators snicker, sly triumph in their wide grins.

Watching the customers come and go, their plates heaped and steaming, the lion thinks about how slow it is to build a business. Not that he has any experience, but he knows gators have a good instinct for profits, even though they are bad at paying bills, keeping payroll, and making any outlay of funds, which they tend to stash out of sight and then pretend do not exist. Why this self-destructive habit, left from their own days of food capture, continues when they are now living above ground and in the open, is hard to say. Still, seeing them arrive for their shift, he figures the place has a good chance of success.

Some instincts persist. The lion, wiping his jaws and washing his paws, knows that he is a hair's breadth from grabbing the attending fowl by the neck. He restrains himself but wonders if the gators will be as correct, especially if the chickens complain to the ostriches behind the gators' backs about the risks they are taking committing to this line of work.

The lion slinks off a little farther away, as the noise of a band of roughneck possums, who work in the rubbish business and come by after hours to demand payment, give the geese and the gators a scare, and accept their protection payment from the ostriches.

The Wheels of Commerce
Outskirts of Melbourne

WAKING IN THE MORNING BEFORE THE stand is open and poking around the garbage area, the lion spies a mass of surplus money stuffed behind crates of cabbages and lettuces. He tiptoes toward the kitchen trailer and finds the pantry full of mason jars rattling with coins. The checks and balances are all off. The books have gone unkept so long they are blanketed with dust and debris. Other matters are out of balance as well. An intervention is clearly required. No wonder the possums are clamoring for payment.

The gators arrive to open the locks and start the day's food processing. A squadron of storks, lean and humorless, also arrives ready for action. They surround the food truck, its tiny office and outlying grill, and stand guard. A fleet of mongooses follows, driving armored vehicles. They commandeer the ledgers, fill heavy, gray burlap sacks with the loose change and enormous quantities of bills. The cloth heaves from the bulk and is hauled off to secure sites to be counted and sorted. The mongooses are independent contractors, but they serve both the tax agencies and the private customers they are sent to assist. The experience is not particularly uplifting. The gators are peeved at having their autonomy violated. They are not interested in being reprimanded for their successes. Their younger, slimmer cousins, a group of caimans educated abroad, show up within an hour to take over the business side of the restaurant chain. Their arrival, with their continental sophistication, slightly foreign ways, accents acquired in charm school or finishing academies, annoys everyone. The chickens are dismissive. The geese are hysterical. The gators puff up and imitate the little arrogant rascals. It all looks like a setup in which the storks are partners.

Still, by the afternoon, the caimans are planning to put things on a solid footing. They even develop a plan for expansion into a whole variety of new markets. Within two weeks, the wheels of commerce will be spinning nicely. By the end of July, and just in time for their yearly trip to St. Moritz or Capri or wherever it is they go to relax with others of their kind, they are planning to get a mongoose team to sit down with them and do a final accounting of what is owed, saved, and still outstanding in terms of liabilities. As to assets, right then and there, they give the gators a fair-ish share. Being caimans, they have an inflated sense of their own importance and contributions, and as a result, they justify taking a substantial portion of what they have not earned. Bad feelings grow over the vacation period, and when the caimans suggest returning to take charge, a general uproar rings out. Service industries are difficult. The cycles of boom and bust are rapid. Infrastructure is neither permanent nor dependable but a constant struggle of maintenance.

The lion is quite content to have other species do this—and any other work—for him. Even at his worst and weary, the idea of a startup, of service work, or of entrepreneurship are all deeply foreign to his nature and his self-image.

Fish Woes
Suburban Pennsylvania

THE MASS OF RECENTLY DEAD FISH is technically garbage, but it is also fresh kill, and as far as Callie is concerned, the bounty in the pet store dumpster is a windfall. She has the benefit of a favorite food without murder charges and an opportunity to eat her fill.

She has found her way through a gully that cuts through a small suburban town, and now is in the alley of a strip mall where a pet store is flush with new fish. Some arrive in bad shape, very bad, and thus go into the dumpster instead of the tanks—in which she can hear, even through the half-closed back door, the sounds of an arrogant carp speaking out of turn. Which turn? It has none. Goldfish are nothing like minnows. They care not one bit for collective action. Their natural inclination toward autonomy is positively obsessive. They are completely self-involved, and their attitude of superiority is irksome to say the least. They learn too much from looking through the glass and then not enough from looking at themselves in its reflection. Or maybe it is the other way around. But they indulge in a fantastic amount of gossip. Callie listens attentively. She is careful to keep her distance, aware that the smell on her breath could betray the contents of her recent dumpster meal. But fish soap operas are always amusing.

Among the newly arrived shipment is an old matron, an absolute celebrity with a twisted tongue and sniping spirit. She is vicious, viperous, vituperative, and vengeful, and this distorts her looks, eyes bulging and popping, her mouth so pursed she can barely breathe. The other goldfish swear she will be the first fish anyone ever knew to die from disdain, and it happens before their eyes. She gives a burst of outrage in every direction. Her mouth distorts from dismissive grimaces, her brow lifts so high her forehead disappears into her fins, and her cheeks suck in and puff out in alternating throbs of repulsion all to such a degree that she cannot get air into her little lungs. After half an hour of spasms, she dies of a rare form of asphyxiation associated with vile temperaments.

The matron's funeral is quickly arranged—within half an hour of her demise, the fish finalize all the details and make all the arrangements. Never has Callie witnessed such an eagerly attended funeral. It is a very strange affair. With all the trappings of mourning and none of the sentiment, it is attended by the sincere and the furious alike.

When it comes time for a final eulogy, the company falls silent by unspoken and accidental consensus, and this is embarrassing except that even the immediate family—and she had quite a brood or two in her youth—breathe easier knowing the sharp lash of that harsh tongue is now silenced by its own bad behavior. Mothers hold her up for years afterward as an example to their young, frightening the little whippersnappers with images of quick decease if they speak meanly or badly of each other.

The gossip networks continue to thrive, the unkind edges softened. Though they are not quieter—goldfish cannot shut up—they are much gentler in their commentary and exchange. Compassion filters through, like dye tinting the water, among the burbling, gurgling company. Questions of the social meaning of kindness bubble up in the gossip mills, giving them much to reflect on and consider about their ability to determine or self-determine outcomes and behaviors.

Callie is particularly impressed with the rate at which social change occurs among the fish. Though it was at least a week before a new generation hatched, the shift in attitude happens as dramatically as if it has been processed through several generations. She finds the mismatch between speed of transformation and genetic mutation interesting, though she processes this knowledge intuitively through observation. Washing meditatively as she reflects on the events of recent days, Callie knows something significant is occurring in the aquarium culture. She continues to avail herself of the dumpster contents and makes a few new friends among the older fishes while watching the hatchlings avidly, pretending to be interested in their progress.

Kangaroo Communications
Melbourne

BACK IN THE SOUTHERN HEMISPHERE, THE onset of fall is accompanied by the same intermittent but pervasive transformations that punctuate the spring landscape in the northern half of the globe. The coordinated harmony among the species continues, always without any possible anticipation of the extent of the shifts ahead.

The lion, amused by the novel surroundings down under, watches as the kangaroos, always so remarkable for the elastic energy in their tendons, spring into the air with endless grace. Their tiny joeys, the newborn babes, small as beans, blind and red, wet as jelly, crawl into their mothers' pouches in the same way they always have, and spend months in that comfortable chamber. The peek-a-boo actions of the young play well in their social group at close quarters. But the adults take up a new game of signaling across the wide distances of the open Australian outback. The lion, at ease in the heat and grasses, chases spots of light as the kangaroos develop their new game.

One of the adult kangaroos plays with a hand mirror, a small reflective surface edged in pink plastic with a handle delicate enough for her forepaws to grasp. Like any other jill, she has need of it for cosmetic purposes, of course, but that is not the task to which she currently puts the thing. Instead, noting the strong light that flashes from its surface, she sends a series of short bursts at random outward through space. The lion's winces from the sharp light, but he instinctively follows the movement.

At first, nothing happens. The unfenced view of the outback returns the same brown expanse of openness through which the kangaroo is accustomed to bounding, using her easy capacity to cover distance and graze freely wherever there is food. But after about ten seconds, the lion sees something strike her eye. Light, sharp as a needle, returns from a distant point, too remote to make out anything about the source. The kangaroo flashes two short signals and then a steady stream. The same comes back, amazingly, in perfect imitation. So it begins.

The lion, halting his chase, watches as the kangaroos' signal code builds rapidly. Do different signs identify a major food source or watering hole? Kangaroo telecommunication has begun. As in any true ecology, other activities shift to accommodate the new phenomenon. The lion sees a passing crowd of skinks and goannas—for whom the idea of constant conversation is anathema. They show their disdain for this new social media in very concrete ways. Their methods are crude, but the message is clear. Maybe the geckos can make up for that. The kangaroos, in their innocence, are absorbed in immediacies, hypnotized by the rays of light they are able to generate across the open spaces. Innocence will soon be a rare quality.

Though enjoying the view and amusements, the lion feels pricked by anxiety. He is worried in this odd place, not sure about his security. The kangaroo light attracts attention, and the lion worries he might find himself the object of it in ways he will not enjoy. This is not his continent. And he is not growing any less weary, so with a nod of thanks to the long-limbed marsupials, he strikes out toward the coast, feeling the need to recover his sea-legs and the refreshing smell of salt air. His taste for cruises is becoming sophisticated.

A Stint of Work
Northern Virginia and Elsewhere

BY THE SPRING EQUINOX, WHEN THE world is waking in the temperate zones and passing out of the summer phase in the southern climes, the trade between chill and warmth seeks a balance among the atmospheres and across meridians. The downdrift hangs a moment in the balance, and for that moment, it seems the whole process might, even could, be reversed. Some long-legged stork-hoppers, insect-like in flight but bird-based in their cries, readjusts proportions and their hatchlings have a suspicious tendency to resemble one or the other of their ancestors. Hybridization recedes like a tide for a few weeks. Callie allows herself to hunt rodents without any twinge of conscience and the lion dines on fresh killed rabbits, abundant in the outback on his road toward the coast. The musical instruments taken up by the various animals lie idle, and the revenue streams of the energetic winter activities slow to a trickle.

But nothing stays in equilibrium. The balance of light and dark hours tips over, and the longer days in the north revive the momentum of the downdrift, even as the shorter ones in the southern hemisphere exert an undertow of darkness. The momentum revives. Some populations stir and others begin to finish their supplies, hoarding final bits against coming storms.

Having been chased from the pet store dumpster by an outraged carp and told in no uncertain terms not to return, Callie finds temporary asylum by volunteering at a shelter. The faith-based organizations have changed their policies to allow support from a wider range of species. But Callie still prefers to work for secular humanists and milk their ample liberal guilt. The shelter needs some simple secretarial assistance, and though the work is beneath her (she lies on the papers to keep them still), she is quite content to see the regular appearance of food in a bowl.

Asked how long she intends to remain in the "job" she is doing, she equivocates, her face twitching between whiskers and brow, noncommittal. Like any cat, Callie feels a need to complicate the very things dogs simplify, like relationships. She encourages her feline ability to elaborate upon ambiguity, coming and going to and from commitment, keeping her options open, as if they were a door.

Callie's loyalty is directly proportional to the contents of her dish. She is doing epistolary work for the shelter. Stretched out in the sun, limbs reaching to their limit, belly and fur absorbing the fresh heat of the early season, she uses her nails to prick a lazy message from the air, scratch it in the dirt, and bury it. The shelter organizers are a bit unsure about these missives, who they are addressed to, and why there is so much secrecy about them. Callie smiles.

Settling in at the shelter, Callie assumes a lazy posture and a sense of smug satisfaction. Then, early on the fifth or sixth morning of her job, she gets chased from her sinecure rather abruptly. The regular feline officer at the shelter returns from a personal leave and is shocked by the presence of the interloper. Tail fluffed, back arched, whiskers stretched by a hiss, the returning cat is having none of the whole "sharing" thing and contrary to the letter and spirit of the organization for which he works, turns our poor errant feline back onto the road, where she follows the trail of some of the letters she has posted during her brief respite.

On the move, she skirts the urban areas and heads toward suburban yards and patchwork fields, annoyed, hurt, angry, and once again, constantly hungry.

She could not metabolize, as I could, from basic compounds, and my byproducts offer little sustenance without considerable processing. My bulk continues its expansion, but according to an imperceptible scale. She relies on higher order foodstuffs and thus must organize her foraging more skillfully.

Humming Communications
Tropics

HALF A WORLD AWAY, THE FADING autumn lapses. In the tropics, the equinox hardly matters, especially to the masses of hummingbirds. Masters of flight and navigation, agents of rapid communication, skilled at surveillance and mapping, the brilliantly colored birds can signal the location of anyone, anything, from anywhere, almost instantly. They are the wireless network of the new universe, and their communication lines function invisibly at almost quantum speeds. Parallel processors, they telegraph their information across a matrix of nodes and edges, and having no central hub in the system. They let emergent connections happen as they might, and simply supply energy and information so that the network hums away with a warm buzz.

Amazingly, the activity resists entropy, in part because the birds are full of light sugars and nectar that do not weigh them down, so they don't flag in their energy or the supply it provides. The substance of their communications is only evident when a leak occurs.

The birds begin to exhibit new tendencies—deferring to each other in flight, sitting and watching each other feed, and engaging in other forms of turn-taking—and the ripple effect is profound. Any hint that the downdrift might recede has vanished.

Among the insects, only the hymenopterans, ants, wasps, and bees, subject themselves to the rules of social order. But now a gnat, usually a free agent, acts in accord with others in a way that is not only staggering but charming. A few of the grasshoppers in the Nicaraguan neighborhood signal their approval and a very senior, highly decorated male, looking like some gaudy figure from a medieval armory with spikes, spots, red-and-gold segments in his articulated body, makes a sound that is distinctly laudatory. Social connections are evident.

No one expects the phenomenon to last, and the dear old grasshopper, having offered his approval, turns discreetly back to his own affairs as if wishing to avoid the embarrassment of failure the gnats will experience when they revert to their habits of old.

Rockabilly
Central Virginia

CALLIE FEELS LIKE AN OUTCAST BUT is also a willing audience to whatever scenes she encounters. During the winter, the raccoons went in for rockabilly in a big way, and now the all-night events flood light through the cracks in the barns and other buildings they pack with noise. It makes them happy, and Callie is drawn to the raucous scenes, eager for distraction from her own troubles. She watches their fat little bear bodies sway, black lips and sharp teeth in motion to the howling sounds. They are comical and grotesque and the camaraderie among the group fills her with yearning as she peers through the slats at their performance, wondering if they would let her dance in the chorus or not.

The parody of their bulky shapes is amplified by a threat from the dark-ringed eyes and black noses, paws, and claws. The screeching pleasure of the songs promises to turn violent. The raccoons look as if they will shred the air in a moment of frenzy. Mad things, they are brazen in their appropriation of sentiment, and play the broken-hearted lovers, the betrayed husbands, and lonely, truck-driving, hard-working men of their musical universe with pathetic irony, thick bodies acting out moves that possess them.

Initially, this was bizarre, disturbing, and then, like the rest of the downdrift, it has become routine, the new norm of activity, so that passing a nightclub downtown about midnight no one is surprised, looking in, to see the stage occupied by the ring-tailed critters. Their attempts at tune blare through the amplifiers attached to the bass and guitar.

Callie, taking a seat in one of their sets, is dismayed at the amount of raccoon scat on the wooden dance floor. They have no sense of when or how they drop the trail of defecation. The floor is littered. Callie finds it offensive that the animals can play chord progressions and still ignore basic hygiene. She knows they are used to their wild habits and link odor to survival. The generation that shifts into public spaces and entertainment culture faces a few steep challenges. The small mammal house stench lingers almost every place that is part of the drift zone. Callie realizes this is just part of the experience of watching the raccoons play guitar and croon around the microphones. A few microorganisms treat the molecular structures of odor as food for more than thought, and benefit accordingly.

Songbird Music
Central Virginia

LEAVING THE CLUB JUST BEFORE DAWN, with the other all-night revelers, Callie is witness to other dramas. A flock of sweet songbirds migrates back from their winter retreat, and they pitch their melodies against the traffic tapestry in the background and the low hum of too many machines. Home home home, they are happy to be home! Callie appreciates the sentiment, watching the birds delight in the familiar branches. The bare-limbed trees are just beginning to leaf out and the birds pick at the still-hard earth, scrambling and scratching for food. As the sun edges over the horizon, they pump their lungs with joy and laughter.

In a few hours, the world overwhelms and catches up with them, swallowing their tunes in the tides of noise that break through the rhythm of their songlines. They hop down from the trees and look around in bewilderment at the scrambled ground. They are baffled. The habitat they share with the humans is plowed under—by the humans themselves. They cannot understand the motivation to take the trees and bushes, bungalows and yards, and churn them into a chaotic mass of earth and rubble. They profit, temporarily from the upheaval, gathering seeds and worms, bugs and grubs, and all the other foodstuffs the overturned earth dishes up. But the bounty is short-lived.

The birds retreat by afternoon, into the places where quiet can still be found. They search out the small zones of consumable peace, the little areas in which vibrations and disturbances are at a minimum, and then they tremble the air with their songs, expressing an exuberance of being, temporary, ephemeral, resonant, profound. They are the darlings of the upper atmosphere, audible from on high, and they cherish their relationship with each other, carving a soundscape into sculpture through the arc of music they exchange.

The cat, leaping into the air in a futile attempt to catch their tunes, falls with a thud and picks herself up with bruised dignity. Someone brandishes a broom at her and she flees, unable to take the time to reflect on the multiple dimensions of injustice to which she is being subjected.

Archaean Views: New Woes

I HAVE BEEN LYING LATENT, DRIFTING passively, letting the forces of distributed energy wander where they might. But now, in a random surge, my attention focuses again, intensely. I feel the pangs in the cat's empty belly along with a renewed appetite of my own. I want to take initiative, make a choice, act on my own behalf, or, at least, inhabit some being

I can monitor more directly than these errant felines. If I don't do something decisive, I will never know my limits, my own boundaries.

My consciousness is steadier, a dull point of awareness I can count on. I sense my own agenda. The outlines take shape. I am gaining strength, ready to test my metabolic mettle and take an active role in the downdrift. My chemistry pulses and twitches, and molecules transact with my membranes in a pleasurable way. The changes intensify.

I see no point in giving warning of the inevitable; all the living things will find out soon enough the price they will pay for their impulses of mutualism and community, boundary crossing and dissolution. I still am not sure if the "I" making these observations is a self or myriad selves. I move between singularity and multiplicity. I cannot edge myself into view, but only possess sensation in the general sense.

I sink into the hot sharp fissures of iron oxides and hypersalinated rocks in a deep-sea trench and breathe deeply. My kind are not photophilic. As I have noted many times, we thrive in the fetid toxic wastelands, without malice and without any ill intent. Banal environments that are too normative threaten our well being, extremophiles that we are. I love a shot of radiation now and then, but it is too harsh to share with almost any other creature.

At least I am immune to the blue-eyed disease, for obvious reasons, though narcissism takes many forms. From time to time, I feel something aggressive at my edges. My instincts to flight are enhanced—but to a distributed organism, this means nothing. A cluster of cells gathers from time to time on my distributed perimeter and sends a common signal. To me, code is chemistry, not signs and glyphs. The attempts are weak. I am fine.

But just as I relax, a prion turns in my cytoplasm, hijacking the strands of DNA that fold and float in suspension. I repair the breach in my cell wall, gathering phosphates to bind with the carbon, but the raping actions of the folded protein take a toll. Its aggression goes unchecked, as it inserts itself into the replicating structure of my being. I sigh, twist, writhe, all in vain. Because it is not alive, exactly, I cannot kill it, only work at making the conditions for its presence unfavorable. Cell invasion for self-propagation is such a crude form of social life, but prions cannot be shamed into good behavior. I am most happy when I am the object of no one's interest.

April

Weasel Crimes
Richmond, Virginia

ON A SOFT SPRING MORNING SOON after her encounter with the birds, Callie gets some amusement from a bunch of exceptionally well-groomed weasels performing cosmetic and hygienic work. Always spiffy, they sport tawny spring colors. Their white fronts are spotless, and their very good posture shows off the defined patches of fur that reflect light up under their sharp chins and into their sparkling eyes. The cat is jealous, for a moment, knowing her own fur has suffered from sleeping in rough spots and eating less well than she likes.

One particularly fine weasel is headed to a salon. She waves and a driver instantly appears. He is just another weasel, not a poodle or a hound, so Callie gets some satisfaction from that, but still, the weasel's sense of entitlement is a bit much to witness. The fine weasel sweeps off to her appointment in a streamlined luxury vehicle whose bubble top protects against the elements. She parades en route, smiling from side to side like a movie star. But when the scent of warm rodent trickles into her nostrils, she cannot resist the smell. She dashes from her vehicle and onto the scent trail, killing the smaller mammal without a moment's hesitation, sharp teeth to gullet, ripping throat and arteries open in a swift yank. Callie is shocked, truly shocked.

Such behavior makes socializing awkward now, anywhere along the species spectrum.

The driver does not stop or cite the murderous weasel, just turns a blind eye to the stains of blood on her jaws and hands. As she returns to the vehicle, the driver casts down his head, avoiding her gaze, ashamed of his complicity.

The weasels' old association with misfortune has passed away, but a rumor persists that a small cult group among them keeps alive the habit of destroying brides' apparel in recompense for having been metamorphosed from girls jilted at the altar. Somewhere, though Callie never gets a glimpse of it, a vault of repressed treasures is supposed to exist, filled with scraps of lace and strings of pearls ripped from silk and satin bodices, shredded trains and mutilated veils. If it is ever found, it will prove beyond a doubt that the customs still prevail. She thinks the weasels are probably capable of anything.

The attendants at the salon clean up the bloody weasel, discreetly. They oil her fur and dig the remains of flesh from her nails so that by the time she is ready to leave, only an expert can sniff the evidence of the violent crime still clinging to her underfur.

Waiting on the curb for a ride (her weasel driver suddenly had another commitment), the weasel has a good view of passing drivers, most of them working human shifts. A poodle, the most sought-after of the chauffeurs, catches her eye. She waves him down. He has hold of modified pedals from his booster seat and handles his customized gearshift with a cocky look under his perfect, shiny-billed cap. These affectations are very fashionable and the caps are so popular that the supply has almost run out. The shape of the visor sits just right on the puffy curls.

He glances at the weasel and it is clear that the bright-eyed pooch knows how good he looks. They are a nice match, vanity for vanity, though no poodle has committed felony murder for generations. White poodles are particularly vain, taken with the profile they create behind the wheel, and what they lack in skill they make up for in style. They keep many of their regular habits and are not the first creatures to do so.

The poodle returns the spoiled weasel to her home base, then parks the car by a lamppost, gets out, and misbehaves. He cannot resist the tagging. With a studied air of nonchalance, he waits for his next ride, sniffing the hydrant, the base of the mailbox and the ground around a tree. Every few minutes he pauses for a squirt. Then he pulls himself up and becomes the very image of an elegant poodle standing tall by a shiny, well-polished car, with the casual grace of a well-trained domestic. Old habits die hard.

Irreverent Behaviors
South America

THE LION HAS ARRIVED AT YET another continent in yet another hemisphere, steaming north along the eastern coast of South America. He sleeps through the call at the port of Tierra del Fuego, decides against jumping off in Montevideo, finds Rio too congested, and Barbados too overrun with tourists. But somewhere north of Panama City, near the famous canal, he gets offloaded, without his volition, by an over-conscientious crew who purge the deck of everything, including the crate full of coil ropes that has served as his bed and lair. The zealous team might have been pelicans looking for a surface on which to play shuffleboard or a mess of gulls getting ready for a dance marathon, but the result is the same. The lion, now on land in the Western hemisphere for the first time, tosses his head one way and then another and picks north as the direction of his journey. Why he doesn't stop to converse with the macaws and the monkeys is a fair question, but he knows mainly chimp and bonobo dialects and feels at a disadvantage outside of his culture.

The lion happens onto a group of chimps, sitting on their butts laughing and grinning as simians are inclined to do. They pretend to work. Really, that is what they are best at anyway, acting like they are busy and making fun of it at the same time. Everyone loves them for that. If a situation gets too heavy, bring in the chimps. Put them in school uniforms or white lab coats or chefs' hats and the mood rises immediately.

But the lion happens on them when they are in nuns' habits, which is a little dicier. This is near a small lake in a tiny town near Managua where a modest nunnery serves the poor and the sick. The monkeys have stolen the habits (confused about the use of the term) and once attired, are putting on an extraordinary show. Not everyone appreciates it. The swans are very religious and think some things are sacred, so they get their necks in a twist and won't talk to anyone for weeks afterward. The buzz in the swan press is really negative. For a while it looks like they might impose sanctions, which would be a disaster.

Getting a monkey to apologize for anything is a hopeless task. They flash their butts, cover their grins with their hands, and jump up and down like little hooligans. Undercuts any of the seriousness or substance of regret. They don't experience regret, in fact, unless they are caught at something that will lead to deprivation or humiliation. Jokers, yes, but they are super sensitive. Slight a monkey and it sulks for days, falls into a depression, lies on its side curled up and crying. Terrible. No one wants that. Makes the whole social mood very grim.

As the lion passes through the fertile spring rain forests, leaving the raucous chimps and their bad behavior behind, he can feel the vitality of the unfolding seasonal cycle of things. Hatchling creatures populate the spring pens and the houses and the newborn chirping, cawing, crying, mewing, bleating, barking, baying welcomes the rains in freshets and song. Renewal is on the way and he feels more invigorated than he has in ages.

Archive Work
Central Virginia

CALLIE'S BRIEF SPELL AS A SHELTER volunteer has given her a taste of document-related work. She finds her way to a Species Historical Society, a venerable institution in a stately home in old Virginia, where some arrogant felines pretend to be suited to the role of archivists. Wary of some old prejudices against the treatment of cats in the past, she tiptoes around them to get an idea of current codes of ethics. The cats who have jobs won't let her work, but they have a flair for southern hospitality and Callie figures free food at a stocked buffet beats hard labor any day.

The archive cats are agnostic as to the local politics. They wave away any idea that legacy issues are a problem. As long as they have a professional title, they occupy the archival positions. Their approach is to lie on the papers—stacks of them—and swish their tails to rearrange the order of things. Cat classification systems. Not precise and not good for retrieval. They don't care. They roll over, bellies exposed, staring out over a broad expanse of documents. When asked, even politely, to do something that might be of use, they blink. Layers of sedimentary disorder are interleaved with fur. Cats will shed in the course of things. A little nasty, really.

The secret indolence (they had tried to pass it off as the lesser sin of laziness) of the cats is apparent; they loll and lie about, without any sense that anything they do is slacking. The archives, they assert, are safe, very safe. In fact, they are mainly warm and comfortable places, with piles and piles of pillowy papers. They look at unemployed Callie with disdain and tell her they want praise, praise, praise, even though they act with complete disregard for guidelines. Callie obliges, eager to be invited to the daily mealtimes.

Cats are not wicked, as Callie will explain, just luxuriously lazy. Once in awhile, one of them stands, shakes off sleep, and saunters off to take care of business. When that happens, a SWAT team of pipers sweeps in, gathers up a long abandoned stack of paper, and whisks it off to the sorting station. In minutes—literally!—months and years of back inventory is ordered, numbered, given its unique ID and its place in at least two classification systems (World Feline Format, WFF, or Protocol Information System Standard, which they call by its acronym to make clear their disdain). The birds should be in charge, Callie says. Her hosts are not impressed.

The sandpipers are deft and efficient. They do the filing and the system runs very smoothly as they swoop down on any abandoned pile. In short order, they deal with the backlog, set up a front desk, and pull a curtain across the front of the room for drama. History, they say, belongs to the victors, strutting on their temporary stage for all the world as if they have conquered the mass of legacy documents.

But the archive cats, coming back from their meal, look

around astonished, annoyed at the opening made in the piles. Scanning upward with their whisker radar, they launch into space and land on a multi-layered mess of unsorted papers. Sliding home, they destabilize the whole mass under their weight. A paper avalanche occurs. The pile topples like a slagheap. The cats sled down, front legs stretched outward, tails up, backs arched, registering as much surprise as felines allow themselves to do, ever. They enjoy the long, slow motion of paper slipping over itself in a stream of gathering momentum. Coming to a halt in a new mess, they settle back to the all-consuming tasks of grooming and napping and lying around to be admired while maintaining a steady state of disorder. They love it.

Callie is appalled, but she is an outsider and her comments mean nothing to them. She feels cheered by the encounter with the cohort of feline professionals. The image of long afternoons sleeping among piles of paper with others of her species offers an appealing promise for the future. Though she has no credentials, she tries on the title of archivist to see if she likes it.

Ferret Brutality
Central America

THE LION'S TASTE FOR DESERT HARES is now tempered by tamales as he leaves the southernmost part of Costa Rica and moves into wetter zones where plump pigeons and moist frogs are ample, if contraband. Meandering north along small streams and rivers of forestland, he revels in the smorgasbord of ample offerings. His relation to prohibitions is softer than that of other animals (who can stop him?), and he feels justified by the fact that his natural range is not available—and may never be again.

On unfamiliar ground, he has a very distant encounter with a jaguar, whose throaty growl puts him in his place, whatever that is. Unsure of his footing, his social standing, or of pretty much everything else, the lion does his best to skirt disputed territory and remain as invisible as possible. Scents and profiles give him away, but the courtesy extended to strangers counts for something. He is left alone to wander.

In spite of the rush of vigor he got from seeing the thriving creatures of the region, he is battered in spirit and body, his energies sapped by the endless traveling and the uncertainty of his future. Passing through a small, once-colonial town, he takes an unplanned turn into the middle of a public square and comes face to face with a scene so dreadful, he realizes how naïve he has been about the larger effects of social processes and development.

A golden eagle has been brought out in chains. The magnificent animal is almost unrecognizable, her plumage so badly damaged she looks like caked mud has been patched onto her hunched body. Her head is withdrawn, cowed by abuse, and her dulled eyes stare from behind a battered beak with cold, dead hatred. The ferret captors hiss and spit at the pathetic bird. In turn, they are attacked by the civet cats who accompany them, taunting all along the way. In the face of the public's disgust, their mutual animosity is nothing to their loyalty to each other in their despicable undertaking.

The martyred bird, still proud but so badly beaten she is not likely to survive, stands without a sound, chains chafing her ankles and mutilating her talons, which are rubbed raw. The bird is a female survivor of nestling rivalries, the murderer of her sibling a few days beyond the hatching. Ruthless in their own right, the birds do not hesitate in that act of atavistic selection, though they no longer need to continue such actions to ensure survival. Other methods are available. But the impulse to kill is present in the hatchlings. Eagle parents watch, sanguine, nonjudgmental, passive in the face of fratricide. This has been the case for generations and generations. This female is a killer, a bird who has triumphantly determined her own fate.

Now one wing droops and drags, gone limp from the abuse to which it has been subjected. The other is tied to her body. The signs of torture are paraded by the flagrantly vile ferrets, who have the opportunity for reform and refuse to take it. They are vigilante ferrets, willing to be hired as mercenaries for the basest tasks. They take some pleasure in the repulsion they generate, in being spat on and disregarded by the general populace. Their main motivation is cruelty, to create a spectacle of humiliation for a bird whose species has often robbed them of their young. That was a generation ago, and this young bird had no role in those crimes.

The stinking civet cats, a random band, are beneath disdain. They have accessorized themselves with long whips of barbed razor wire, which they cut through the air in a facile motion. To subdue them, careful tactics must be deployed.

An ugly sight, the entire parade, and the worst is that no one steps forward in defense of the bird. The ferrets sashay in public view, daring anyone to put a stop to the monstrous torment they enact.

An argument could be made that in the old times, when the notion of a natural order reigned among the wild creatures, such behaviors were rampant and no higher law of any kind existed or was invoked. But that is specious as well as romantic. Order has always been part of the world, just that regulations were local, among communities and between them. Ecological equilibrium is always being recalibrated according to the additions and subtractions, assertions and transgressions that are the daily business of being.

In this new order, where legality is meted according to terms of an administered justice, damage can be done with sanctions, out of sight, but not outside the limits of the law. The fate of the eagle, who dies slowly in public view, causes an outcry and galvanizes a movement for retribution.

Terrible events transpire. The ferrets are hung out to dry, the civet cats stretched on wires above the public square. The laws will change, but slowly, too slowly for the noble birds, who withdraw to the highest altitudes, go vegetarian, become thin and ethereal and extremely spiritual. They were never religious in any orthodox sense, and so withdraw into contemplative modes, reflecting deeply on the nature of the universe, the limits of justice and judgment, the causes and effects of behavior, and the need for a civil society. They write lapidary treatises and distill their considerable wisdom into dense, haiku-like statements they dispense in airdropped pamphlets, not to proselytize, but as an offering, wisdom falling as gentle rain. The martyred bird becomes the emblem of their dedication to reform and regulation, and to the higher order of compassion as the only route to justice. The time for real transformation is almost upon us, pressing. Sick at heart, the lion, like most of the animals, turns away, unable to conceive of how to act in the face of such events.

LATE APRIL

Possum Literacy
Near Richmond, Virginia

LEAVING THE ARCHIVE, CALLIE DECIDES AGAINST gainful employment, slightly piqued that not everyone saw her recent contributions in that light. She figures she can continue in public service if she can find someplace to be conspicuously useless. She has a bounce to her step. Spring is in full swing, the air is fine, and she has packed a cache of tasty morsels from the buffet under the watchful but benevolent eye of the generous archive cats.

She prances around a corner to a small local school. On the steps of an old repurposed Carnegie building, she encounters a group of fast-reading possums on the outdoor benches. No one invites them inside. Ever. Their bad eyes, red-rimmed in their unattractive faces, hairy in that spiky, wet-looking way, are charged with a voraciousness that defies belief. They live to read, blinking in the light, and consuming everything in sight. But they could benefit from a little serious pedagogy.

They have helped themselves to a few of the final books on the school library shelves. These are mainly in disrepair, their paper substrate disregarded, their old bindings chewed. Or their pages are folded into lampshades, tricked out as devices of distraction, or other monstrous misuses of once venerable objects. Absorbed in the texts, the possums don't look up at the cat.

Still, sitting so nicely on the benches in the spring air, the possums, light shining through their round, veined ears with skin thin to the point of translucence, are like posters for the repose and rewards of reading. Clearly they are just pretending not to hear as Callie makes polite inquiries. The saucer-like capacity of those ear cups is astonishing. They can hear footfalls a mile off and any whiff of intention focused in their direction.

At this moment, they actually just want to be left alone to wrangle with the densities of Euclid, the perversities of Faust in versions by Goethe and Mann, and to paw their way through the poems of Elizabeth Barrett Browning, of whom they may be the last living readers, dedicated as they are to recovery of textual remains. They are the salvage eaters of language. When they get overwrought, their teeth chatter, their eyes get bright and feverish, their naked hands go raw, as if scraped by contact with so many genres of composition.

Poetry has a funny effect on their digestion, as the lines pass so fast before their eyes. So different from scanning the heavy tomes laced with formulae and mathematical notation. Some days, they see all of this textual matter the same way, as code ripe for the taking. Filling though it is, it always generates as much appetite as it satisfies. Byron and Keats and Shelley produce particularly acrid chemistry, the aftertaste of longing. The sharp edge of intellectual drive mixes with aching melancholy suited to their nervous imaginations. Shakespeare goes down well. But Emily Dickinson must be eaten on an empty stomach, preferably after a fast, to be fully appreciated in all of its nuance.

Callie is so impressed with these model readers that she suggests they join her in the classroom. So many public-spirited impulses are just wrong. What results is not just confusion and noise, as the other students object unkindly to their presence, but Callie hears distinctly some very unkind remarks about paws on the desks and tails on the chairs, as if they are less than clean. One student draws a caricature of a possum on the chalkboard, and they all hurry away in shame. Callie takes an early recess.

Musical Entrepreneurs
Near Richmond

AS ADAPTATIONS GO ON AT THE cellular, the genetic, and the social level, some changes are causes of upset, as when the shepherd dogs are dismissed from the driving pool. They think of themselves as the most likely candidates for the task of chauffeuring, better than poodles, even. They are shocked to find they test as too distracted, too intensely aware of the trails they are following and perimeters they are guarding, to respond well in traffic. They are still sulking.

The small-minded and mean-spirited Pekinese are keepers of some particularly fine bits of genetic code, which explains their mania for test-tube cultures and cultivation. They are paranoid about potential thieves and hackers. They lock their labs and sanitize like mad. They wear silly little anti-contamination booties when they work, in an officious excess of conscientiousness. But they are tipplers on the side, and drink pure vodka and chartreuse, their favorite liqueur. They are less than steady on those little feet, and sometimes they slip and slide when they are alone in the cold storage units. In the presence of others they are completely uptight, sneer, and try to cover the scent of alcohol by cultivating a very distinct brand of dog breath.

Unbeknownst to the dogs, a side business in smuggled Pekin, the rare ingredient they guard so jealously, has sprung up. The pirated substance is marketed in alleys and back rooms, and used to keep any number of noses stuck in the air. Better than Botox—or at least, that is the hype. A pinch of Pekin tightens the cheeks, nostrils, lips, and other unmentionable orifices. As part of the hybridization phase, the Pekinisation of rhinos, baboons, wild hogs, and a whole host of pygmy rodents is characteristic of the early summer season.

As the air warms and outdoor cafes begin to fill, sidewalks throng with animals on parade and the desire to look a bit Pekin becomes a trend. The aftereffects of the pinching are a counterpoint droop. The inability of slack skin to regain tone gradually causes enthusiasm for the contraband drug to diminish. But the little dogs never admit to either the rise or fall of their genetic material in the market of public opinion.

Thankfully, however, they do not take up singing in public as a way to compensate for their losses, but the giraffes do. Zoo-bound, they are filled with passion and longing. Why they begin to croon rather than use their flutes isn't clear, and the sound is awful. Maybe it is because the little jerboas have abandoned them for other amusements. The giraffes often imitate the sounds of oboes, woodwinds, elegant clarinets, and other instruments by using those long necks, but now they make bass foghorn sounds, dull, flat, and without any hint of musicality. Their enthusiasm for the gluey duets and triple harmonies is nothing to their wild love of the quartet, and the sight of four heads bobbing in unison, their brown eyes rolling to the apparent heavens, their lips moving with the liquid velvet smoothness of their loose, wide jaws is a wonder to behold but a kind of horror to the ears.

However, no animal wants to disappoint the deeply innocent giraffes, and for a while the neighborhood communities consider creating an orchestral accompaniment to assist in mutating the sound. But the giraffes are onto that from the outset and sigh, saying *no no no,* they just cannot, will not, under any circumstances allow their a cappella purity to be polluted. The cafés are full of their ensembles, and for a season or two it seems one cannot have a cup of coffee or a dry martini without that background roar of noteless music.

Recordings spring into being and their label goes global, Gi-Riff-Raf-Recs. This is very nice for everyone, really, because the revenue stream is ample. The business in slacks and tics for the long-legged beasts skyrockets, which means that the squirrels are as busy as they can possibly be, running up and down the gawky heights for fittings and adjustments. Plus, the volume can be turned very low if the tuneless numbers are played on a device. That means that everyone gets what they want, more or less. If a combination of dreadful music and marketing success counts as a triumph, then this is it.

Specialty Niche
Virginia

THE NEED FOR DISCO AND NEW groups for nightclubs is exploding. So many of the animals like to go out, even dress up a little. The entertainment industries are booming with raccoon rockabilly and songbird quartets. Tuxedos are very popular among the penguins and the felines, who would corner the industry if it weren't for a few of the slim and long-limbed émigré gibbons with superior style. They just have an elegance that even the most agile feline cannot match. The gibbons are graceful. They dance. They have rhythm. They have *style*.

The gibbons bring a dignity to the way they lean into and out of a waltz or a turn in the ballroom that the poor penguins will never achieve. Combined with the sleek, black-and-white combinations, the gibbons are unbeatable in the wars of fashion, and when they take up stickpins and carved-handled walking sticks, the game is essentially over. No penguin can stand to wear jewelry (never say "pin" in their presence), and cats, though they love all accessories, cannot drape themselves around a long-handled, mother-of-pearl cane with anything like the nonchalance of a senior gibbon.

Lemur Bling
Near Washington, DC

HAVING ABANDONED THE POOR POSSUMS TO their reading, Callie assesses her food situation. She has exhausted the little stash from the archive, and a not-quite-fresh bowl behind the school is not encouraging. She does a little cat math and figures the situation requires movement. The lion, still moving north and west along the angle of Central America, will soon turn in her direction and begin the leg of the journey that brings them together. His view of the state of things is also not improving. Nowhere does he spot a living wage or sustainable housing for his species, let alone sites for homesteading habitat. How can the lions have been left out of these new civil codes?

Still, Callie is in a cheerfully reflective mood. She has managed pretty well in recent weeks and has ample energy for forward momentum and inward reflection. Her feet are muddy from the roads, but the recent rains provide plenty of fresh water. She feels confident, inconspicuous, and blends into the urban environment. After all, the once-human landscapes are not foreign to her as they are to the lion, and so the bustling shopping street, lined with boutiques and busy animals, does not intimidate her. And in the city, no one will bother with a passing cat. She feels safe taking in the changed scene and feels pretty sure she can find some leftovers somewhere.

Very few of the animals wear actual clothes, she knows, unless it is for an occasion, like when the raccoons perform or the rats don disco gear. But they do accessorize. Oh my, how they accessorize! The market in baubles has clearly escalated. Not only shop fronts, but stands and street vendors abound. The lemurs, in spite of their dubious immigration status, set up displays in front of their offices. From the way they dash back and forth that morning, they look like they are dealing law in the back and jewelry in the front. Their tastes are conservative, a little upscale. The cat notes that the prices of the lemurs are much higher than at the crows' stands. But everyone knows the crows pick up anything, dust it off, string it on a bit of chain or elastic, and lie to your face about what it is. They are shameless, but so cheap that they do a booming business among the young.

Some adolescent bunnies are frantically bedecking themselves with complete abandon, as are a cluster of swaggering beaverettes. Pushing ahead of them are a few still-slim piglets and a few young giraffes (diplomatic brats), whose graceful necks and elegant ankles can be stacked high with contrasting strands of glass and shell and silver-plated beads. They are doing their best to empty the lemurs' stands. The lemurs prefer to work with an exclusive clientele. Not that they refuse anyone service, ever—they are too egalitarian for that—but the individuals who enter their storefronts are usually prepared to pay for the sophistication of the collections. The floors in these spaces are softened with local moss, dry grass, and imported banana leaves. The giraffes, too shy to say much, are flush with foreign cash and somehow manage to transact plenty of business. Given the proximity to the capital, Callie is not surprised to find a cosmopolitan and ambassadorial crowd.

She is a bit envious of the bling and glitter being traded and displayed and wonders if a little adornment might be in order. Something shiny, sparkling, and discreet? She looks longingly through a window to where a passel of little aye-ayes, originally imported as exotic pets, are busy working as attendants in the shop. They have very cute accessories, with exotic banana flowers worn like caps on their small, well-shaped heads. Every half hour or so, one of them suddenly leaves their post and runs off, abandoning their employment. Callie finds this baffling until she realizes that they are so addicted to grubs that they would rather enjoy the bounty in the city park than gain the small reward of pocket change in sales commission. In their home environment, they forage in the trees of the canopy, a little drunk from coconut milk and ripe mangoes. Here, in the mid-Atlantic, they just lean seductively against the cases in the shops, waiting to get enough cash for a drink or two with their grubs, pretending interest in the quasi-glamorous work with velvet-lined boxes and satin-draped displays.

Rejection
Washington, DC

THIS SEEMS LIKE A GREAT OPPORTUNITY to Callie. She is willing, very willing, to handle jewels and baubles for a while, especially for a bit of an allowance. She offers to do temp work during the aye-ayes' breaks, just minding the counters. But the indris and the sifakas, the most serious legal minds among the lemurs, prefer to train their own kind for every job in the shop. They enjoy the prattle of the young and flatter themselves that the little aye-ayes respect them. They don't see what the cat sees immediately, that the sashaying sway of the sifaka, for instance, is being wickedly imitated among the mocking younger set. They would insist that imitation is a fine form of flattery.

Business is truly thriving. The cat is impressed. The passing months have changed things dramatically, and Callie realizes the lemurs would have grown rich, except that they do almost all of their legal work pro bono. A group of not-very-good-smelling bears, now nuzzling their way through the adolescent shoppers, heads toward the legal offices to see if they can take advantage of these free legal services. One of them wears a judge's robe, but they have no legal training, none at all, and this masquerade offends the studious lemurs. The conversation does not go well. The lemurs try to be patient, but they are night workers, heavily lidded in the light of day, and tend to nod off if conversations get tedious.

After a few professional exchanges, the lemurs close their books and tell the bears to look for partners closer to their native land. Everyone ignores the bears as best they can as they snarl and snap their way through the shopping strip. The cat, among others, wonders if the problem is that they got up so early that year. If so, that situation may get worse before it gets better.

More Legal Matters
Washington, DC

THE NEXT DAY, THE WEATHER TURNS cold again. And rains, usually heavy that time of year, reach record-breaking amounts. Callie takes shelter in another city archive, where she finds common goals among her kind and another regular, if uninteresting, food source supplied by management. Civil work is looking like a sinecure. But among the animals in the wild and even the suburbs, food supplies are scarce. Hoarded stocks shrink and quarreling breaks out in some quarters. The dogs (a committee of border collies, to be specific) make an enormous number of rulings to keep the squirrels under control. They design a civil code of ordinances that has more subsections and constraints than the hybrid offspring of a Napoleonic law book. The squibs of an ancient bureaucracy get tangled in ceremony and dispute.

For days at a time, the dogs pore through the documents they are designing for the squirrels. They struggle with wording about paw prints and speed of chatter, rights of passage over and under branches and gutters, the rules about when and where and for how long a raw peanut might be buried and to whom the rights of removal could be transferred on occasion of loss of property titles or in the event of liens placed and terms bartered. The squirrels lobby heavily. But this is a dog document, filled with the characteristic revisions and returns, reworkings of passages and twisting sections that stop, pause, and then go nowhere. The dogs are capable of clearer work when their brains are not flooded with passion, but when it comes to squirrel legislation, they go bonkers—in part because it is so very, very evident to all concerned that not one single line, word, dot, jot, or tittle of that juridical language is going to have even a whiff of effect.

The longer the legal file the shorter the squirrel patience. When served with papers, ordinances, subpoenas, summons, or citations, the squirrels stand stock-still, spread-eagled. Their noses up, eyes bright, tails momentarily frozen, they twitch with just that look of express disrespect they can never repress. Then they spill their high little chatter until the poor dogs, full of attention and sincerity, have to give in to their bafflement, give up, and go back to refining the writs and mandates with the most innocent belief in the power of the word to assert authority over the mad will of the disobedient rodents. Given her instincts, Callie would have exercised a very different kind of authority, but she knows that is no longer acceptable, not publicly.

Archaean Views: Protein Battles

THE ILL-INTENTIONED PRION CONTINUES TO TRY to use its misfolded proteins to convert and pervert my own cellular operations. I keep the process under reasonable control, but the nasty opportunist is undaunted, persistent, and highly annoying. Time is not an issue in our universe. My concerns are neither seasonal nor geographical. Just as some overt symptoms are universal, a behavioral pandemic, others appear as localized effects. Similarly, some events occur in specific moments, but others are widely distributed, hyper-events, with unbounded duration. Seasons have no impact on me, and I understand geography only as terrain variation, not boundary zones. My presence breaks out like a rash in a half-dozen places all at once—in a smelting pot in South Africa, a polluted marsh in the Philippines, lying on the floor of an abandoned water tank in the Russian steppes, and soaking in the tepid, cooling waters of a radioactive basin in a plant in southern Utah. I could list other sites as well, since I can feel each location like a tingle in an extended but oddly disconnected limb. What connects these sensations is a network of charges, passing through the nodes.

I am in the dry earth and also watch from the wetlands. I hang out in the sewer lines and tailpipes, in exhaust vents and runoffs, aware, always, of my rapidly changing coordinates. But the prion that has penetrated my defenses stays close to the fluid medium in which it travels, continuing to produce its wretched chain reactions. That is one site of my existence, but I also find myself on the edge of a chainsaw blade poised for action and held at a dangerously careless angle by a totally reckless monkey with a lovely face and wild grin. They cannot be trusted with chainsaws. Not because they mean mischief, but because they laugh too much, wave their arms, and throw the flat paddles of the blades around in the air with a casual abandon. I have no chance of controlling them—not that I am at risk. At my size, I am too small to slice and dice.

Now the chaperone proteins show up to assist the prions, and soulless, DNA-deprived and depraved things that they are, they continue their attempts to hijack my workings. I decide to expunge them through a dose of radical toxicity and have the pleasure of feeling their ribboned forms shrivel into impotence. What a relief. I have no desire for a prolonged zombie afterlife as the vehicle of some genetically challenged protein.

MAY

Among the Frogs
Costa Rica

SUMMER, STILL YOUNG AS A FLEDGLING, has arrived. A hawk, ready to leave its nursery nest, takes flight with a gold stud and nose ring to celebrate its independence. He has no idea he is being played as a medium of downdrift symptoms.

Enough of adolescents and their discontents. The lion is now reduced to near beggary. He reviews the inventory of sites he has seen, while a platypus crawls onto the bank of a slow-moving creek with his harem in tow. A bunch of salamanders stop their swimming to watch the peculiar family. They are clearly inspired. Polygyny, practiced among the platypuses, threatens to spread with viral fervor among the amphibian populations in the small streams and ponds where these marsupials dive and cavort.

The lion watches in amazement as the quiet platypuses, known as an isolated species, take out their cell phones and start texting and talking away. Long into the afternoon and evening, they indulge in the joys of late-night phone calls that reach from their vast subcontinent to other regions of the now-known world. Their influence is spreading so fast on social media that they have established an Institute of

Potential Geography, with the belief that more places and spaces lie beyond their current mapped coordinates.

The Leaf Green Tree Frogs are aghast, since they are so discreet about their own reproductive behaviors. They feel the mammals ought to practice more decorum. They know nothing of the strange sex lives of microorganisms. But they witness polygyny and find it vulgar, crude, and potentially polluting. The frogs depend on the purity of the water in which they lay their eggs and carefully watch their tadpole offspring until they reach maturity.

Though so many of the frogs are endangered, they do not stoop to the habits of the platypuses. An odd case of species disdain, crossing boundaries of hierarchy and behavior. The frogs are developing collective governance, for one thing. They meet frequently and croak out some of the rules by which they feel their various communities should be governed. They have no archives and no place to store documents, which wilt in the moist air or dry and go brittle in the blazing heat. They feel superior to the awkward, duck-billed animals, with their webbed feet and fat tails, looking for all the world like some bad medieval illustration in an ancient bestiary. Frog perception is linked to a narrow range. They know little of the larger fauna and nothing of the micro-world on which they depend. Typical. But they did not see the larger downdrift, breaking in wave after wave across species.

The lion moves through the mountains of Costa Rica where frogs are abundant and diverse. He looks on their parades, their elaborate family gatherings, their world congresses, and wonders at their differentiation, the colors of skin and nuances of voice and song. The growling grass frog and the common mist, the magnificent brood and the torrent tree variety are all different from each other and

from the green-thighed, the Cooloola, the giant barred and
the neglected, the stubbies, the swamps, and the cannibals.
They all lay their eggs dutifully and watch and wait for the
mottled green-and-gray, the yellow-marked and blue-spotted,
the rich-brown, and black-speckled features of their skin to
blossom forth with maturity.

They do all of this without any kind of misbehavior
among the males, the lion notes. He feels a twinge, knowing
that his own behavior has been far more brutal, more com-
promised. Frogs do not toy with the affections of one after
another of their species.

One afternoon he surprises a small committee of the
frogs discussing the intolerance laws that are just coming
into being. The little amphibians all nod in agreement.
These will be passed by the next season or soon after. They
use their elegantly long fingers, knobbed and supple, in the
arduous process of writing out civil codes that justify behavior
and regulate the worst of it back toward consensus.

As the meeting wears on and the details proliferate, the
lion struggles to register the implications of these changes. A
few poor young sloths, ignorant of the disdain in which they
are held, are gamboling and playing in the waters nearby.
They behave or misbehave according to their whims, which
does not raise them at all in the estimation of the frog committee. "Mammals," say the frogs, with a tone of voice that
says everything.

Overhearing these comments, the lion sighs. His mood
droops. He puts his head on his beat-up paws, off his guard.
The next thing he knows he is under a net, being dragged
unceremoniously across the dirt and pulled into a cold,
metal-barred cage. Incomprehension and trauma set in
immediately as adrenaline races through his body. What has

just happened is incomprehensible. Incomprehensible. He has never before been in an enclosure, except for the open hold on board the ship, never subjected to the control of others, never under constraint or locked into a space and out of the world. What are these bars, lines across his sight?

The shock nearly kills him. He is stunned. The chill of the steel on his paws goes right into his heart, gripping what is left of his spirit. What now?

Half a continent away, Callie is jarred back into action through the line of communication that connects the felines. She remembers she has somewhere to go and something to do.

Conflict in the Foothills
Blue Ridge Mountains

CALLIE IS DETERMINED TO IGNORE THE gaudy newt with flamboyant gills, who is decked out as if for a formal occasion. He is bidding for attention, flaunting his elaborate, bright-blue breathing apparatus as he struts among the damp leaves. The early summer forest has a slightly moist smell with a very fragrant undertone and light and delicate top notes. The newt strikes one show-off posture after another, his vivid colors stark against the dark earth.

A swaggering group of bullfrogs—major bullies—begin to bad-mouth the newt. The noise comes through the stream water. They claim they are mounting a beauty contest, but have the bad taste to make a meal of flies and drop bits of wings and legs all over the edges of the pond. The newt, concentrating on his elegance and photogenic preparation, refuses to participate in any pageant unless the stream surfaces are spotlessly clean. The frogs take umbrage, so the newt slides away to a nearby pond that is perfectly fresh and quiet, certain that photo opportunities will arise. A fresh batch of newt hatchlings, programmed for beauty, starts their posing and posturing as soon as they can twist their little tails enough to act sassy.

But Callie's course is now charged with urgency and she forces herself to turn her back on all of this. Later she hears from some gossipy starlings and sparrows that the bullfrogs' event was a flop, and their backers, mainly owls, are so annoyed by the insect eating incident that they threaten to withdraw from a newly formed nonaggression coalition just out of spite. This gives the newt and hatchlings a fright. A tremor of unease runs through the group. Dark forces are gaining strength. This time, the threat comes not from bacteria, viruses, or prions, or even destructive humans, but from social forces that cannot be kept at bay.

JUNE

Coyote Encounters
Richmond

CALLIE'S COAT IS PATCHY AGAIN, HER pink nose a little dry, as she follows the impulse driving her toward the lion. A coyote trails her. Though their missions are different, their paths coincide briefly. The coyote is in fine shape, heading home to one of his sleeping dens. The spot is among some human settlements, which are becoming intolerable. He is anxious to leave the places where the fatty humans, foul-smelling and pasty, stand outside the inconspicuous entry. They are oblivious to his presence, mostly, and the spot is safe enough during the day. He finds it unpleasant to be so close to the bipedal species and wonders if he can learn anything from listening to them wave their stout hands. The site is on a road where the stench of exhaust and diesel fumes gets caught in his nest among the tangled vines. The day's rising traffic stings his eyes and they burn from the vile smells. This is as close as any animals go, voluntarily, to the humans—except for those bound by domestic fealty. Callie's perspective has changed since the start of her journey and her view of the world has tilted, though she still feels loyal to the human order of things. The coyote's ability to move between the wild and the human systems fascinates her.

The odor of a woman ripples across the sidewalk, polluting the morning air with unwelcome exhalations and exuded products of her glands. The coyote finds the stench unfortunate. At night, coolness soothes the sting and he rambles at will in the quiet streets, plucking the squirrels from their slumbers and enjoying the pleasures of the water features and wet grass. His violations are noted, but go unpunished. In the bright daylight, he skulks close to walls and brush. The coyote sports an earring, a beautifully wrought silver clip decorated in the style of his species, with an intricate pattern of tracery that marks him among his peers. The silver circle catches the light as he runs.

Callie follows. The coyote's path is so different from hers. He moves with skill through yards she does not see from the street, and into passages sheltered from view. He looks constantly from side to side, watching everywhere for possible prey—and threats. She is impressed with his speed and knowledge of the urban environment, and when he reaches his hidden sleeping spot, Callie is worn out. The coyote, ignoring her but without any hostile vibe, puts his head down between his paws. He is tired from his run, but also, from the dirt and stress of the urban environment. He tries to nap in the mid-morning, not sure if he can let go of his vigilance enough to pass into slumber. Callie has no interest in the naps of others, and though grateful for his guidance through the city, takes off on her own again. She could get a major crush on a coyote like that.

Under the Soil
Virginia Woods

A FEW MILES AWAY, JUST BEYOND the edge of the city, where the freeway streaks into the landscape, Callie happens on a pack of goat-dogs actively searching for food. These are genuine hybrids, one of the few cross-species to actually survive and propagate. They snort constantly, since their sense of smell is acute and their appetites are eclectic. They snort frenetically around the culverts and drainage ditches that divide the roadbeds from the cultivated land, the tended areas from the abandoned ones, trying to satisfy their omnivorous appetites.

They are not pretty to look at. The front and back ends are mismatched and their gait is off-kilter, revealing the difficulty of integrating their mixed genetic source material. They are the first and second generation, still smoothing out the kinks in the mix. The muzzles of the dogs and the long jaws of the goats come together in an overbite. Tails that want to wag up often flag against the wind, or else stand so feather tall that getting any communication from them is impossible. They are simply pennants flown from the arching sinew of a long appendage, inarticulate and semi-comic.

Some of the hybrids are awkward and trip as they move, their hoof-paws getting stuck in the mazes made by moles and worms. The ground is soft in the summer season. An altercation that would not have been public earlier in the year comes as an audible echo through the opening of one of the underground passages. A worm has raised its tiny voice in protest to something handed down by a mole, and one of the goat-dogs pauses to listen. Callie pauses too.

The worms are protesting administrative decisions made by an old mole. They have a right. Their survival depends on it. The worms are not libertarians, in spite of the freeform action of their intestines, and in fact they are more cognizant of the social life of others than most of the burrowing rodents and varmints. The warm-blooded animals want heat all the time and the worms are casual about that, except in winter when the mudpack is so hard they cannot turn easily. But worms get sullen under pressure, feeling rotten about the way the earth is treated.

The moles are quiet, poking along, and their occasional mumbling seems pointless to the worms. Why talk to oneself in the dark when the moist, soft, fragrant soil clinging to the body offers its redolent scents for consumption? Vocalization seems like a crude form of communication to the worms and to microorganisms thriving in the earth.

Today the worms have found their way through the detailed flavors and varied composition of the dirt. An incident has triggered the commotion that caught Callie's ear. The worms have broken into the hideous chambers that hold their annelid brethren in suspended states of poisoned existence, waiting for the mole bureaucrats to determine the just distribution of the inert but living bodies to the hungry family members. Moles seem inured to real relations; even in immediate families they don't seem to be able to show preference for one member over another. Yet, just this morning—and this is what has caused the upset—one old mole judge led one of the many offspring from his litter into the underground larder, taking advantage of the oxygen stored in their systems. He and the young one performed a grotesque act of consumption, gorging themselves on the poor worms. Messages reached the surface. Though the worms have always known, vaguely, about the moles' hideous practice, this event is too monstrous to ignore.

The worms in the larder are passive, filled with the toxins the moles use to keep them from getting away. Half paralyzed, they cannot resist, and they watch as their fellows are subjected to the horrors that precede their ingestion. The moles are fussy and do their work with a thoroughness that belies any claim that they are hampered by their blindness. The cat, listening to this dreadful tale, wonders at the moles' capacities for cruelty, as if she has entirely forgotten her own past behaviors.

Meanwhile, the worms, their culture active and thriving, continue their protests. They feel superior to the moles, who for one thing have never developed a poetry of their own. They borrow lyrics from the worst of the popular stuff that circulates among the rodents, and as they lug their bodies through the tunnels, shapeless as their aesthetic sensibility, they mumble low-culture verses that wake the worms just enough in advance that sometimes the worms can escape the clutches of those weirdly shaped paws, with their creepy polydactyl features and sickle-shaped thumbs. Bad singing among the moles is an advanced warning system for the worms. But nevertheless, they are often overtaken as they flee. The worms who do not want their guts squeezed clean by the moles before being eaten simply contract and expel, emptying their guts in an act of defense. Not pretty.

Under traditional rules, the tradeoffs kept the populations in balance. Now the circumstances are different and administrative rules are being imposed. Callie feels divided loyalties, unsure how to deal with such complex systems of cultural conflict. Worms have rights. Moles have needs. She is too impatient to sort out these moral issues and is unsure of her ground.

During a Primary
Rural Virginia

THE SOUTHERN ROUTE TAKES LONGER THAN Callie expected, though she makes good time. She passes through rural Virginia during a primary election where Chihuahuas are working the polls. Feeling a call to civic responsibility, Callie takes a few hours off to check political trends and refresh her geography with the map of new districts, just redrawn. The abundance of muffins at the polling place doesn't hurt either.

She can see that the Chihuahuas are doing a very good job in spite of the jealousy of one of their old rivals. Soon after the polls open, a small, very vocal, very spoiled, and extremely destructive Pekinese gets ahold of the clipboards and the buttons and the ID cards. He makes the whole process so untrustworthy that it is not at all clear that the elections are valid. He registers some voters twice, or three times (they can't count very well), and sees nothing wrong at all with giving a vote to a deceased relative if the price is right. Bribery, to which this breed is not usually prone, is flourishing in this small, unruly, and irresponsible pup.

Someone calls spaniel security, which steps in and tries to sort things out, putting the Pekinese under basket arrest, but it is too late. Nothing can be fixed without calling in the storks, who are the only ones with the right combination of accounting skills and patience. They go through all of the voting rolls and figure out where the duplicates are and who is still living and what addresses can be matched to what names through which dates and election cycles. But how this is to be done in time to shorten the voter lines isn't clear to the cat. Meanwhile, the Pekinese is deeply offended and threatens a lawsuit. He has no grounds. The bears, who are working the local circuit court, agree to hear the case immediately and just as immediately dismiss it with a grunt and a fart—a rarely invoked but sometimes very useful statement. Callie, held temporarily as a potential witness, also shows her impatience in unseemly ways.

So many legalities tangle the process. An additional chorus of mockery is mounted by a line of trilling finches, who ask over and over again what is meant by enfranchisement. They pipe their disregard throughout the precincts, which does not help one single bit. The spaniels look at them with real frustration, but they can't be cited just for mockery. But after all, it is the Pekinese they should be mad at, not the birds, who are just silly and opportunistic. Seeing a chance for cheap humor, finches will go for it, in their tasteless, shrill manner. To be honest, the noise levels in the neighborhood border on intolerable during the hours of the elections.

Callie sits out the rest of the day in the crosswinds, trying to sort out who is running for what and why. The traffic around the polling place is terrible, and she figures she should wait for it to die down before she heads back into the woods. In any case, it is interesting to stand around with the spaniels and talk about who is standing for election, who has funds, backers, and a decent campaign strategy.

In the evening, the air fills with a bloom of bees in formation, spelling the outcome of the elections as a script across the fading sky. Callie finds this a beautiful touch and, now rested from her day of lounging, heads off into the dusk.

Possum Meddling
Southern Towns

PRIMARIES OVER, THE CAMPAIGNS DIE DOWN. The billboards are needed for other promotional activities. Callie could not care less. Passing through one town after another, she has ample opportunity to figure out which of the cows are the best painters. A few can edge a wall without taping and do trim so exquisitely they are in high demand. Their skills at scaling up the poster designs are also unparalleled. But they cannot stand on scaffolding without trembling. So they supervise a crack team of squirrels and send them aloft, brushes in hand, to cover the outdated signs.

Callie watches a skillful group cover the face of an old harbor seal who has just run for sheriff in one of the outer districts. His face disappears under whitewashing, and the cows are happy to see it go. The old seal was not a favorite among the locals. But since they are hired to paint, not to editorialize, they keep their opinions to themselves, chewing steadily while the subcontracted squirrels do the work. The squirrels are careless, as usual, and do a sloppy job of painting. Passing underneath, Callie has to be careful not to get dripped on by white paint.

Still heading south, the cat hears a miserable racket from a parked set of trailers, close to the road, that comprise a minimum-security camp. A node of recently liberated monkeys has taken up residence there. Liberated from incarceration but still far from their homeland. This is a known spot on a safe route, a place to touch base, find food and shelter. The cat spends the night and hears tales that make her fur stand on end, but she also has a hint, for the first time, of the whereabouts of her feline cousin. The monkeys make sure of that. They know more than Callie and have seen much more of the world. From the shape of her whiskers and profile they know she is a species match with the lion. They have no idea what the business is that drives one feline toward the other, but they encourage Callie on her quest.

No money is needed in the camp. It runs on a combination of gift economies, barter, and an enormous philanthropic endowment established by pachyderms and cetaceans released from land and marine circuses. These are refugee environments, and on account of their own experiences, the older, larger mammals promote a tradition of philanthropy. They establish foundations to fund schools and training programs, entertainment centers, and health clinics at a scale no government, established or emerging, can afford. They hire adders as accountants, taking advantage of the pun. The snakes work in the business offices of the clinics, keeping the books straight. This is an enormous improvement over the work of the possums, which is always sloppy, suggestive of malice and even criminal behavior. Forgiveness is essential in all cases—otherwise relations across species remain stuck on fantasies of retribution. The pachyderms let the possums off with just a scolding. But that is not the end of it.

Callie learns that night that a certain percentage of revenue is being shaved off, and the possums, always guilty-looking, waddle away in a pique, annoyed, they say really quite, with these suspicions. Everyone knows they fix tables and manipulate machines in their establishment. They also issue loans with exorbitant rates to cover losses. So it isn't hard to figure out where the startup funds have come from for the gaudy lights and fixtures. The possums could have been charged with larceny, probably, or at least, with embezzlement, but the lifecycle of folly is well enough understood by the rest of the community that they simply watch from a distance as jackals move in on the gaming tables and clean up the place. Some forms of justice are swift. Even if they are not fair, exactly, they feel appropriate. Not all methods of achieving equilibrium are subtle. The evening has left an impression on Callie and strengthens her resolves against gambling in any form.

Kidnapping
South Carolina

THE COYOTES TERRORIZE A HUMAN NEIGHBORHOOD—THE first organized action aimed at getting human attention. It works and suddenly ups the ante of downdrift behaviors. The lion, incarcerated and powerless, hears reports of these events from the birds, of course. He is hypnotized and horrified.

Early summer is in full bloom and the coyotes pick a week with breezes gentle and fragrant, so the small-town windows are open and welcoming. Lean, dark-faced coyotes start skulking (an unkind word, but there it is) along yard fences in the dark, just before dawn. Their loping gait, so completely characteristic, gives them away instantly. No dog walks like that—light, agile, and so deliberate. Coyotes give off an aura of awareness, strong as body odor. The freshness of fear becomes palpable.

The inconceivable happens. The coyotes take a human baby and hold it hostage. No threats, no real demands. So provocative, they paralyze the community. Their lockdown is swift, terrifying, and successful. The coyotes police the borders and let no one in or out. They make no threats, and careful, bold, strategic action gives them an advantage. No one expects anything or sees it coming, and then the coyotes completely and immediately control the perimeter. Leave if you like, they say to the humans, but do not return. A few do, but then realize their mistake as the perimeter seals behind them.

A stealth attack on the animals is impossible. The coyotes are prescient, know what is being thought or planned. They have all the advantages. They have observed the humans for generations. They move the baby constantly and then take another and another. Panic is an understatement. The human population sweats all around their mouths, upper lips soaked, brows dripping. The babies get their milk, their cereal, their clean diapers. The parents get fear, huge chilling loads of it. This, too, saturates the soil and the atmosphere, soaking into the earth. Fear does not filter well and the microorganisms are affected by the psychic toxins.

The coyotes don't want anything. They don't care for human flesh, even young flesh, and the still-fetal smell of the pampered, helpless children turns the stomachs of the more sensitive among them. But they want the humans to know they can control urban territory if they choose. They are fast, ruthless, cunning, and relentless. Though not without compassion, they are unflinching. They establish boundaries and post their sentinels. The humans imagine it should be simple to do a strategic strike, get the babies, and eliminate the coyotes. But how? They have infiltrated the fabric of the neighborhood. Gas of any kind will hurt the humans. Shooting is impossible—the coyotes are too quick, and they blend into the yards and curbs, edges of property and underneath porches and cars. They are the shadow portion of the visible world, its animate capacity for action made into agency.

Release
South Carolina

THE WHOLE EPISODE LASTS ONLY THREE days. Just long enough for the humans to get really nervous about food and work. As a community, the coyotes are organized, collaborative, and single-minded in their actions. As loners, they are quick to grasp the higher value of a common cause. They do nothing to the infants—nothing harmful, that is. Coddle them a bit more than necessary, actually; even if they hold the fat pale things in disdain, hairless and toothless as they are, they don't bother to harm them.

Then, just as suddenly, at the end of the third day, they release the children, leaving them in blankets and boxes on the patios where they found them, or on the curbs, or in the swing sets. One is left on a front stoop, since the window locks to the baby's room are too hard to pick. Scenes of abduction and return are the same, and the distraught parents get the message to do nothing. Make no attempt at retribution for the minor crime of babysitting without a license. After all, other canine sitters have been working that system for generations. To act all of a sudden like the coyotes have second-class status on account of their outsider birth seems just wrong. And potentially dangerous.

As swiftly as they shut the neighborhood down, the coyotes abandon it. They made their point and they know it. But the chill of the lockdown causes a new level of recognition of the control of which they are capable.

Callie skirts the edge of the coyote's domain during this incident. She uses the distraction they cause to take a bold step. She enters a convenience store and takes milk from the fridge while the clerks are discussing the kidnappings. She has never been so bold, or resorted to outright theft, but these are not the best of times. The clerks are noisy and vulgar ducks and geese, wagging and quacking creatures. Some are crude rural geese, some of whom are slightly intimidated about being in what they call "see-evil-a-zation" and thus act with a little restraint. But hanging out with their cousins, the ducks, the whole gaggle is impossible. They have neither conscience nor constraint.

They swipe credit cards like nobody's business, and with their heads cocked and eyes bright, appearing to take account of each transaction. Turns out they erase more information than they keep. But they refuse to leave their clerk positions. They have plans to take over one convenience store after another. But they can't handle anything more complicated than a single room full of commercial goods and a single checkout counter. By the time they empty the shelves of unsweetened cereal, the place is a complete shambles. Callie, somewhere else entirely by then, is spared the sight of the mess they make.

Assembly Lines
The Carolinas

SCENE AFTER SCENE PASSES BEFORE CALLIE'S eyes. She sees into houses and schools, into churches and shopping malls, into hospitals, factories, and places of high and low activity across every possible species and spectrum. She finds out that old-style assembly lines are being managed by many of the smaller bears, but they have no work ethic and yawn in the summer dawn, waiting to fully awaken. They sit in place, watching rotors and gears, belts and conveyors, and space out. In some circles, the general consensus is that this is deliberate. The bears may be saboteurs, passing themselves off as mild beings. They have a good sense of humor about all the mess they make, but for finer work and, frankly, any project with a deliverable, they are not the creatures to put on a line. Their notion of assembly is strictly mechanical, and they do not deal in social organization or chemical compounds. Any attempt at firing leads to "accidents." Ball bearings get loose and tangle the chains. A screw goes missing here or there and a whole section of a conveyor system sags. Renew their contracts and the machines work again, just like magic.

Callie has taken to waiting by kitchen doors, hoping for scraps of southern hospitality. In her scruffy state she does not risk adoption, or capture—quite the contrary. She gets glimpses of the food industry's use of power tools and finds them scary. She watches chef raccoons with carving knives animated with a spirit of mischief and a huge, hairy javelina pushing a salami through a slicer as if taking revenge on an entire family line. Another day she glimpses a peccary trying to keep a giant mixer from going awry after it is afflicted with arrhythmia. The irregular beat is the result of a stealth attack of a flock of flippant, nihilistic penguins. They are reading the dark philosophers, the ones for whom existentialism is the bright wing of their intellectual palace. They struggle with the forces of despair that level out sunlight and flatten all optimism until there is no place for future planning. She catches the references on the breeze as she passes, processing information with her intelligent whiskers, golden eyes squinting to keep her path straight ahead. Poor penguins, she thinks, opting to skip most of what is on their reading list.

Swamp Conditions
Southern States

CALLIE FINDS HERSELF IN A SWAMPY creek bed, where a family of crayfish volunteers sort through known evidence of every species. Like their crab cousins, they have a keen ability to pick through weeds and distinguish viable from useless matter. The mud is thick and the stream is lively, and Callie is enthralled by the soupy water full of nutrients for which she pays nothing. But swimming and slithering prey is also plentiful, so she takes a break from her good behavior and her travels, helping herself at the expense of others. These are misdemeanors, not felony offenses.

On the back of a truck, the lion has passed the border of Mexico, confined to a cage. At least he is not in chains, but he is understandably abject, submissive to his fate

Callie watches a whole host of gators—massive numbers of them—getting off buses, trains, and flat-bottomed river boats. They make their way toward an outdoor arena in the subtropical zones. This is the first time the gators have held their council, and as it unfolds, they behave preposterously. The amount of bombast they produce fills the air with the sour stench of gastric juices escaping from a tightly packed bladder, and the sound is about the same as that of a high-pitched leak from a bad valve.

None of them shuts up. They hold forth with the breezy, easy air of an endless summer afternoon, enjoying the close-ness of the summer solstice. They speak a language of languor, oddly tendentious given how vacuous it is, and they loll around the edge of the swamp pools with the sloppy indulgence of their lizard race, doing nothing but soaking up the ample radiant heat through their bellies, which they show off to one another and the rest of the world as if—as if what? As if the whole point of their assembly is just to demonstrate how little they have to offer. Callie is an advocate of inertia, as a rule, but this is an affront in the face of all the work that might be done just then, that particular season, to repair damage from the flood waters of the spring rains in their native homelands.

The gators care nothing at all about repairs. They make their way through the warm mud, leaving trails behind. Their big old tails swish with no regard for the effect on the ducks and geese, who are up in arms (wings) and totally

peeved, racing around in klatches aflutter with their annoyance. Who thinks, they say, that this kind of wanton disregard
for decorum will be tolerated? But of course it is just that
kind of behavior the gators have come together to address
for the sake of community relations. It takes a while—as in
days, not hours—before they empty their brain sacs of gas-
eous matter and get down to the business of regulating
transit through the mud-flooded plains and banks. Then
they put themselves on a schedule that can be anticipated by
the flocks with whom they supposedly "share" the swamp.

Toxic Gas
South Carolina

A MASSIVE RELEASE OF METHANE, BUBBLING up as swamp
gas, intoxicates the scene. The toxins make the night noise
impossible. The ducks, who come to help out with the
catering, pull their ducklings under their wings to keep
them from being tempted by the rhythms of the wildly
dancing reptiles, who stagger from exposure to the high con-
centrations of gas. The frenzy is understandable—a simple,
spontaneous, collective protest against the horrors of reality,
an outcry of desperate impulse toward something more than
survival, as if a life force might be generated from the enthusiasm of their little bodies for the sheer vitality of motion. A
party is in full swing until morning.

After the convention, instead of improving their lot and
their attitudes, the gators become disgusting. In just a day or
two they drift into sloth and slovenliness, as if they don't care
at all for hygiene. The older males, untypically, decide to
continue their council activities and hang together, something extremely rare among the usually solitary beasts.
Perhaps they have caught a bit of aggregation fever from the

flies and wasps in the area. The younger ones start a club and lounge on a nearby bank, coming and going into and out of the fetid water that gathers around the group. They just finished their first season of spring mating, during which they put up with the bellowing chorus of the older males and were relegated to the margins at the dances.

Summer nesting brings piles of rotting vegetation. The tending females slow-cook their eggs, incubating the hot-tempered species by keeping the clutch warm in the heat of decomposing leaves. The older males are particularly voracious. The males eat their spawn without any particular discrimination, absorbing their own genetic material with a swift crunch as they pick out random young for breakfast. It isn't nice, but self-regulation within a species is difficult to enforce. Just ask the salamanders.

The smell of their part of the swamp is astonishing—heavy with slow, swirling gas that bubbles along the edges of the waterline. A froth of excess releases through the liquid at the same slow rate the gators' energies seep through the days. They burp their exhalations into the same air they breathe back in a few minutes later. Callie is disgusted and barely able to disguise it. They take these habits to extremes as the summer goes on, as if to set a standard of behavior against which everything else seems an improvement.

Who do they imagine cares? They have few witnesses except themselves to note the stench that washes over their activities. The storehouse of their food supply—the muskrat and nutria bodies that they stash in the water to rot so that the chunks of flesh soften and come off easily in their jaws—contributes its own vile odors and unseemly sights. No one in the natural world feels quite right commenting on the habits of others and passing judgment, since all beings are equal. But the Councils on General Hygiene take note. The gators are shamed for the effect of their repugnant ways on others. They would wallow in their filth endlessly. But their polluted waters threaten other populations, so they are controlled by law.

As it happens, the gators have to hit rock bottom before they notch it all back up again, little by little. By August their parlors are as appealing as those of the rock wrens and spider monkeys, both renowned for the domestic arts. Seems they took a vote, which is odd considering they have no ability to design a ballot, and reached a very, very lazy consensus.

Callie drifts too, letting the lassitude of the gators and the southern climate lull her into momentary sloth. This feels satisfying, and she lets herself drawl a bit in imitation of the idle lizards.

Archaean Views: Chemical Memory

I HAVE NO TASTE AT ALL for organic matter and seek heavy chemistry in the dark depths far from the gator waste. The darkness in my retreat is combined with high pressure and cold. I feel a momentary relief after being in the fetid organic stew of the swamp. But something is still gnawing at my membranes—either from the inside or the outside. I am prone to hypochondriac episodes (a socially sanctioned form of narcissism) when I feel excluded from social groups. I drift into oblivion to forestall any breach in my defenses, psychic as well as chemical. We all have our points of sensitivity. But neither salt nor heat nor lack of oxygen can damage me. But it is possible that a social force of the lowest kind is seeking any replicating mechanism it can find. Mine is basic, but very efficient, since my genetic material floats, completely unprotected and vulnerable, like a drifting ribbon in the fluid of my cell.

I barely control what crosses into and out of my interior. But I know I am expanding, feeling connections increase across so many spaces. Sentience networks are my area of expertise. I feel a tingle that makes me realize one of my ribbon-shaped brethren is nearby. Mobile, connected, free, present, increasingly aware of infiltrating myriad zones and multiple populations, I am not immune to sadness. I am aware of the lion's disintegrating spirits, just one among many cases in the massive epidemic of animal melancholy. My spirits are low as well, and the archive of memory, stored in my cells, resonates with histories of what may and may not come again.

The Crisis of the Whales
The Carolinas

CATCHING A SALT SMELL IN THE breeze, Callie gives in to the impulse to head to a beach again. She listens to the whales and indulges in a little illegal seafood. The waters are more heated than usual, clouded with organisms taking advantage of the bath to breed uncontrollably, vulgarly.

Walking on the sands, she catches the whales' complaints on the wind. They are tiring of life among riffraff such as algae and plankton, and think nostalgically about their oldest cousins, the hippos, who live with their heads above water. The whales love the depths and blueness of the cold waters and for generations they have been more than happy to plunge into its cool dimensions. They are far more serious than their dolphin kin, who laugh through the days. Whales often mused and were amused, in the times before the killings and slaughter. But as their species has thinned and lifespans have shortened through extermination, their sense of humor has worn thin as well.

Some ambitious and well-organized sperm whales are running a training program to attempt small forays onto land, combing the edges of their migratory paths to see if they can learn to use their vestigial limbs again. This has been coming for a while. The cat watches, spellbound, as the young whales attempt to "walk" in the shallows near the edge of the shoreline. They know that the mutation cycles are long, and change will have to be accelerated by artificial means.

They sing among themselves. Theirs is still an oral culture. They pass history from one generation to another through the long night tales they tell and the daytime accounts they share with each other and their young. They have fantastic memories, which they organize encyclopedically rather than according to myth cycles or narrative forms.

A nursing mother whale, just a little offshore, pulls her calf tight to her teat. She is passing the knowledge of their classification systems to her offspring through thick milk, fatty and rich with cells that contain nucleic bits of inventory. These assemble knowledge structures in the young one's mind in a novel but effective transfer of information about the world, the cosmos, history, and belief. They are not religious in the least, and unlike the hippos, who demand a certain amount of conformance to the rituals of their (unfortunately) primitive church, the whales (who had in part broken with their cousins over this question of pseudo-orthodoxy) do not require observance. The calf shifts its position, smiling as knowledge fills its gut, appetites of many kinds being satisfied at once.

This season, in response to a low-level anxiety, the whales

convene their pods and then convene conveners from their pods, and ask whether they are making the right choices. The distinctive sounds from the vocal clans are marked, and themes echo through the group. The family units are all led by females, though on this occasion the males float within echo range, wanting to participate. Their social skills have been badly damaged by their mating habits.

A watchful mother keeps a close eye trained on her calves while the event unfolds. Knowing her young are more inclined to socialize than in the past, she is still surprised by the frenzy of mediated exchange that takes hold. Devices are still extremely rare and expensive. The few calves using social media are surrounded. The females have not bargained on this side effect of swarm behavior among their offspring. The pathological effect of social exchange is becoming more and more clear, but collectivity is in their genes.

The afternoon is trying. The whales make every effort to organize their congregation, but they are constantly disturbed by activity among the young. In an effort to take advantage of their latent roots, they send a small delegation in search of the older hippos on the other side of the ocean and the world.

The hippos, occupied with their own encyclopedic undertaking, are folding reeds and pounding them flat to create a paper-like substance. Their industry is also domestic, though they pay the river birds well to supply them with materials, realizing their own efforts are better suited to beating the fibers than to plucking and gathering.

The whales on the diplomatic mission arrive at the river mouth. Two of the most prominent venture toward the hippo clan, asking for an audience. The hippos do not care for these cousins and find their blowholes unseemly, their tiny ineffectual limbs displeasing, and their constant vocalizing and song so sad that the hippos turn their backs.

Still, the whales pitch gently, rolling in the muddy channels, asking for an audience. The hippos pretend to be too busy to hear them, too involved in their own activities to be bothered.

The beginnings of cruelty are hard to bear, and whales have no capacity for unkindness, so they are baffled by the disregard these once-close creatures have for them. They wait, hoping the sheer gravitas of the delegation will register on the hippos, but their cousins prove frivolous beyond belief, turning their large backs on the giant, graceful, patient blues, who finally accept the social slight and turn around for the long swim back to their traditional waters.

The whales have a moral economy, as well as a practical one. They return to the larger congress downcast, uncertain that a future back on land is possible, given the cost of real estate and the difficulty of re-adaptation. Other discussions follow in the months ahead, as the waters cool in some places and heat up in others, causing consternation. A creeping edge of resignation casts a filmy pall on their collective mood. The males, waiting to mate, keep to themselves. The females, with calves pulled close, dispense increased amounts of sustenance in the deep waters. They nurse them with doses of small factoids and miscellany, sparks to the spindle neurons of the nursing young.

Otter Rescue
The Carolinas

BACK IN THE BUSY, BUSTLING OFFICE worlds on land, out of sight of the whales, though within their hearing range, a pair of graceful storks pounds for hours across twin keyboards of ancient mechanical typewriters. They did so the day before and will do so the day after, producing page after page of prose without a single error—as long as they are interested. Disinterest comes over them like sleep, and they suddenly collapse, knees bent, heads dipping, and topple into the water. Accurate and unreliable—a bad combination, fatal to the sheets of paper that rolled through their antiquated devices.

This is the sort of thing Callie cannot ignore completely. She is in fine fettle, having eaten and slept well for several days. She is prone to distraction when her whiskers are clean, eyes bright, and fur fluffy from leisurely grooming. She has standards, after all, even when conditions are adverse. Today she holds her small head high and steps with precision along the edges of the marsh, where two herons are disentangling themselves from their typewriters in the wet grasses. She welcomes a chance to show off her superior experience in office work to the slow-witted herons.

Coming closer, she realizes their keys are rusted and sticking and the gears in need of oil. An officious otter, happy to oblige, appears on the scene. He loves nothing so much as to make a little motor hum or a gear engage with the silky smoothness of a butter churn on a warm afternoon. Maybe that is not the metaphor he would use. Otters, in part because of their mechanical gifts, are not inclined to figures of speech. They prefer the literal, which they understand intuitively.

The storks stand at a correct distance, preening as if it matters. The small, stagnant pools by the otters' lodge swarm with paramecium, but the otters pay them no attention whatsoever. Making a poster child for cuteness from a *caudatum*, that standby of biology textbooks with ciliated cell walls and asexual division, is hard. The lovely transparency of its appearance, its ability to show its vacuoles and membranes has a certain appeal, but they never sit up straight at a table and are lousy conversationalists.

The otter works, the cat lounges about watching and wondering what she can gain in the situation, and the vibrations of the single-celled creatures imitate vocalizations in the summer landscape. The throaty song of the frogs, the hind-quarter-orchestration of the crickets, and the rubbing wings of cicadas and hum of bees inspire their efforts. But all to no avail. They cannot produce sufficient vibration to make an impact. Nor is amplification of any use. The problem is fundamental. They are tone deaf, dull to the sound of any music, even their own. Their aspirations to melodic harmonies can only be fulfilled by listening and by the passive participation of their species in circumstances where they swarm in a liquid medium used to pass sound waves safely from one place to another. In this situation they find they can be useful, keeping a filtered watch on pollution in waves and particles. Clever souls, they are virtuous in their attention to duty.

The otters finish their repairs, pack up, and leave the scene. The storks go back to typing. Callie decides to look for amusement elsewhere. Unfortunately, she cannot sense what is happening among the micro-organisms, where a temporary uprising is taking place to combat psychic ills. This requires an injection of mild electric shock, received from a benevolent eel, whose training in cellular medicine is nothing short of remarkable. Though already well advanced in years and career, the eel has a sensitivity to these matters that combines discretion and strategic insight. Within a few nano-cycles of electrolyte exchange, the paramecium population exhibits signs of repolarization, a distinct uptick in attitude and well being. Though the eel does not see it, the communication centers at the surface of the water are humming with the news of improvements to the system. A massive surge of self-fertilization occurs in the population in the next round of reproduction. The waters swarm with a thriving renewal of species, whose extrusomes fairly sparkle with wit. And to think that the cat misses all of this excitement!

Left Behind
The Distant Savannah

IF THE LION WERE BACK IN his ancient kingdom, he would see the antelopes taking advantage of full summer light. They are gentle and learn to read and write as the days get longer. They pause on the plains, sit down, open books, journals, and anything in print. They are conservative that way, clinging to paper substrates marked in ink. Generous to a fault, they read aloud to invalid children or rapt audiences of small creatures of all kinds, and spend hours by the bedsides of the ill and elderly, just reading, reading aloud with a sing-song intonation that modulates with the emotion of the tales. Something of their athletic grace enters their delivery so that their voices pronounce the stories with a melodic through-line.

This has a captivating effect.

Suddenly, in keeping with seismic codes, vibrations shake the earth nearby. But it is not the earth moving, but instead, woolly mammoths. No one wants them around. The prairie dogs shrink and keep safely out of the way, but the rumbling comes through the openings of their tunnels and the odor of the ancient beasts fills the air. The mammoths stink and are completely incoherent. Their language died out ages ago, but it is still programmed, a residual genetic strain living in their saliva. This contorts their utterances. An aging penguin, a member of the faculty of Paleolinguistics, who is tracking the mammoths, dedicates himself to the study of mammoth-speak. The penguin is an idiot, which everyone knows, and he is pompous beyond belief. He is their sole champion, but this does not improve the lot of the mammoths.

The mammoth incident is brief. Soon their carcasses are strewn everywhere, attacked by pathogenic agents. Felled by viruses, they are rapidly consumed by the bacteria, then mildew, fungi, and predators of all kinds. The opportunism is a bit unseemly. But no one has suggested that microorganisms should be brought under control.

Shoaling Syndrome
Southern States

FURTHER SOUTH THAN SHE HAS EVER been—or imagined—Callie is forced to take shelter from a violent summer rainstorm. Amid the other sounds in the noisy warmth of southern nocturnal orchestras, she catches grumblings on the wind. A beaver, whose dam is close to the bridge under which Callie shelters, is so late coming home that his family gives up on him and mutters about it aloud. Before they go to sleep, they hold a meeting. Nothing can be done, really, but they struggle to make a decision about the undecidable situation. The uproar is raucous and goes on for a really long time. Finally, to Callie's relief, they put paddle tail to water and slip toward a secure location for sleep.

A couple of the animals keep half an eye open. One leans on a crooked arm above a sleek black paw, though most of the others just tuck in, wrapped up tight, as their minds fall into dreams. Finally, the late-night rambler arrives, stumbles in, blithering. Beavers are calm by nature, so his exaggerated affect disturbs the tribe. His thermal balance and his equilibrium are off, so they dose him with bark poultices and wrap him in a water blanket until his shaking stops.

He needs a while before he can talk about what happened, and even then, the trauma-speak of his encounter seems sheer gibberish to many. Something about fast food, off-gassing, and other matters that suggest rapidly moving toxins in a bath of hot oil. Incomprehensible indeed.

That night, the cat's sleep and the beavers' calm is disturbed again. Their dozings are ripped by sharp, swift, grotesque screams that break the back of their slumbers. The sound of eating, inevitable in the course of things, but repellent to many, penetrates their dreams. Hunger is intolerable but the impulse to rip into hot, sweet flesh, ever-present among some species, is almost always repressed. Vegetable slaughter does not produce the same thrills, and so the intermittent murders continue. The thrill of the hunt and the rush of the kill have driven a coyote out that night. The coyote's marauding has a particular violence to it. The cat is shaken to her core, realizing no law protects her from this or any other menace. Social life and the presence of others is probably the best security.

The violent acts weave into the dreams of the cats and beavers, make them part of a shared semi-conscious recognition that only some things change. At dawn the coyote skulks along the underside of the bridge, neck dropped between his shoulders, loping with a slightly embarrassed gait. He seems almost ashamed of his night activities. This is progress. The look on his face is vaguely apologetic, and he is careful not to keep scraps of his evening meal anywhere in sight. He knows his business and his rights (some predators have found a loophole in the law), his capabilities and his abilities, and does not stop.

A few hours later, shining in the sun, Callie sees the coyote's footprints in muddy patches on the pavement of a parking lot. Here, among the rolling carts and stacked baskets of what the humans call a supermarket, Callie witnesses a curious phenomenon: an outbreak of human shoaling, seepage into the *Homo sapiens* from the minnows and sardines. Though the activity has been identified before, this case is more acute than in the past. Human family groups cluster around each other, and a form of motion transfer takes place, affecting other random individuals as they come into and out of the supermarket. Spontaneous grouping patterns orient their movements. Perhaps a sense of defense against predators, subliminal but insistent, motivates the small crowds.

Something in the coyote urine may have provoked the cluster formation (he marks every bit of territory he passes through, drunk on murder and fast-flowing blood). More likely, the latent bonding impulse is activated not by the coyote, but by delayed triggers of the fish oils, patterning the shoaling impulse. Perhaps a swarm behavior is instigated by a desire to give up responsibility in the face of difficulties. When direction is set by a group, the stress load on any individual is reduced. But if the influence is from fish, and the source was food—direct absorption of genetic materials— why hasn't this happened before? The explanation is too literal. Shoaling has to be a symptom of communication disorder, not an organic disease. The humans have been resistant on account of their oblivion to other species, but perhaps their immunity is wearing thin—or the downdrift is reversing polarity.

The Lion's Path
Texas

HORNED TOADS AND BASKING LIZARDS WATCH with wary eyes as the truck with the lion passes through their territories. The truck pulls onto the side of the road and the silence in the darkness provides some moments of peace.

The lion lifts his heavy head and many things appear in the delicate landscape. A pair of desert tortoises is engaged in a slow, artful courtship ritual, stepping carefully this way and that while avoiding a show on the sands put on by some predatory arachnids. The tortoises glow in some ultraviolet light cast by an errant source. To the lion, they seem illuminated from within. The scorpions, by contrast, though conspicuous, are trying to avoid the limelight. They get enough recognition not to need attention while they mate.

The tortoises perform an elaborate courtship script. The lion can only make out part of what they are doing, but he sees them nod their helmet heads together on the long extension of their wrinkled necks. Their eyes crinkle shut. They obviously think whatever they are doing is extremely clever. They look around, hoping to find a critical audience for their debut.

They walk toward a tiny settlement where some neon signage from the roadside joints shines vividly through the velvet-dark night. They set up a makeshift stage at the edge of their remote world. Beacons of passing headlights signal the sleeping fireflies to wake, and even the underwater fishes whose lanterns light the way in the darkness respond through some telepathy of their own, far, far away. Changes are now being communicated in a quantum way.

Neither the lion nor the scorpions—or even the horned toads—can make head or tail of the old tortoises' stories. If this is courtship, thinks the lion, it is nothing like his method of grabbing a lioness by the neck to subdue her. Around the dramatic pair, however, a small audience clusters. Some desert rats and nocturnal spiders sport portable and wearable illumination. They quickly turn a small profit in selling the blinking signals to the assembled crowd. The lights disturb the cloak of darkness and the desert community shows up in a satellite image on a large map of global events. By midnight a handful of lizards and prairie dogs, hard workers, have inventoried the stock and measured the impact of the event. The tortoises are thrilled.

The lion catches the mood rather than the substance of these entertainments. He is grateful for the diversion and to participate in the sense of joy that the tortoises generate. But his sense of betrayal and collapse keeps increasing and the momentary pleasure is an inadequate antidote to his dark mood.

Construction Work
Mississippi Gulf

CALLIE FOCUSES ON HER PLANS FOR the rendezvous she knows is coming. She keeps heading south, and all over the landscape she passes through areas where enormous developments are underway. This particular morning she is particularly impressed by seeing the hard work of a group of highly capable badgers and patient hounds. They are breaking ground, laying out the strings and plans, thinking through the connections of sewer lines and electrical cables. Their smarts and skills are evident and they work diligently, pulling the twine taut between spikes. They don't quarrel once in the course of the morning, and Callie, having plied them with questions about the financing for such a large project, is content to watch with amazement at their efficiency.

After lunch, to which Callie is invited as a reward for her enthusiasm, a chase breaks out. The hounds' limbs are a bit weary, and the badgers are a bit testy. Paws and paw pads are a little sore, she imagines, watching the work slow down and the gestures of the workers turn a bit clumsy. The hounds pant with exhaustion as the afternoon heats up. The badgers, ever attentive to the cost analysis of things, start to look in Callie's direction, figuring she owes them something for the meal.

Averse to hard labor, Callie keeps a discreet and respectful distance. When the badger foreman starts in her direction, she suddenly remembers her quest and, thanking him profusely for the hospitality, speeds off toward a nearby beach.

Here she amuses herself for a few hours, first watching a small terrier follow a scent at the shoreline. The dogs have longer memories than the fish, who are programmed to forget in advance of their experience, or so popular opinion states. And as a medium, water is different in its densities and communicative effects than air or land. Rhythm and sound, rather than sight, provide cues to social behaviors among the fish. But the terrier neither knows nor cares about these fine points, happy as he is to roll in some wet seaweed and kick up sand.

Bounding along the beach, at a safe distance from the little dog, the calico nips at a jellyfish stranded on the sand. Never the brightest among the sea creatures, the jellyfish are very, very slow to show any sign of change in their habits. They are hard to motivate. By contrast, the plankton floating in the waves are happily cultivating a variety of seasonings and flavors from their surroundings.

Callie is intrigued, but she prefers not to wade into their presence, even if they do advertise themselves to her as a renewable food source, guilt-free. She shares the terrier's meal, focusing on the edibles among the clumps of redolent seaweed.

Lots of aquatic mammals have language, and some under-educated barracudas come dangerously close to shore, claiming they want to advance their linguistic skills. Callie is skeptical and keeps more than a conversational distance.

Rumors come racing toward her from distant reefs and deeper waters. Some sharpfins and sawtooths and yellow-mouths start jabbering away, far from shore. The disturbance in the depths is dreadful. The aftermath of the afternoon of gossip creates eddies and sound waves stretching for miles in the open seas. Callie does not engage in these exchanges. But the rhythm disturbs transit routes and distribution networks. Having none of this, the calico turns her attention to the fine motions of a group of groupers, who are edging toward the rocks where she watches, poised.

The groupers are proposing that the barracudas be fitted out with glasses and given the chance to improve themselves through exercises in silent reading. But reading what? Here even the groupers, sage and wise with age, are stuck. Fish literature has not advanced much since the early sagas and origin myths, the stories that every fish and flounder, every baby eel and adult fluke, absorb with their first drink of salt-water. Keepers of more ancient, supposedly authentic, tales have to be sought in the cold, dark depths where the stories of generations sink and are safeguarded by the archival dragonfish. They have no active storage facilities, but they keep track of all falling matter. Filtered and salvaged narratives manage to drift through the many layers of thermal change, away from the surface light. Callie is not skilled in reading these archaic forms and struggles to make sense of the waves.

Some dragonfish, far offshore and way beneath the surface, lighting the deep with their luminescent barbells, take pity on the poor confused cat and send her a text message all in lights. As witnesses, they are particularly sensitive to the impact of the photophores, but they are generous to a fault. Normally unsocial, the dragonfish, who spend the long, unlit hours of their nocturnal lives prowling the depths, are suddenly motivated to share the inventory of their story banks with Callie. Some grouper ambassadors show up to try out this novel mode of reading. Callie watches with fascination as the narrative strands twist into ropes of saltwater slime and silted matter. These lie on the sea floor, a veritable palimpsest of tales, one lacelike layer on top of another, out of her range of sight.

But the dragonfish continue their efforts and brighten the way for the groupers, who follow them into the depths. Going so deep, they get too cold and out of sorts. Their eyes suffer from strain, unaccustomed to the extreme absence of light. The big, slow-moving fish are grateful for the hospitality of the deep-sea dwellers, but they are eager to return to the upper layers where the thermal conditions are milder and the general atmosphere cheerier. Thus their happiness at being in the warm shallows that afternoon. The June light, heating their environs, feels almost as good to them as to the cat. They revel in the outpouring of krill and plankton that come with the increased warmth, but also feel a duty to set up a steady workflow to bring the archive of ancient tales to the eager barracudas. These take the form of primitive gelatinous films, impressions from the seafloor tracings, which have fossilized and ossified enough to have the texture of old vinyl. The new impressions, though not so permanent, are flexible and can be rolled up for easy transport. That is what they had brought with them to share. To the cat, all of this looks like so much fishful thinking and tail waving, but she cannot see the tales below the surface well enough to read them, so her opinion can be taken with some of the grains of salt in the swirling waters.

Callie plays at the edges of the tide pools, splashing slightly and sniffing the fish-scented air. Everything has consequences. The job of the barnacles is aided by the secure rocks on which their sharp protrusions are anchored, and starfish, who are not reliable, sometimes roll the rocks in exchange for a slight narcotic supplied by local whelks.

None of this is legal, but street and seabed economies are thriving in the era of new possibilities. Stoned out of their distributed minds, their complex nervous systems pulsing with hallucinogenic pleasure, the starfish pry the barnacles free from their posts and set them adrift. This is cruel, doubly so because the poor barnacles are attached by their foreheads and get wicked headaches when they are pulled loose. They struggle to reattach, but the effort is futile. Their tentacles are sensitive, with super-delicate hairs on their ends, modified for feeding, not for holding on. Every population has its little crosses to bear.

Lion Tribulations
Sonoran Desert

THE LION KEEPS HIS PROFILE LOW as he is driven across the open landscape of the southwest. The flatbed truck has decent shock absorbers, but sometimes the road is rough. Daytime is blazing hot and the sun parches the dry domain.

He is heading north and east, toward a scent of unfamiliar water and unknown distraction and a rendezvous unimaginable within the terms of his prior experience. The new world smells strange to him.

The desert is full of creatures, novel to his eyes. Arachnids, hairy and arcane, insects adept at survival, and reptiles of every kind, thick-skinned and ignorant. The snakes also are everywhere, and they are insinuators, skilled at inciting suspicion and disturbance through their sometimes sinister moves. They hiss at the lion and among themselves, insidious in their unkindness. They can be insightful through successive efforts at sustenance, sensitive to the seasons, but mostly they sleep successfully in their silent coils.

Such sophistries as they indulge in, however, soon try the patience of some of their reliable brethren, the lizards and toads, who are the more erudite among them. Those with a bit of spleen turn a touch savage, at least temporarily. The killing congresses are scheduled and canceled, scheduled and canceled, many times over. The problems are with jurisdiction as well as authority. Cooking gets modified more quickly than expected. The sight of flies roasting on a spit, turned by a salivating group of salamanders, creates a controversy. At the very least, the cicadas and crickets complain, a tent or blind of some kind should be put up to keep the spectacle from public view. The whole business of who eats whom is still complicated. Details of preparation are the first line of negotiation, but soon followed by increasingly selective execution.

Who has the right to call the legislative assembly together, let alone set the guidelines for discussion in such matters? That is not a question, just a formulation of uncomfortable and inconvenient fact. The cast of thousands has no coordinator, every animal goes where it wants to slither and slide without supervision. Their impulses, neither vicious nor vapid, are vicariously expressed in the glint of their eyes and the twist of their sinews, and they move with such grace that their prayers, such as they are, are lost in the tracks they leave behind.

The lion, unmoved by metaphysical reflections, yawns and sinks dolefully into dreams, wishing for release. He longs to take shelter in a nearby clump of creosote bush inhabited by a team of banner-tailed kangaroo rats and have them suspend their swing-band rehearsals to let him sleep. He loves their music, but the camouflage is what he craves, and the feel of earth, not metal, under his body. He is stuck in the metal cage, rolling through the world without volition.

July

Archaean Views: Labors and Social Pressures

YOU MUST HAVE MEMORY TO INDULGE in a vision of the future, paradoxical as that sounds. I inhabit an extensible present. Retrospection is not in my arsenal. I do not have memory. I am memory, immediately present in my code. But I know the difference between now and other moments.

I seep into the simple cells of plankton and they glow and shudder, knowing that identity and memory are intimately bound and equally vulnerable. They are adept at storing minerals that spice the waters. Though they are consumed at a great rate, they are treasured for their service to culinary arts and for their willingness to hold their lowly place in the food chain.

I am careful of fast-moving solutes, those particles that carry too much thermal energy. The bacteria, virus, and prions have done their work. My immunities are robust. My receptivity to hazardous molecules is one of the few remaining threats to my metabolic well-being.

The "unis," as we are called, act as the border collies of the disputed spaces. We police boundaries, keeping limits intact. Unbeknownst to the bulk of the other creatures who benefit from our attention, we even work constantly to keep the sounds directed toward the appropriate destination. I won't join forces with bacteria, but I help passing plankton or amoeba any time I can. What we do is often thankless work, because we are too small, too diligent, too completely dedicated to be noticed much. Often the only benefit we reap from our actions is the satisfaction of knowing we have been useful.

Like all unicellulars, I was raised without religion and so have no larger moral framework within which to judge behaviors. Self-worth is an elusive quality, even among us.

The personal economies of esteem are not easily managed, and when winds of desultory ennui blow through the liquid medium in which we often do our daily tasks, the paramecia fall slightly ill, their effectiveness drops off, and the signals of communication suffer more loss than in many a season. I race in with restorative charges of sewage-gleaned gas and pump them up with laughter as well as I can. A swarm of like-minded unis joins in. I am happy to see so many oblong and triangular relatives and friends, so many methane producers whose novel lineage I share. A kind of delirium sets in, accompanied by a manic desire to replicate. I am a micro-hyper-organism in asexual heat.

I have a yen to visit the black smokers, to harvest carbon dioxide, and breed among my own kind. I track an elusive object of attraction cycling in the marine sediments—as happy to see me as I am to recognize its thermal fingerprint.

I find I can move at will, under my own direction. My tensions have eased, but social demands are rising, threatening my autonomy. Have I morphed beyond recognition to my earlier self? I feel confused, trying to keep the distinction between normal adaptation and hybridity clear even as I guard against having my replicative machinery hijacked. I am, after all, the most ancient of species, with an enviable pedigree many opportunistic young organisms might like to latch onto.

I can feel the endpoints of my awareness, like tips of a microfiber, light up in their connection to my general will. When I move, masses move with me, coordinated in their outlook, at least briefly. When the mood subsides, the living beings release themselves to their own cognition, and I do too.

Fish Schools
Gulf Coast of the United States

THE WATER IS WARM AND FOOD abundant as Callie lingers for a few days by the coast, her sense of urgency tempered by the vacation atmosphere. The fish school with the enthusiasm of eager participants in the social world. They are too short-lived and simple to mutate much individually, but their collective rate is considerable and their productivity increasing.

The school year is a long way off, but all summer, the fish register pupils for elementary instruction. Callie watches one tiger minnow mom after another, eager to get a jump on the whole business, showing up with their young ones. They are full of aspiration, hoping to gain advantages for their offspring later in life. Given that they live about twelve months, this seems a little odd to Callie. The bubbles of exhalation crowd the water and make it hard to see.

But every animal has its own perspective. A line of preschool and early childhood applicants files into formation, offering Callie a distinct opportunity, of which, contrary to law, she avails herself. The minnows roll in the lapping waves and clear water, and the admissions officers sort the young by size rather than ability—perhaps not the most accurate predictor of academic success.

The group is mixed. The fatheads and bluntnoses, shiners with emerald streaks, long-jaws, and suckermouths are all lined up, waiting to receive commendations from the general superintendent for their contributions to the schools. The cat helps by eliminating the slower pupils, which speeds up the process. A few others go to the head of the class, swimming artfully in the lead. Callie pauses her plunder, giving priority to the educational mission.

The superintendent is in a mild mood. The warm water eases his standards. A few of the minnows express somewhat unpleasant thoughts about discrimination in the standards. They are a little jealous of their guppy cousins, who lead an easy life in the brightly lit and well-kept aquariums where they breed without reserve. Living the life of luxury, the minnows gripe. But those guppies are content with their lot and keep to themselves in their fancy glass residences.

On this registration day, the schooling motions of the swimming fish produce a living tapestry, a silvery, flashing field that at a certain distance resolves into a pixilated image in constant motion. The gulls see it and take note, watching as the minnows swarm. As they school, their moving image is picked up by satellite cameras and projected onto screens all over the world. They self-orchestrate, and the sheer reality of the situation makes infinite variety and constant change a factor as they move. They are an afternoon sensation and make the evening news with congratulations spilling in from everywhere about a successful first day of school. The dance of symmetry and difference, order and deviation from it, produces a spectacle of entropic process that fascinates audiences for weeks.

Later, they rest, content, as the moonlight flickers on the waves, silvery as their scales. Callie watches, equally content, happy with the richness of her food source.

The popular taste for minnow dancing will fade as quickly as it came on. The very next morning, the mild weather is troubled by storms. The seas go cloudy and waters rough. The obedient minnows go back to their work in the schools without asking too many questions. They have no memory to speak of, and when shown the recordings of their performances a few months later, they are quite amazed and surprised. "Us?" They said, "Us? Well, what do you know," and they flash with all the silver grace of their species and go on with their lessons.

To Callie's amazement, even at this late date, a huge sector of various populations does not believe in evolution. She conducts a few random interviews among the fish and finds that the lookdowns are curiously resistant to the notion of change. They are strikingly beautiful, pancake-flat silver fishes with supercilious expressions and utterly transparent bodies. They cannot even understand Callie's question. They look at her with disbelief. They are perfect in their design, they tell her, so utterly self-assured by the organization of their parts and aesthetics of their appearance, that they cannot imagine either an earlier, less aesthetic condition, or progress that could possibly lead to improvement. Theirs is not narcissism exactly, rather a belief in perfection of form. Their form. They are, perhaps, simply more susceptible to the ideas of the humans than some other species.

As to the jellyfish, though considered mindless, Callie sees they are very actively setting up a whole system of transistors and resistors essential to undersea communication. In fact, she trips over some of their wiring, which leads to a whole new line of questions. Turns out they have been rewarded for their efforts by being raised to the stature of "most valuable citizens" and given a place on a postage stamp. Unfortunately, it's on the backside, as part of the mucilage. They do not appreciate the slight and are considering turning off their lights, leaving the ocean depths in the throes of confusion. A very assiduous and determined delegation of dolphins spends much of the day arguing with them, trying to bring them back into the fold, affirm their value to society. They finally coax the poor beleaguered jellyfish into starting up again by recharging their useful filaments. The jellyfish are not fools. They put a sin tax onto the bills for months ahead, gaining small but steady retribution by exacting more for their services than is absolutely fair. Who is going to stop them? Callie, who has taken the dolphins' side, feels she can do nothing more in the way of argument. The dolphins have been splendid. She really does appreciate the rhetoric of others almost as much as their kindness, though nothing trumps food.

Summer Holidays
Texas, near the Gulf

NOW IN A STATE OF HYPER-AWARENESS, Callie tries to manage her own expectations and the drives that bring her to this point. She is not sure how long she has been traveling, but she senses the destination is near. Feline communications work in mysterious ways, but she has information from a rodent network that affirms her upcoming rendezvous with the lion.

The Gulf Coast is in full holiday rush. She has trouble finding accommodations, and the things she needs are in short supply. The summer brings a need for temporary staffing. Some birds talk their way into a whole host of jobs. Whistling ducks and emperor geese, pintails and mergansers are to be found in every all-day-all-night convenience store.

The mallards and golden-eyes are busy stocking shelves, placing most of the goods lower than in the past. Stopping to see if some milk would like to leave with her, Callie is somewhat surprised at the reorganization.

General chaos reigns in the shops. The smaller birds are taking pleasure in disorganizing the stock, mixing Nutella with motor oil and hanging hairbrushes next to the hotdogs. They don't know the alphabet and they don't have much idea what any of the goods are good for, so to them freezers are just cool places to hang out, and the idea of inventory is beyond them. They are opening boxes, carrying things here and there, and moving around with an air of utter importance and purpose.

All of this is a sham. Their irresponsible behavior is threatening to undermine an entire sector of the economy, not to mention the fact that their habits with regard to bodily functions have not changed since they took jobs indoors. The health department is coming to close them down. They ban the whole *Anatidae* family from clerking. Ducks and geese are far from quiet about their discontent. But they are given the option of training or being barred from employment. They leave in disgust, quacking over their shoulders and giving backward glances filled with vitriol and disdain. The poor inspector hardly knows what to say and shoos the cat away instead. She leaves without paying and enjoys her stolen goods in an open field.

By now, Callie and the lion are within miles of each other.

More Woes
Texas Plains

THE LION'S STATE OF MIND DOES not improve as he is transported across state lines. He hears complaints from all sides. Prairie dog housing is at a premium that summer.

When the grasslands dry and go from green to gold, their villages are packed. Underground tunnels are essential, but increasingly, so are front entries, doors, and even windows. The little ones want to play, having gotten into the habit of cards, board games, and even video games from hanging out with mice. The lion watches their games turn to gambling, and had he the strength, he would have reprimanded them.

New patterns of activity threaten the old ways of hibernation, and if the old ones now choose to sleep in the summer, the littlest ones want to go in and out across a threshold, have sash windows, and take advantage of the daylight. The nursery chambers in the burrows have been renovated with air pockets to protect them in case of heavy rains. But the towns are overcrowded, and the need for new developments is a topic of constant conversation. The lion catches snippet after snippet on the wind, including news of a huge scandal. A transient prairie dog clan takes over a span of property just at the edge of the colony and creates an entire housing project on speculation, throwing up one identical entry after another. These look well-enough crafted, with their portals and lintels, but the burrows are shallow, shoddy, and not suited for habitation.

Near a bit of shrinking marshland, where Callie sits, an old heron, worn out from aspirations and respirations, weary in the knees and defeated in spirit, simply lies down among the reeds and grasses and sinks into the combined darkness of mood and mud. Callie interprets this as a bad sign. Cats are inclined to superstition.

Random Encampments
Near the Road, Texas

OFFERED FOOD AND WATER, THE LION barely partakes of anything except the remaining tidbits of experience that pass into his mind. Parked at night, he witnesses a sudden rush of crazed activity, like the last spurts of fuel running out in a system. An encampment has sprung up along the railroad tracks, not for refugees or the homeless, but for a revivalist group of hedgehogs and blackbirds, who see a real benefit in using the rails as an instrument of proselytization. They are good-natured enough, just noisy. They create a major disturbance every time a train goes by, hopping and shouting and asking for alms for a cause they make up on the spot. They are rascals, not brigands, and have a wanton attitude toward civil order.

The problem with these encampments is that they attract riffraff, lazy raccoons too sloppy to appear in public, ragged possums who neglect their flossing and grooming and stink rather more than is acceptable. A few toothless coyotes, old and half-blind, who just want company and a cup of soup now and then, hang around the edges of the cooking area, rewarded by the softhearted and deeply religious hedgehogs who serve them with the patience of nuns ministering to the poor.

The core staff of hedgehogs is joined by a group of mendicant monkeys, heads shaved, faces rubbed with ash to subdue their appearance, who have decided to dedicate themselves to service. Some show signs of earlier lives, self-administered tattoos and gang markings, lots of piercings that are now healed over. But they are still visible as scars among the many other thick, dark areas of tissue where a fight or brutal treatment has inflicted slashings, burnings, or other mutilations. They are damaged in body, but they purify their souls with fasting and meditation and now wish for nothing more than to assist others. They make no judgment about whether those are individuals more or less fortunate than themselves. Long abandoned by fortune, they abandon it themselves and now work only in immediacies. They have a homing instinct for need, and gravitate to where they sense it—whether this is a crying young mole, lost and groping, eyes still shut, or an elderly crane doddering and barely able to make it to the water. If a gap opens in the social structure of support, they move in to fill it, ask nothing, and stay as long as they are useful.

Within sight of these unraveling and rebuilding safety nets are a set of high-rise apartments populated by elite loons and a few noble cormorants. Stability is setting in. The loons stay put, sometimes calling across the empty spaces from their balconies. The cormorants launch from the rooftops, hang suspended, and glide slowly downward just to enjoy the movement and the gradual shift of perspective. They no longer eat anything they catch or find themselves, but order in from a vegan menu. When they watch the hedgehogs catering to the suffering and lonely outlaws at the edges of their camp, they feel moved and send supplies though they do not go among the poor, as afraid as if their condition were a contagion.

As the truck moves in the early morning, the lion rides through areas where there are stretches of new homes and tidy gardens filled with tricycles for small badgers and swing sets on which young refugee penguins play, guarded by their goat nannies. He catches glimpses of the well-tended and over-watered courses on which thoughtless but skillful geldings play long games of golf and think nothing of opening a split of champagne and enjoying the changing colors of the light while listening to the distant sounds of the city. All of this is foreign to him. He does not know it is foreign to the others as well.

Life is not as it had been. Sitting in their chaises, old limbs stretched out, with their friends the loons for company, the cormorants wish only to just go on awhile and to enjoy the slow fade into their ancient days. The lion would be glad to be with them, if he had any idea of the peace they felt. His desire to stop moving, stop being moved, across the endless roads and open spaces, is overwhelming.

A Bug's Life
Southern Woods

ON CALLIE'S PATH THROUGH THE SCRAGGLY brush of the southern woods, she lives on fat grasshoppers, who are momentarily put out but quickly silenced. She is exposed to the culture of a whole new region. The sounds of country meows twang in her ears as they come across the airwaves. Sometimes the caterwauling of her kin is almost unintelligible to her, so thick are the southern accents.

Meanwhile, a rash of religious zeal breaks out among the country populations after the summer solstice, as if caused by sunspots and too many days of beach exposure to direct rays. A sanctimoniousness appears among the older toads, who take to wearing prayer shawls on non-holiday days and shushing all the cheerful little rodents dancing in the streets during the long nights of summer. Rodents are more or less secular; though some stick to the faiths of their forbears, they do not parade their allegiance in public. Some Sundays one could trip over an assembly of mice chattering in unison and perched in the crevice of a psalm book or hymnal of a vaguely recognizable denomination of some sect or other, but they do not make a thing of it and are utterly incapable of proselytizing.

No one troubles too much about the toads until they take to broadcasting and buy up all the early morning program time. This upsets the children of all species, who love their cartoons and counting shows. But the toads are operating within the guidelines of the communications regulations as they and the other animals understand them. The only solution is to shift the schedules to asynchronous media and let the young ones access whatever they like on their personal devices. Somehow this seems to destroy the sense of social solidarity that creates bonds in the playgrounds and schoolyards. So many things change and so fast that this phenomenon is not the highest priority.

Toad popularity wanes quickly. They are monotonous and their message doesn't play well. Advertisers withdraw support. The tele-congregations dissolve. One or two of the better known among the amphibious preachers manage to commandeer a huge following, but they leave the airwaves free again for new forms of entrepreneurial entertainment.

Southern woods are full of life, especially in summer. But vermin are vermin and parasites are extremely difficult to reform or retrain. The cat, picking fleas from her coat, is all too well aware of the struggles this involves. Get a leech to do a little bit of homework or housework? Take a tick to the movies? Let a mosquito date your offspring? Not likely.

The bedbugs are the worst, with their insatiable appetites and skin-piercing mouthparts. They offer to do some office work, collating tasks, pinning sections of papers and publications together, as if they can resist their own impulses. They go months and years without a blood meal, sometimes only to celebrate some random holiday with their traditional public acts of lust and bloodletting. But trust breaks down almost immediately. They cannot be trusted to stick to a job description. They are redirected to jobs in the corporate sector where risk is not shared by the taxpayers. A parasite is a parasite, probably changed less by the downdrift than others, since some of the seeping human traits are ones they already possess.

August

The Pink Fairy Armadillo
Texas

SPRING IS WONDERFUL IN TEXAS, FULL of flowers and wild blooms, where decent desert creatures revel in the sweet fresh air. But summer is hot and deadly, and the lion, even used to African heat, is almost overcome. The sight of new creatures like the exotic armadillos barely rouses his interest. His caged condition subdues him.

Shy like crazy, armadillos can barely talk to themselves let alone to others, and yet, they have a real sense of purpose and work ethic and so, without making eye contact, they band together to work on the roads. They jump beautifully when startled. Once they realize they should stay off the highway and keep to the edges and hedges, they increase their survival rate considerably. The shoulders and break-down lanes have never been so pristine, the hedges so clipped, the wildflowers so abundant. They are not gardeners exactly, but pruning and weeding come more naturally to them than they imagine. Having daily tasks and concrete accomplishments gives them a little bit of confidence.

The armadillos' breakthrough is followed by other improvements, in particular, the start of a break-dancing

ritual that creates a celebrity culture among them. One individual in the diminutive pink fairy species gets so popular
that a European tour is arranged. For a species that has its
origins in the Americas, this is huge. The international recep-
tion is tremendous. Concerts, appearances, social media
campaigns bring sellout crowds, all eager for a glimpse of the
delicate, dynamic performer.

But the tiny star longs for home. She is cold the whole
time she is abroad and refuses to wear fur or wool. So future
performances will all be done virtually to spare her from
the traumas of frigid temperatures and long distances. She
was bred in Texas and raised in Louisiana, so her musical
tastes run to country and western. But dancing, not vocalizing, is her strong suit, and that is what she is known for, at
least in the early stages of her career. Her publicist thinks
she can expand her range, but he is an opportunistic llama
and not particularly sensitive to realities. The blushing
armadillo interviews an alpaca as a possible alternative. He
looks down his nose through his gold-framed glasses and
refuses to take her on as a client. Bad decision, because the
little armadillo has a mega-career following her initial mete-
oric rise to stardom.

The alpaca regrets the loss of residuals and has to be content with priding himself on the illusion that he has good
taste, really, much better than the common folk who flock to
her performances. He thinks he can live from his superior
knowledge but is proved wrong. Half-starved and mangy, he
gets work managing minor contracts in smaller markets for a
touring a cappella tortoise quartet. To say business is slow is
an understatement.

The lion, worn out by his travails, lies mildly tranquilized
and caged. His sighs break through the dull air and are

heard for miles by any with ears to listen. Callie, though distracted by mews from another quarter, hears him and orients herself in his direction.

Snakes and Birds
Deep South

DETERMINED TO GET TO THE LION, Callie focuses on finding him. This quest has dominated her entire spirit, but she bravely faces the dangers and challenges. He is still further off than she realized. She dodges trucks and traffic, bad children and worse weather. She goes through afternoon downpours to filthy drainpipes and is soaked through by summer storms. She manages, just barely, to escape from a garage after inadvertently getting trapped inside by the lure of food and a dry bed. A door slams shut on what would have been her prison, just as she leaps through a half-open window.

The lion's sounds and scents keep Callie on track. Both are far from their ancestral or domestic homelands and much has happened. The records of the changes are legion. So many versions of what occurred have been produced that it will take lifetimes to read through them all. The titmice prick their tales into dried leaves, lacework Braille, delicate filigree texts for which one has to have the code. The penguins etch their stories into the air through exhalation and catch it on flat pieces of glass to produce fine ice patterns on the newly frozen panes. They store these upright, lest they rub against each other and do damage. The last intact pride of lions uses an old reel-to-reel recorder, loving the sound of the smooth tape running across the humming heads. Their grief is palpable in the deep-voiced solemnity with which they pronounce their own passing. Among the smaller felines, no such sadness reigns. The archival cats connive to

produce accounts that feature their value in undue proportion to their accomplishments—but that is feline logic for
you. Conscience never troubles them. The fishes write long
lines in the sand and let them vanish, not bothered by any
idea of permanence. The sandworms and coral create elaborate silicon trails that can be captured and kept for study.
Deciphering the scripts of various crayfish and lobsters is a
challenge, as is reading the writing of the drunk Chihuahuas
who have taken over many of the libraries and local history
museums, perhaps jealous of the beagles' earlier efforts.

The list goes on indefinitely. Every species makes an
attempt, inadvertent or deliberate, to assert the authority of
their version of history and the effects of downdrift. But the
larger dimensions of that record are manifested in the living
bodies of the beasts, in the shifted patterns and structures of
behavior among the fauna (and, it was hinted, among some
of the flora as well), their newly formed associations, part-
nerships, and their dissolved loyalties and frequent
renegotiations of all lines of partisanship. A sense of the
whole cultural ecology seeps into their general awareness.

A Bad Python
Southern Shores

RACING ACROSS A TREACHEROUS BIT OF swamp, Callie
trips on a barely recognizable water moccasin. He is on the
lam, the cottonmouth, and moves his anxious coils as fast as
he can to get away from any party trying to find him. He has
been caught in deceit, working at a food truck not far from a
playground from which he has been explicitly banned. The
moccasin is a pederast, though the county authorities failed
to tag him in the tracking program. He let his parole bracelet
slip, cruelly cinching it around the belly of a young frog who

refused his advances. Unkindness and reprehensible behavior come in many forms. The frog PTA is up in arms, and for a while, vigilante action seems imminent. The moccasin asks for protection. Instead, a program of systematic reform is proposed for playground zones. Now he flees, one step ahead of the vigilante mob.

He is in wretched shape from a botched protective surgery. The moccasin was caught on a security camera looking for a surgeon to do a cosmetic transformation—his only chance at a normal life. No responsible physician would do it, but the black market in scale removal and fang caps is rampant. A month before Callie crossed his path, the moccasin met a wet, nearly unidentifiable rodent in a very dark place and in exchange for an inordinate sum was given a kit with which to work. The moccasin checked into a motel and out of sight. After about three weeks, he snuck out through a back door and under a dumpster, leaving a check for the room bill on the bed. The bedclothes had to be burned, the bathroom drain was clogged, and the poor snake was barely able to move, his skin was so sensitive.

By the time he is healed, he has shrunk to nearly half his original girth and is reduced to a liquid diet. This does not keep him from making smoothies of the most abominable sort, a mix of swamp water and living things whose protests he refuses to hear. He is an outcast, willowy and wan, defeated and desperate for company, as well as a criminal with a bounty on what is left of his head. He foolishly agrees to appear on a talk radio hour, which outs him as he gives advice to various mutants and misfits who cannot sleep on account of their consciences.

Callie turns tail after this story, flashing the snake a disrespectful farewell. The following summer, when his memoirs appear, the cat recollects their accidental meeting. She only reads part of the book, which is published just before he dies. The snake's writing is censored, but even then, the uproar over the audacity of his confessions probably contributes to his demise. The publishing industry, with its usual hypocrisy, openly condemns the book and secretly profits from it, but too late. To the cat's amazement, the moccasin develops a following as a martyr to something—but what exactly? His crimes? His self-inflicted punishment? Or is it just that his longings, so clearly unfulfilled and wonderfully expressed in the tender passages of the book, touch a chord with others for whom emotional satisfaction proves elusive? So many conflicting feelings drift through the species that they hardly know how to act or what to think much of the time, torn from their once-firm foundations of identity and behavior.

Spider Song
Deep South

IN THIS TIME OF LONGER DAYS and shorter nights, light spills into drainpipes and shadows pool among the foundations and crawlspaces, attics and caves. In all of these secret spaces, the spiders sing beautifully, artfully, almost as well as they craft fiction and webs. Though a chamber group is very close by, Callie does not hear them. The sounds are too small, too closely uttered and without intervals. The tightly packed instruments of their vocal pipes hardly open to the air. The tremulous strains of their tongue-less song are pitched in a place so high they escape notice among all but the glitterati, those esoteric arachnids whose hearing is akin to the old crystal sets of another era, multifaceted and perceptive beyond the wildest dreams of creatures heavy with the dulling effects of mortal flesh. The spiders have a way of being, swift and creative, and they double their time by making it move according to their own pace, not letting the oxygen into their blood.

The spiders' musical production opens and closes without the cat hearing a note. Callie has other thoughts on her mind, but the spiders play away, lost in their own performance. Earless, they do not need to hear, but catch the tunes in their claws, bending the tarsus and metatarsus elegantly to manipulate the sound. Bending the songs to meet the occasion, they pull the notes against the bow of their palpus, stretching strings across the parts of the mandible, and take up each other's refrains to play one variation after another of the tiny pieces. They call it singing, but really, the pulled notes are a kind of play. The vibratory mechanisms of their trachea are the launch sites for an elaborately orchestrated combination of compositional moves and amplifications, but so esoteric they remain a well-kept secret.

A set of ticks takes up playing the smallest violins imaginable, playing with articulate fingering as well as with their bows, holding the tiny instruments against their wide, flat abdomens and fiddling for all they are worth

The fleas love all these sounds. Though Callie has been vigilant, she knows more than a couple of them are traveling with her. A few hop off to dance to the spider and tick music, shaping the steps into a kind of Busby Berkeley imitation. They act out a living score, striking a figure against the ground on which they stand. Flea jumps, a particularly artful form, increase the amplitude on the wave of their little leaping bodies. The spiders gather at the edges of the scene, entranced by the dancing fleas. Their tiny footsteps mark the ground in one arabesque pattern after another. Weaving and hopping, bouncing and twirling, making their hard-shelled bodies move with pinpoint precision, or close enough, the little tribe comes together just by sheer force of the music's offering. When the tune finishes, they disperse, without an energy field to hold them, seeking heat and blood in the true spirit of their kind.

The scribes writing down the spider song cycles are not the usual suspects. The monkey scribblers, usually so adept, are too far away to be hired for the task, and send messages expressing disinterest in ways that only their display of back-sides and other rudeness can communicate. The badgers, usually reliable in the matter of recordkeeping, fall asleep when asked. One is still snoring, annoyingly, nearby. Not a single one of the reptile secretariat deign to pause long enough to listen to the arachnid chorus, and the birds keep their hungry eyes focused suspiciously in ways that no one thinks particularly reliable as a prelude to musical notation. The squirrels are impossible, flighty and silly, making light of the serious business with insults and disrespectful chattering, so that in the end the sheer deftness of attention required is left to a single species of moth, a wild relative of the domestic silkworm.

A brave and independent *Bombyx mandarina*, a noble and somewhat lonely creature, has arrived just in time. Her patience is inexhaustible. Pale, gray, powdery, and incon-spicuously elegant, this shy worker weaves recordings on small strands of raw, silk-like thread and later stores them in an archive arranged by theme and musical structure. The eyes of the moth archivists turn blue, very, very bright blue, clear as azure and striking, which makes the caste of the scribal *Bombyx* conspicuous among their kind, and much respected. They show no sign of the narcissistic disorder, not at all. But from generation to generation, as long as they ply their craft, the unique pigmentation remains, a living memory of onset, permanently recorded in their kind.

Like others of her species, she operates at night, in silence, her motions muffled by the scales on their clumsy wings and furry bodies. The lone *Bombyx*, heading back to the archive, takes her new recordings with her, bundled onto a spool of silk. No one knows what the whole industry of moths is even doing until they reveal the encyclopedic inventory of the spider songs in one dramatic gesture. A cluster of moth archivists takes flight and leaves the entire range of shiny cocoon recordings in full view. The spiders, needless to say, are ecstatic. But even they cannot predict what will happen to their native music with the advent of amplification.

Lion Dentistry
Southeast United States

A SMALL NUMBER OF OLD LIONS are freed from zoo cages by their passing kin. Ours is not among them. His incarceration is unofficial. But in the quiet evening, as his flatbed rests in a parking lot behind a strip mall, he glimpses the life they are living. A dental practice is flourishing in a former coffee shop, and as he watches the comings and goings, he realizes it is being run by a few of his distant, aged cousins. The released lions are not teachers, though they could be, knowing what they do and having the disposition of the elderly, mellowed and calm, kind and unflinching brethren of a true humble church. Instead, oddly, within a few weeks of their release, they opt for dentistry, a task for which their large soft paws seem ill suited. Their pads are cracked and worn with age and the scale way out of proportion to the tiny patients. But they focus on the pediatric set, wanting to use their skills for assurance, relief, assuaging the fears of the young by offering the soft shelter of their wide flanks and deep, plush pelts.

Hard to even fathom how they manage to manipulate any of the fine tools and necessary implements, except that they do, quite miraculously. Through a crack in the door that he can see from his cage, the lion watches one of them holding the neck of a child steady by turning his ancient, magnificent head sideways and using the rubbery cushions of his by then near-toothless gums. Black, moist but not wet, and very velvety, they function like a cushioned vice to cradle the young head and hold it steady.

The child lies back in docile splendor, admitted to the warm cavity, and sleeps almost immediately. Something about the lion's breath, warm around the ears and neck, and a sense of that whole powerful beast behind them, makes the child relax. It goes mildly limp and quiet, while the scrapers and polishers do their swift work.

What an oddity it is, that brief episode in the downdrift spiral, with the leonine caretakers at their tasks. The noblest of beasts, their capitulation signals the beginning of the final phase of onset. The thick-pawed animals maneuver their instruments in silence, their breathing the only sound in the cool rooms, once sterile. Now they sigh like the rest of the crumbling structures. Keeping clean is an aspiration, not a possibility—though oddly, sepsis and infection have waned, rather than increased, as the use of antibiotic treatments subsides. The smaller organisms, like the larger, have accepted their place, more or less, and do not aggressively mutate, since they have less need to and can spend their time on aggregation and its benefits.

The colonies of single-celled animals live a leisured life. In the middle kingdoms, the predatory migrant flocks of colonial flagellates and some of the smaller multi-cellular organisms are consumed with competitive attention to success. Domination is an atavistic approach. The gentle, aging lion dentists slope off after a day's work, spent but satisfied, licking their forepaws and washing their pelts in true royal manner, undisturbed by the deterioration of the world around them. Profiles are struck against a fading sky; they hold nobility in their blood and posture, and refuse to lapse from dignity even to the last of their kind. They do not pause to look across the dark parking lot to their caged cousin, knowing they are powerless to help him and feeling ashamed for his plight and theirs. The terrible truth is that they know he is there.

Bear Shops
Louisiana

LATER RENOWNED FOR HER EFFORTS AND success, Callie shows amazing persistence in the final weeks of her saga of tracking the caged lion. No dog could have done better.

Utterly oblivious to the drama unfolding elsewhere in slow time and distant space, and completely absorbed in their own narcissistic activities, some bears, brownish and blacker ones, take over in vacation spots where the ducks and geese have abandoned the shops. This is mostly out west, but also they come down from the hills of northern Alabama and take up residence where the cat is passing west toward the lion.

Stopping for a milk raid, Callie finds that the bears have seized an opportunity to take advantage of the summer tourists, doing their best to be shopkeepers. They are not inclined to handouts. A single bear is in the store when the cat comes in. He is managing the register, watching the surveillance cameras, issuing lottery tickets, and still checking out the customers, eager to get back to stocking the shelves. Like all bears, he has a tendency to eat the profits, so to speak, and is even then making his way through a bag of chips with mild salsa, along with a morning orange juice and pastry. He woke up hungry in the spring, and seeing the opportunity to trade a little bit of work for a lot of access to snacks, figured it was a pretty good deal.

Once in a while, he gets irritable and smacks a customer across the room with the sweep of a paw, or gets mad and goes up a tree for an afternoon of peeved sulking. But mostly, like today, he is happy to hang out inside and watch the register, huffing and moaning with the piped-in tunes. Recently his musical tastes have become sophisticated. He's gotten into serial and minimal tracks and now he finds the customers will often not leave the store. A weird repetitive motion disorder sets in, and the rippling cycles of twelve-tone sequences trap the shoppers in one loop after another. The bear is confused too, and it is not at all clear what should be done except to change the track. Callie takes full advantage of the hypnotic drone, and while appearing to look through the magazines, waits for the bear to nod off. Her departure leaves the store down a few cartons of milk and a few cans of the better cat fare.

September Again

Railroad Yard
Outside of Baton Rouge

THE CAT AND THE LION EDGE toward their encounter. Each has witnessed vast changes in the cultural ecologies of other species and developed new sensitivities of their own. Callie has seen everything familiar turn strange, behaviors she never imagined are everywhere in and among the domestic world she inhabits. The lion has left everything familiar behind and wanders in a landscape where everything he has known is gone, missing, lost. He understands that his habitat was vanishing even as he left it behind. Now that he has ventured beyond the open plains, he sees the hemmed-in condition of an existence he once believed open to all horizons.

Weary Callie, so long in pursuit of the lion, at last approaches the place where he is being held. She sneaks through a gate, a fence, a sluice, and a doorway to approach him. He sees her from a distance, and with what is left of the life in his eyes and breath in his chest, lifts his voice and spirit in her direction.

Wretchedly thin and a bit bedraggled in spite of her milk, paté, and cricket breakfasts, Callie confronts the lion, who is terribly worn and wan. Cautiously, the cat steps close to the cage. None of his human keepers are in sight, and the cat, whose wariness is now habit after a full year of travels, is relieved. The lion feels optimism as a possibility for the first time in months. Is it too late?

Callie sniffs, then jumps and grabs at the door latch. She fails. The lion puts his head back down and watches without moving again his head or his heart. The cat, now sure of the task she faces, jumps again, and again and again, until little by little the latch begins to move in her unskilled paws. She works it free, aching as the sounds of creaking metal pierce the air.

Miraculously, suddenly, finally, the bolt releases and she presses herself between the door and the cage with the same sinewy movement she used to leave her house, launching her journey.

Nose to nose, muzzle to muzzle, their whiskers quiver. The old lion stands up, the cat backs away. They make no attempt at easy friendship, have no assumptions about sentimental connections or obligations binding them. But a transaction occurs, a cool feline acknowledgment. What passes between them is at once profound, miraculous, and banal. They have an instant of recognition, of the similarities that bind them and the gap that separates them across the many lines of evolutionary shift and change. They know they are related, but not the same, that what they share is a species bond. But it is only enough to bring them together, not keep them linked. They do not share a life, only an ancestry, though their conditions of survival are entwined. The fate of the wild and the future of domesticity cannot be reconciled, not in them as individuals, but neither can they succeed independently. Then, the cat hisses, the lion swipes with his paw, and the cat bounds away, her fur up along her spine. His teeth are bared. They stand frozen for a few minutes, and then, slowly, ease out of their defensive postures. The lion takes a few long strides, turns to Callie, and nods.

They exchange a mutual recognition, a calibration of sentience. Callie wonders at what moment she came to represent herself to herself, know she was a being, aware, sentient. Her identity as a feline is instinctive, keyed to behaviors and capacities. Nose to nose with the lion she registers the force of the downdrift, the transformations at work in every aspect of their lives. They recognize that awareness in each other, and the inevitability it carries with it. No going back. The species seepage and mutation of identity will continue and the changes these bring will be irreversible. The lion cannot go back. His cubs are into social media, his pride has opened a casino, and the gazelles run a small buffet with a lunchroom for employees. The hamadryas baboons have settled their disputes and now stage wrestling matches on cable networks. All that was wild is now processed and managed. As for Callie, she is certain that home is not far off, and that she can find her way, now that her task is fulfilled.

Was she meant simply to release the lion? No. The moment crystallizes her understanding. Their resolution is the same, as they both recognize the two extremes of the downdrift and its effects on the identity of the animals within the global ecologies from wild to cultivated, once natural to fully domesticated. Neither is spared. The lion has no illusions. Callie still clings to hers, imagining that the changes she is part of are less tragic than the lion's. She can hardly bear to look on the worn beast, with his skinny flanks and the bald patches on his pelt, and she reserves her emotional energies for self-preservation. She cannot save the lion. His survival requires more than she can provide. He will have to fend for himself, now that he is liberated, and now that they have shared this epiphany, the impact of which will have long-term effects they neither live to see. Knowing what they do, they have released that knowledge into the downdrift, and their ability to recognize change and themselves within it will become a feature of the future. They will have to accept the changed conditions, but not without mourning the loss, or recognizing the costs. Hard to predict what changes lie ahead, but the old lines are gone and traditional zones and definitions do not hold.

They do not leave the scene together. Each goes separately. The lion finds his way to a road and then a stream and then a river until he is back by the gulf and can watch sea birds and eat minor mice and outcast frogs while he regains some strength. Mostly, however, he indulges his preference for cornflakes and puffed rice and an occasional can of tuna, all provided by ministering pelicans, even if the more gourmet among his acquaintances think the combination of milk and fish is not really a sign of cultivated taste.

Callie recovers that long-repressed capacity to find her way home, and she returns to the place from which she started. An anticlimax? Or a realization of the need to preserve what is left of the order of things? She thinks of the lion and all of his travels. But he considers a life by the gulf to be a luxury in contrast to a caged existence and any outcome to which he was being led. He asks for very little else than to be left in peace for the time remaining to him.

Archaean Views: New Regulations

A MOMENT ARRIVES, ANNOUNCED LIKE A bolt of lightning through my system, and I know I have crossed a line. Change that cannot be undone has mounted to a critical peak. I am fully aware and yet massively distributed. I am in the

creatures and of them and also independent. In the fiber of
plants and the pulsing saps that moves through their veins I
feel my own presence as an aspect of their being. They sigh in
their bending and waving motions, and the symbiotic fluid
that connects us is filled with a rush of what must be
emotion.

Some part of all of this is me, connected in my loose but
definite network of communication. My nodes do not have to
touch, do not need physical or literal contact through which
to send their signals. I project in little quantum bursts across
gaps and distances, creating a massive sense of sociality. The
effect is stimulating, a vibratory condition that is something
like contentment, as long as it stays in equilibrium. But the
critical mass of connectivity, though vulnerable, is robust on
account of the distribution. I can route and reroute from
one message center to another, and because my networks are
virtual, not literal, they can be repaired by wishing.

The executive branch of my being advances more quickly
than the legislative or judicial. But I have no need of regulations or constraints. I feel the taxes on a being of my size,
scale, age, and complexity ought to be paid in reverse, since
the social benefit of my presence has such high utility. Not all
the organisms agree, of course, and if I have to make a case
before the Assembled Congress of Life Forms, I will try
humor, rather than logic, to build my arguments. Still, I
escape that fate, since the "I" that will have had to appear
before the legislature has no more corporeal unity than loca-
tional definition, and mere species integrity does not provide
standing for a civil case. These are minor matters, since this
means I cannot be subject to any codes of law unless I want to
be. On balance, I feel most of the benefit is mine except that
I am absorbing all of the worst kind of language in having to

think this through. So, farewell to bureaucratic language and back to the soaring, surging flights of energy through time and across space and all the exuberance therein.

Panoramic View

THE SUMMER SEASON PASSES, AND SHIFTS of moods and activities register in the air and foliage and behaviors. Fall looms again, with its closings and shutting down, its endings. In the northwest, the open spaces of the plains are marked by the changed attitude of the cattle, banding together to take stock of their own situation. They are acting on their increased capacity for collective action. The horses sniff and stomp and begin to think of seating arrangements that can work in their stalls, and that in itself is so radical it takes everyone by surprise.

In the pens closer to the barn, goats are stirring, ready to go forth and campaign for office, and not just school boards and city council positions. They aspire to participate in the state assemblies, at the very least. The idea comes to them while they eat and wash up and put away the dishes they do not use but still put out as a ceremonial gesture toward their own future public profiles.

Along the creek beds and streams, and among the clustered lines of trees, the songbirds produce a steady stream of aspirational music. The sheep sleep later and later in the day, using the time to dream and think, to imagine their next stage of activity along a peculiarly nonlinear trail of change. This cannot be called evolution; it is too rapid, too lateral, and not genetic.

In the swamps near the bayous, way to the south, the water moccasins receive more of the radio programs that float through the vapors of the night and make them restless, eager for wider exposure to forms of music and culture they have missed out on in their provincial enclave. The fireflies dance and their writing against the dark is full of portent— undecipherable, but specific.

Fetid waters seethe with bacteria and microorganisms, all working through their collective guilt and trying to get beyond it, wanting to understand their place in the elaborate universe articulating itself before their eyes, or within range of their ganglia and sensors. Or, at least, some of them do. Turtles, those wise, wise souls, feel a calling toward spiritual ministries and educational offices, which everyone agrees makes sense.

The establishment of local academies is the first step in a rapidly escalating cycle of knowledge exchange and cultural stewardship. These are the positive effects of the initial downdrift. In the mountains, the eagles, alone with their mates, sense change in the life below, and spying as best they can, read the movement of the others on the ground. They have their own brilliance and skills, but are so far removed that it takes a while for them to be influenced by any other species, or to even feel what is happening among themselves. The fledglings are the most susceptible, and yet, out of loyalty to their noble parents, wait to show their interest in experimental physics, quantum math, and organic computing in a slow unfolding, rather than abrupt confrontations.

Time will come, and soon enough, for all of that to register and resonate among the insects and reptiles, amphibians and flies, the ciliated and the smooth-skinned, the hairless, the harmless, and the adeptly camouflaged.

The desert creatures, always a tight community, act rapidly in their many transactions. The prairie dogs set up a newsfeed and social media site that functions adequately by late spring and early summer of the second year of the downdrift. Every species seems to be addicted to communication. Meanwhile, the so-called domestic animals (a term that is challenged, questioned, examined endlessly in the reviews ahead) advance the issue of individual rights and collective responsibilities. They are able to access all kinds of information sources very close to home and happy to share their sources.

Final Encounter
Boston Suburbs

THE NO-LONGER-SO-SKINNY CALLIE, FILLED WITH WONDER and bewilderment, plays in the field near the home she left more than a year earlier. Much altered in mind and spirit from all she has seen, learned, and witnessed, she moves slowly one afternoon toward something that stirs in the golden grass. The lion has come to find her.

He has sought her out through an inexplicable sentimental impulse. He is done in, finished, his energy nearly gone now, but he comes toward her with the gentleness of wisdom rooted in a surplus of experience. What he knows he knows too well. He is no more or less innocent than the cat. He seeks her company without expectations.

Too exhausted for conversation, the lion approaches the delicate calico. A glow of maturity deepens her beauty. She gazes on his archaic face, wasted now. Wisdom has drained from his body, his skin hangs loose, ribs protrude, and his sorry, sad carcass makes him seem the final witness to the fate of his kind. Nobility is ascribed to him by humans, but their love of charismatic creatures spawns from their own aspirations. They adopt the animals as role models, as if the animal kingdom is a metaphor whose purpose is symbolic, not lived or real.

The cat knows nothing of this. Only, in the moment of contact, eye to eye, nose and whiskers trembling, she feels the resignation of the old animal. Face to face once again, their unmatched profiles emphasize their ancient common ancestor. They sniff each other and the air between them. The gap is impossible to cross, but their breath mingles, their whiskers share a frisson of exchange, and the air in which they tremble, trembles with them.

Like all other species, felines sometimes have an immediate, intuitive understanding of relations. But this will not save them from the rising tides of difficulty and transformation. Behind her, the noises of domestic life, her safe household, secure food supplies, regular routines, obscure the tragedy in the field behind the house where the lion sighs and gently lowers himself to the ground.

Callie tiptoes closer, skittish, careful, and then more certain that she can approach, gently brushes her whiskers against the worn brow of the ancient lion, who now puts his weary head on his faded paws and leaves this life behind.

Lacking power or knowledge, the cat has no idea of what to communicate or to whom in the face of her overwhelming sense of loss. A little later, called to dinner, she goes back into the house, bewildered, at a loss. When his body is discovered, she will keep her own counsel. Some experience is too personal to be shared.

Archaean Note: After

A TWINGE IN THE EAR OF a rat, the sting on the skin of a toad, a strange feeling of something bitter on the tongue of a frightened donkey—these, all, are connected to me. If I have limbs, I do not feel them. If I have ears, I cannot use them. If I have edges, I do not know where they are. And yet, I am at once all and many things and a single awareness with feeds and source points all over this world.

So I come to the dark and frightening awareness that my complex organism, with its distributed capacities and ancient codes of knowledge, is being hacked. I feel an upsurge of panic and anxiety. A struggle is about to commence, not for survival—I have lived too long for that—but for preservation of whatever identity I have come to possess. I have been radically reconfigured by the downdrift, made into a new kind of communication system, a social medium. I have no idea what lies ahead, as I lose the consciousness I have obtained.

The winter comes again to the northern climes, sweet summer to the south, as the winds of change blow over the landscape and once again the animals sense that something is in the air, their air.

And you, do you feel it? Feel my presence in you, notice that I have insinuated myself into your organism, into your fields of energy and communication, become a thought form in your awareness like a wave of passing energy? How will you know when I have finally established myself within your being, transgressed your limits, seeped into pores and soft spots, through eyes to mind. As you read my seemingly passive symbols on this page, do you feel their purposeful engagement with the workings of your imagination? Are they answering the call, the question—who am I?

Waiting, lurking in the sidelines, is a trigger to awake and morph me into you, you into me, as we merge within the universe as a monstrous single organism, aware and not, of its limits and capacities. When the transformation begins, individual awareness will be assaulted. The delusional sense of autonomy, of a self, will succumb to impulses that traverse the circuits of exchange. You will feel a hint of onset, a slight disturbance in the normative fields of behavior. Like the cat and the lion, you sense that you are both other and the same, distinct from and part of some larger ecology. You, too, are a medium, a node in the communication network.

You may feel a desire to crawl, lean over and drag your knuckles on the ground. You may bark at the moon or chase the tail of a rabbit with a predatory hunger. You may catch a glimpse of a busy little aye-aye in the street that used to have only house cats and squirrels. If you pick at your scalp, or that of your mate, will this be the beginning of a habit? The hair may thicken on your face, on the backs of your hands, or appear along your spine one night, sprouting innocently enough and yet serving as a harbinger of radical change to come. The alteration may be subtle, a mere shift of phase as you adopt a rocking motion and a deep squat, feeling contentment with your place in the implacable universe. You may feel that all that comes into your view is already familiar, uncannily so, because you recognize it, are part of it, rather than meeting it anew.

How will you know when the downdrift comes seeping across all the many boundaries that once reassured you of your self? I feel all this extensive being-ness distributed across distances and species, through attachments between one living being and all others. In all of this pulsing, pulsating stimulation and reality of being I cannot say where I begin or finish—or even where life itself begins and resides. In my capacity to be absorbed and run through the connective tissues that make and remake me so that I proliferate within the whole throbbing matter of being, I only know that I do not want life to end.

The very recognition that you feel now, reading this, is part of that and joins you to me as the hyper-organism that I am, distributed, ubiquitous, and, paradoxically, still able to be experienced as a local point of consciousness. Your self. My self.

About the Author

Johanna Drucker has published nearly a dozen works of creative prose, as well as multiple volumes of critical writing. She is internationally known for her work in the history of graphic design, typography, experimental poetry, fine art, and digital humanities. In addition to her academic work, Drucker has produced artist's books and projects that were the subject of a retrospective, *Druckworks: 40 Years of Books and Projects*, that began at Columbia College in Chicago in 2012. She is currently working on a database memoir, *ALL the books I never wrote or wrote and never published*. Recent creative projects include *Diagrammatic Writing* (Onomatopée, 2014), *Stochastic Poetics* (Granary, 2012), and *Fabulas Feminae* (Litmus Press, 2015). A collection of her essays, *What Is?* (Cuneiform Press) was published in 2013 and *Graphesis: Visual Forms of Knowledge Production* (Harvard University Press) appeared in 2014. In 2014 she was elected to the American Academy of Arts and Sciences and awarded an honorary doctorate of Fine Arts by the Maryland Institute College of Art in 2017. Her title, *The General Theory of Social Relativity*, is forthcoming from The Elephants in Vancouver. She teaches at University of California, Los Angeles, and lives with her cats, Coco and Cleo.

RECENT AND FORTHCOMING BOOKS FROM THREE ROOMS PRESS

FICTION

Meagan Brothers
Weird Girl and What's His Name

Ron Dakron
Hello Devilfish!

Michael T. Fournier
Hidden Wheel
Swing State

Janet Hamill
Tales from the Eternal Café

William Least Heat-Moon
Celestial Mechanics

Aimee Herman
Everything Grows

Eamon Loingsigh
Light of the Diddicoy
Exile on Bridge Street

John Marshall
The Greenfather

Aram Saroyan
Still Night in L.A.

Richard Vetere
The Writers Afterlife
Champagne and Cocaine

Julia Watts
Quiver

SHORT STORY ANTHOLOGIES

Dark City Lights: New York Stories
edited by Lawrence Block

First-Person Singularities: Stories
by Robert Silverberg
with an introduction by John Scalzi

Have a NYC I, II & III:
New York Short Stories;
edited by Peter Carlaftes
& Kat Georges

Crime + Music: The Sounds of Noir
edited by Jim Fusilli

Songs of My Selfie:
An Anthology of Millennial Stories
edited by Constance Renfrow

The Obama Inheritance:
15 Stories of Conspiracy Noir
edited by Gary Phillips

This Way to the End Times:
Classic and New Stories of
the Apocalypse
edited by Robert Silverberg

MEMOIR & BIOGRAPHY

Nassrine Azimi and
Michel Wasserman
Last Boat to Yokohama:
The Life and Legacy of
Beate Sirota Gordon

William S. Burroughs & Allen Ginsberg
Don't Hide the Madness:
William S. Burroughs in Conversation
with Allen Ginsberg
edited by Steven Taylor

James Carr
BAD: The Autobiography of
James Carr

Richard Katrovas
Raising Girls in Bohemia:
Meditations of an American Father; A
Memoir in Essays

Judith Malina
Full Moon Stages:
Personal Notes from
50 Years of The Living Theatre

Phil Marcade
Punk Avenue:
Inside the New York City
Underground, 1972-1982

Stephen Spotte
My Watery Self:
Memoirs of a Marine Scientist

PHOTOGRAPHY-MEMOIR

Mike Watt
On & Off Bass

MIXED MEDIA

John S. Paul
Sign Language: A Painter's Notebook
(photography, poetry and prose)

FILM & PLAYS

Israel Horovitz
My Old Lady: Complete Stage Play
and Screenplay with an Essay on
Adaptation

Peter Carlaftes
Triumph For Rent (3 Plays)
Teatrophy (3 More Plays)

Kat Georges
Three Somebodies: Plays about
Notorious Dissidents

DADA

Maintenant: A Journal of
Contemporary Dada Writing & Art
(Annual, since 2008)

TRANSLATIONS

Thomas Bernhard
On Earth and in Hell
(poems of Thomas Bernhard
with English translations by
Peter Waugh)

Patrizia Gattaceca
Isula d'Anima / Soul Island
(poems by the author
in Corsican with English
translations)

César Vallejo | Gerard Malanga
Malanga Chasing Vallejo
(selected poems of César Vallejo
with English translations
and additional notes by
Gerard Malanga)

George Wallace
EOS: Abductor of Men
(selected poems in Greek & English)

POETRY COLLECTIONS

Hala Alyan
Atrium

Peter Carlaftes
DrunkYard Dog
I Fold with the Hand I Was Dealt

Thomas Fucaloro
It Starts from the Belly and Blooms

Inheriting Craziness is Like
a Soft Halo of Light

Kat Georges
Our Lady of the Hunger

Robert Gibbons
Close to the Tree

Israel Horovitz
Heaven and Other Poems

David Lawton
Sharp Blue Stream

Jane LeCroy
Signature Play

Philip Meersman
This is Belgian Chocolate

Jane Ormerod
Recreational Vehicles on Fire
Welcome to the Museum of Cattle

Lisa Panepinto
On This Borrowed Bike

George Wallace
Poppin' Johnny

HUMOR

Peter Carlaftes
A Year on Facebook

 Three Rooms Press | New York, NY | Current Catalog: www.threeroomspress.com
Three Rooms Press books are distributed by PGW/Ingram: www.pgw.com